Cujo, Rabies, and myself,
America's minorities, are gathered in Plum Creek's roadside diner scheming about getting paid big in the land of the free, exercising our rights set forth in the constitution of the United States, specifically in regard to the pursuit of happiness, to our American Dreams.

God bless America.

Cujo, African-American, is wearing his standard thug uniform—a black hoodie. He lays his head low, not wanting to be seen. Rabies—Mexican—is chewing gum, making a mole on his face move up and down. His choice of cover is the pair of gold-rimmed Ray-bans, even though the diner is dimly lit. And me, Chinese-American, ex-military with a Purple Heart, looking like I fought for the other side in 'Nam. I suppose we're all doing our best to act inconspicuous, but man, it isn't working. The waitress hesitates to approach our table, when she does she appears quite amused. She takes a good look at us, up close, probably trying to peg which one of the Village People each of us is supposed to represent, probably thinking we're a second tier cover band, in town to do the *YMCA*.

Shanghai Bandit

by

Eric Qiao

Shanghai Bandit

Cover Art by *Diana Carlile*

The Wild Rose Press, Inc.
PO Box 708
Adams Basin, NY 14410-0708
Visit us at www.thewildrosepress.com

Publishing History
First Mainstream Historical Edition, 2017
Print ISBN 978-1-5092-1248-4
Digital ISBN 978-1-5092-1249-1

Published in the United States of America

Dedication

For my grandmother.

Part One

Chapter One

Five o'clock in the afternoon, right before closing, the bank gets robbed.

I know as soon as the guy approaches Cass's counter, flashing a genuine shitty grin, trotting a gangster walk, which looks like he's either got a cramp, sustained a knee injury, or is mentally challenged. I know he's robbing us because there's a fire up north and that can't be a coincidence. I know what he's going to sound like, too, pretty much. Guy's wearing a bright orange bandanna; might as well stamp the text, *bank robber* on his forehead. He opens with, "My oh my," hands rubbing with glee. Peering at Cass's double D's, then her nametag, he says, "Cassandra Roselyn, don't mind me calling you Cassie Rose."

Cass doesn't get it. "How may I help you, sir?" She pulls her face to a standard teller's smile, her teeth an ad for reasons not to smoke.

"You can start by opening them drawers and show me what you got." Guy tongues his lips. "Sorry to ruin your day, honey. In case you don't know, this is a holdup."

Cass shoots me a sideways glance; her smile turns to a frown. I'm standing at the next counter about six feet away. I trigger the silent alarm. With that fire burning still at north side of town, I know the alarm is a hopeless cause.

He turns to me. "What you looking at, my boy?"

I'm his boy. I'm past thirty. The guy's the same age, if not younger.

Now, in the bank, there's Cass, me, the robber dude in his bandanna, Jim the loan officer at his desk, and Ester the branch manager—she's in the back office away from the action. Jim looks up, dumbstruck.

I say to the robber, "Sir, why don't you just leave the building, right now?"

"Why don't I bust a cap in your ass, right now?" His hand goes inside his pocket and comes out with...nothing. He pats himself up and down as if he forgot where he pocketed his keys, an *uh-oh* moment across his face. "Yeah, uh, gimme a minute." Licks his front row teeth, left and right.

Sirens in the distance.

The guy, still licking, still patting himself up and down his jacket and his pants, backs away. One step. Two steps. A siren goes *woop woop* in short bursts, another one goes *weewoo weewoo*. The dude in his bandanna scratches his head, doesn't seem particularly worried about the police.

Next, two sheriff's cruisers race past the building, not stopping. They're off to contain the fire on the north side of town. The sirens diminish in that direction. Then the door swings open. A young Latina enters.

Early twenties. Curvy figure. No need for her to turn around to reveal her nice can. Her face is about the prettiest thing I've ever seen. Belongs on TV, not in the real world.

The robber shouts at her, "Girl, what I tell you? Stay the lookout!"

She says, "You forgot your gun. Here," handing

over a M1911 semi-automatic, in high heels, in perfect composure.

"Shoot, baby, I didn't forget. Don't think I needed it is all." The guy's calm and playing it cool. He cocks the pistol to a lock and load. Badass gangster ready to rob.

"The police are all gone." She thumbs at the exit. "Where's the money?"

"I'm gettin' it." He returns to Cass's counter and points the gun at her face. "Cassie Rose, meet Mr. Colt. Now please, won't you grab a bag and stuff it full with my goddamn money." To me, "C'mon, you too. Let's go, white boy."

Again, I'm no boy. I'm not white, either. "Just do as he says." I nod at Cass, calm as can be.

As we empty our cash drawers, Jim, the loan officer, pushes himself up from behind his desk. "Cassandra? What's going on?"

The robber turns to him with the gun. "What's it look like, dipshit?"

Jimbo lifts his hands in surrender, sitting his ass back. His eyes are asking me, *Didn't you trigger the silent alarm?* I ignore him. He stays quiet.

Once the bags are stuffed with cash, we concede them to the guy in the bandanna. He chuckles, pleased. "Thank you. Yeah, thank you very much, no doubt."

I shrug. "You're welcome."

The Latina approaches the counter. "Your wallets too. C'mon, take 'em out."

Jesus Christ, she approaches at me like a runway model. Judgment severely clouded, I withdraw my wallet and lay it on the counter. After my compliance, my colleagues follow suit. The bandanna guy snatches my wallet and slides it in his ass-pocket. The Latina collects the rest.

Finally satisfied, the girl beams exhilarated, then she swings her arms around her dude and they start making out right here in the middle of the floor, each holding a bag of money. The guy grabs her ass, putting on a show. I catch Cass rolling her eyes. Jimbo looks to be drooling quite a bit.

Right then, a *third* person bursts into the building.

It's quarter after five. Fifteen minutes past the bank's usual operating hours. The third guy who just entered, is short, has a pump action shotgun at his hip, and he's wearing a black ski-mask. The couple making out disengage, and then exchange expressions with each other, and finally stare at the intruder, appearing absolutely bewildered, seeming to say, *Who the hell are you?*

And I get it, right away.

The intruder's not with these two. Not part of the plan. They don't know one another. Christ, what are the odds? Three years I've worked here, three mundane years as a teller. The most excitement I witnessed was when a stray dog came in and took a dump. That was two years ago. Today, the first time the bank gets robbed; it gets robbed by two separate, unrelated parties—at the same freaking time. I survey the newcomer shaking my head. Naturally, I know what the poor guy is about to announce.

"You! You and you! E-everybody on floor! I-I am banker robber!" His voice sounds old, almost ancient. I detect his accent and his broken English, both are a surprise. The stammering is also out of left field. One simply doesn't expect a bank robber to stammer in a holdup.

No one gets on the floor.

"You kidding me?" the Latina snaps, sounding bitchy. "The place's already robbed. We got here *first*, okay, mister?" Speaking and looking hot. "Us—*el primero.*"

"Yeah, homeboy," her partner adds. "Set your own fire tomorrow and then come back. Or better yet, try a ghetto-ass town someplace else."

The guy in the ski-mask appears stunned. He says nothing.

"Yo, you heard? This joint here, it's *ours.*"

The two parties are standing face to face, but aren't exactly standing off, because the newcomer's right side seems to be shaking, a lot. He looks unsteady. The shotgun at his hip is trembling too. He appears to be having trouble lifting it upright, as if it were an anchor of a boat gradually sinking. So the shotgun lowers, its barrels pointing to the floor. Now the guy's using the thing to prop himself like it's a cane. He stumbles, head snaps back. Then finally his ass hits the floor, jerking. The shotgun grip falls on his knee with a dull *thud.*

"Shit, dude's having a heart attack or somethin'." The bandanna guy tucks the Colt behind his back and surveys the bank: seeing no one's taking initiative, he tends the patient after a short pause. Kneeling beside him, "Man, you all right?"

The Latina babe also comes to his aid. "Take off his mask."

"No, woman. We're like, industry colleagues, you hear? We gots to observe professional courtesy."

The patient is wheezing. "Me...s-str-stroke."

"You having a stroke?"

The poor guy pleads, "C-call...911."

"Get real, fool. We're pulling a bank job and you expect us to dial 911?"

"Let's roll," the girl scoffs, stands, and backs away. "We have the money, let's just go."

"What if I had a stroke on the job?" Her partner rises patting his own chest. "We gotta take him to the ER."

"You out of your mind? We don't even have a *car*."

"Don't be such a cold-hearted bitch. Man's dying. Ain't no ambulance gonna come for him. They up at the fire scene. A fire *we* lit. He dies, it's on us."

"So what?"

"Woman, do as I say." His eyes narrow, meaning it. "Boot us a ride, ASAP. We're dumping him at the ER."

The girl mumbles something in Spanish and turns to the loan officer by the desk. Girl's b-side is sensational. She says to Jimbo, "You there—you seem like a person who owns a running automobile. Hand over your key."

Jim wheels back in his chair, stuttering, "I-no, p-please. I-I'm two months away from paying it off."

The girl places both hands on his desk, leaning over. "I look the type who gives a damn?"

Jimbo cringes on the verge of weeping.

I eyeball the stroked-out dude on the ground, and all of a sudden I'm hit with memories of China Beach during the war. Poor fellow, he needs immediate medical attention, no doubt about it. "Miss, leave my coworker alone, please." I exhale, at the same time I wink at Jim, letting him know I'll take care of this. "I got a car." Producing my key, I make it jingle.

Everyone turns, sights on me.

I got a car but I'm not about to turn it over. I like my car and I intend to keep it mine. So I let on, "Here's what'll happen, my car—I'll drive. The *señorita* is welcome to ride with me."

"No!" Cass objects. "Take *my* car. Please—"

"*Cassandra.*" I motion for her to zip it shut. *I got it handled.* To the robber dude, I resume, "Leave my coworkers safely out of this and you can ride with me as well, asshole."

"The hell you think you are?" The bandanna guy pulls out Mr. Colt. His legs spread and his shoulders lock in, aiming the weapon square at my face. In that instant, I recognize his fire-ready position, his stance and posture are all part of his muscle memory. I know *exactly* what he is, or rather, *was*—before he fell to bad habits. Judging by the way he's licking his teeth, it's got to be cocaine. "Your car key, toss it over." Guy steps closer with hostility in his stare. But his finger isn't on the trigger, it's on the safety. The safety is on.

Unflinching, I address him, "Soldier, listen up, this is a small town and we got a sad excuse for a hospital, a hospital you likely don't know the location of. A fellow like you approach the ER with my vehicle, hospital staff will realize it's stolen. Next thing you know there'll be an APB out for you and stolen autos. You won't be getting out of this town in any type of wheels whatsoever. On the *other* hand, we drop him off *together*, hospital staff would be inclined to believe you're my guests visiting from out of town."

"What you mean a fellow like me?" The way he says *you* sounds like *chew*. His eyebrow goes up and down and he knows what I mean. Shaking his head, he says, "What, we'll dump him at the hospital and you'll let us jack your ride?" His aim lowers.

"We'll drop him off and I'll see how it goes from there."

"Shit, I got the gun, what you gonna do?" He glances over at the wheezing dude on the ground. Time is of the essence and this we both agree. "All right then, let's hustle."

We lift the stroke patient and prop him on our shoulders. The four of us make for the exit with the robber saying to the patient, "Man, you better have insurance."

At the same time, Ester, the branch manager comes out from her office, finally getting off her lazy overweight ass. Coming out not because she heard the ruckus, but because it's time to head home for supper. Taking not a second to grasp the scene, she inquires of me, "Where you going? Aren't you closing today?"

"Well boss, we just got robbed, two, three grand worth." Before she starts, I request, "Cass, help me close today? Shouldn't take you long to balance our cash drawers. I mean, hell, the drawers are empty."

****

The car's AM radio is on, a guy criticizing President Reagan's fiscal responsibility. I turn him off. In the distance, thick smoke rises from a hill, ascending into the clouds. The fire is an inferno and it's losing control, making the desolated town appear more exciting than it is. Excitement is good. Gives folks things to talk about. Keeps their mind off the economic depression.

I veer left on Citrus Street—not a citrus tree in

sight—and pass the closed post office, heading westbound to the county medical. Should be there in ten minutes. Only one traffic light on the way, and if it's red I'll have to run it, no question. Not as if I'll be encountering pedestrians at the crossing.

The pretty babe is in the passenger seat, the stroke patient and the bandanna dude in the back. The dude says, "Shit, you ever met robbers like us, teller boy?" From the rearview, he takes off his bandanna revealing a bald head—by choice, not circumstance. "We're on a robbery and we're saving a fellow human being. That's an act of valor worthy of a Bronze Star, man." Then he leans forward. "Yo, you called me *soldier* back there. How'd you tell?" Before I reply, he lets on, "I got drafted, then dishonorably discharged before I saw 'Nam. Shot an officer in the ass, ha-ha…talk about bustin' a cap." He rubs his head. "It was one of those freak training accidents. But a lucky one, I guess. Most of my homies never made it back." Wielding his gun, he tells me, "I shot him with this, too."

Colt 1911, once army standard issue, now the most popular weapon in American crime. The car's quiet for a spell, except for the wheezing patient. His eyes are closed, arm clutching his shotgun tight. I say nothing. Just here to drive and observe.

"Hey, Cujo," the girl turns back and suggests, "why don't we count the take?"

Counting the take in a gateway is terrible idea, but the guy called Cujo tucks his gun away and extracts some loose cash from the bag, saying, "Yeah, baby, why don't we."

The babe also starts to count, but she stops before getting too far. "Weird. Why is there an envelope in here?"

"*No*, don't open that!" I spread out my right arm, stopping her as if I'm about to grope her breast. "That's a dye pack."

"A what?"

"A dye pack. It'll explode if you tamper with it and dye everything blood red. You won't be able to wash it off the bills, not unless you got the solution from the feds. Try spending tainted *el dólar,* you'll be picked up in less than ninety seconds."

"Bullshit." The girl scoffs, has that bitchy, hot look on her. Her eyelashes are lined with black makeup. Batting her lashes she opens the envelope. "You think this is our first rodeo?"

Soon as her words leave those luscious lips, the dye pack explodes. *Pah!* like popping a balloon. Red liquid splashes everywhere, on her face, on her hair and clothes, on the window and on the dash, and mostly, on the cash.

"Damn woman!" *Damn* sounding like *Day-yam*. The guy reaches forward and seizes the bag from her. "You done ruined the money!"

The girl speaks in hysteria, *español* rolls off her tongue like a Gatling gun. She's obviously cursing, either at me or at her luck. Her hands are all red, she holds them out, trying not to touch anything. Then she turns to me looking like she got shot in the face. Hotness evaporates. "*You*—you put that pack in there, you son-of-a-bitch," more Spanish follows.

"Cass dropped it in," I explain. "We only got one pack."

Midway to the hospital now, Cujo is complaining, the girl is hysterical. I request the latter not to move 'cause she's getting red dye all over my seat. Christ, I offer these criminals a ride and they go about messing up my car.

Straight head, a traffic light turns from green to yellow to red right before the train tracks. The rail line's defunct but the traffic light isn't. The trains stopped rolling in since after the Second World War, after Eisenhower built the interstate highways for the purpose of national defense. Abisko, California, akin to many small towns in America, dwindled and suffered as a result. Now the shanty town is halfway through its death rattle.

As I'm trying to remember the last time a train rolled through here, the word *baichi* reaches my ears in a whisper, amidst the girl's Spanish. I turn my head feeling I'm in slow-mo. Then the sound of a shotgun racking—that one-two action, unmistakable—silences the commotion.

"Stop now."

The double-barrels are connected to Cujo's temple. The stroke patient sits erect, holding the gun. Not wheezing any more, no longer weak on one side. His finger is on the trigger, holding steady. Behind the ski-mask, his eyes are wide open. The man means business. "Stop car," he commands again, not stammering any more.

"Dude," Cujo pleads, kicking my seat. "You hear? Stop the car!" His hands are up.

So my foot eases off the gas and the car coasts to a halt at the red light before a railroad crossing.

The ex-stroke patient takes control of Cujo's Colt and tucks it under his waistband. Now he goes for the money, the tainted bag and the untainted one, as well, muttering, "How you so stupid, *eng*?" He combines the bags into one, easier to hold on to. "You no made for this, *baichi*."

Slowly, the man opens the door and backs out ass first. The shotgun grip is clutched in his armpit, right hand on the trigger, left hand with the money. "All you—*out*!" To me, "Leave me key."

We climb out of the car with our hands up. The two lane street is empty. There's a pawnshop on one side, a tire-shop opposite. The pawnshop has been closed for a month, its aluminum door rolled all the way down and locked. The tire-shop doubles as a used car lot, and is having a buy-two-tires-get-two-free special. No customer cars out front. The owner's truck is gone. Probably off to see the fire, that's where excitement is at its utmost.

The three of us shuffle onto the curb. In her high-heels, the *señorita's* tits bounce, no bra, heaving.

"Thought you was having a stroke, man." Cujo shakes his head, disbelieving and dismayed. "We were saving your *life*. How you gonna play us like that?"

The ski-masked dude hurries to the driver's side casting one last pathetic look at the three of us. Me, in my work clothes, shirt tucked in and wearing a tie; the Latina covered in red dye, in desperate need of a steamy, hot shower; Cujo, his hands up, holding his orange bandanna in a wad. The guy in the ski-mask ducks inside my car with the money. He says nothing. The car door slams and seconds later, the traffic light turns green.

Like that the car crosses the rails leaving a cloud of dust in our faces.

"*Shit*," sounding like *she-it*. Cujo throws his

bandanna onto the ground in a smashing motion. The wad hits the sidewalk with no sound effect. "See, this is what you get for being a nice guy."

Sirens in the distance now, cops finally doubling back to the bank.

"What do we do now?" The girl adjusts her blouse, red liquid drying on her cleavage. Then she frowns at Cujo like everything is all his fault.

To these two, I remark, "That guy—he's Chinese."

They tilt their heads, staring at me as they would an abstract at a museum.

"It's his accent. Plus, I heard him call you *baichi*, which means idiot."

"Man, the fuck you know?" Then in that instant Cujo recognizes, must be for the very first time. "Wait a minute…" Eyes squinting to a line, he points out, "Wait, you're a chink?"

Guy's only saying it the way it is, no insults intended. So I just shrug. "How'd you guess my nickname?"

An eyebrow shoots up. "Your nickname's *Chink*?"

"Name's Chin. Back in 'Nam, men affectionately called me Chink. When I was with the seventy-fifth."

Cujo does a double take, and not long afterwards he appears to be shaking in his boots. "Se-seventy-fifth…em-MP?" He gulps before asking, "Final rank?"

"Major."

The lines on his forehead connect and form into words, the words: *no shit*. Now he looks like he doesn't know whether to salute or flee. At last his feet move with a sound—a click of his heel as if he were in attention.

"At ease, soldier." I try to calm him down.

"Nah-nah, hell with this. Marla, we gotta bail, c'mon." He reaches for her hand. "Let's get the fuck outta here."

"I've been saying that, Cujo—"

"Shut up, woman. Don't say another word, I swear..." He drags her by the wrist. Before he turns his back to me all the way, he relates, "I'm sorry about your car, major. Please don't hold it against me. The robbery was nothing personal, all right?"

Meaning he doesn't want me to go after him. But I just say, "Why don't you call me Chink?"

He keeps quiet. The two flee to the railroad, two pedestrians heading for the vast landscape on the other side. Once across, they run wild amidst the wailing sirens. The girl struggles to keep up in her heels, so she goes barefoot.

I stand idle, watching them flee, hearing the sirens blare louder and louder. I should either chase down these pitiful criminals or return to the bank and assist the cops with what I know. But I do neither. Instead, I reflect on the events of the past thirty minutes. Thinking about the money and the Chinese guy. I can't believe how easy it was for him to highjack Cujo; and how easy it was for Cujo to rob the bank.

Not lamenting for the loss of my car, my mind conjures Cujo's expression when he heard I was in Vietnam. Sidetracked now, I think about 'Nam, about people dying, the killing and the gore. I think about the latest letter I got from Saigon, written by a girl who claims to be my daughter...

I decide to walk home.

Chapter Two

Three hours after the robbery, the bell rings and I tuck away the letter I'm reading for the hundredth time—the letter from the girl who may or may not be mine. I open the door in my pajamas. A man and a woman unknown to me—African Americans—show me their badges. Behind them is Cass. Behind Cass is a squad car parked by the curb. Two sheriff's deputies I recognize are leaning on the trunk of the car, looking to be shooting the shit. Cass is still dressed in her work attire, black pants and white blouse buttoned up, the nametag on her chest. The two showing me their badges are in plainclothes, my-age people.

I catch some letters off their credentials before the flaps close. The man's badge says LAPD, the woman's says something BI. The man is six-hundred miles from home. The woman, I haven't got a clue.

Cass squeezes past the two out-of-town cops and embraces me hard. So very hard. "Boy, am I relived." She lets go of me saying, "I looked everywhere for you, Chin. The county medical, back at the bank and at the sheriff's. I thought you got kidnapped for good and we'd be getting a ransom note." Staring at me with those green eyes, an ounce of disappointment in her gaze. "You could've let me know you were okay."

"I was gonna." In my PJs, I shrug. "But I fell asleep."

"Mr. Chin," the woman makes the introductions, "I'm Agent Reese from the California Bureau of Investigation. This is Detective Grayson from the Los Angeles Police Department. May we come in?"

So I back away to let the law enter. Cass too. Before she comes in, the first thing she does is kick off her shoes on the welcome mat. She knows the drill. Reese sees this and nudges her partner, and they both remove their shoes. Agent Reese is in black stockings, legs smooth and not bad looking. Both of Detective Grayson's socks have a noticeable hole.

"Bureau of Investigation. Where's that?" I make the small talk.

"Sacramento."

We get situated in my living room and I offer tea. They all decline. Grayson is curling his toes, visibly uncomfortable without his shoes. "I suppose we'll get down to it." He clears his throat before asking, "What can you tell us about the robbery, Mr. Chin?"

So I give them a rundown. Then Reese asks, "Can you describe the perpetrators?"

"The guy called Cujo is 5'8, 5'9, a lanky 150 lbs, wears an orange bandanna, thug looking—"

"Ethnicity?"

Fine—I omitted that part. I figured Cass filled in the details back at the bank. Plus, detective Grayson and agent Reese are African-Americans. *A black guy, thug looking* doesn't sound like the right thing to say in their presence.

"African-American," I finally reply. "The girl's Latina. The third guy…" I hesitate. The third guy spoke my mother's tongue. Language I haven't heard in years. Now I feel a strange kinship with the guy who jacked my car. "I don't know." I withhold from the cops. "He wore a ski-mask." The latter's true.

"Two perps fled on foot, and the unnamed, masked suspect fled in your vehicle?"

I confirm and provide the cops with the make, model, and the license plate number of my vehicle.

Grayson, not bothering to write it down, asks, "Why haven't you reported the grand theft auto?"

"I expected my colleagues to have done so by now."

"The sheriff said they did." He twitches his ass forward and he's nodding at my pajamas—nodding unconvinced. "If you don't mind me saying, Mr. Chin, you don't look particularly shaken up after the ordeal. In fact, I'd say you're downright nonchalant about it."

It's not really a question so I don't really answer.

Cass looks like she wants to explain on my behalf, but in the end she keeps quiet.

Silence for a spell.

"Thank you for your cooperation, Mr. Chin." Agent Reese crosses her legs. "And thank you for keeping the situation under control. We heard from your colleagues, you were brave."

I've done braver things under more threatening conditions. So I say nothing.

"Anton *Cujo* Samuels, Melina *Marla* Ramirez." Grayson speaks their names and pauses for effect, eyes on me with suspicion in his stare.

I shrug, indifferent. I peer at his feet and he curls his big toes.

"Do you read the papers, Mr. Chin?"

"Just the *Abisko Monthly*. The *LA Times* doesn't make it up here."

"These people are hostile criminals." Reese leans forward. "Hostile and unstable. Thanks to you no one was hurt today."

"I don't think they were out to *hurt* anyone. In fact, they took one hell of a risk on *saving* the third guy. Wanted to drop him off at the ER after they done robbed the bank. You want to talk about bravery?"

"But the unnamed suspect was faking it? The stroke, I mean."

"They didn't know that."

Cass gets my back. "He *did* look like he was in dire need of medical attention."

Grayson squeezes his forehead, appears to be somewhat irritated. Probably at me for being unimpressed and nonchalant about what happened today. My attitude maybe belittling his job. So from inside his jacket he withdraws a manila folder and presents the contents on my coffee table. Top left of a page is a mug shot of Cujo—thug looking, for sure. I don't intend to read the file, just stare at Grayson for what is up.

"Anton *Cujo* Samuels," he introduces again. "Conceived by gangbangers in Watts, twenty nine years of age, arrested twenty times in the past nine years, one conviction for some kind of hustle. Got kicked out of the army and was with the New Thugs on the Block, LLC, before he got kicked out of that too and went solo."

"LLC?" I ask, taken aback. "A Limited Liability Company?"

"According to the Better Business Bureau, their rating's A-plus."

"You're shitting me."

"Of course I am." He taps Cujo's photo. "Word out of the horse's mouth is that he got shot so he quit on New Thugs. Didn't know limited liability meant no medical insurance—and no, I'm not shitting you about this. Meanwhile, word on the street is that New Thugs had to let him go. They fired him."

"'Cause he got shot?"

"'Cause he got old. *New* Thugs on the Block. He was old news."

"No equal opportunity?"

"What are we, communists?"

"Detective..." I heave a sigh. "Why are you telling me this?"

"So you would grasp the scope of the danger surrounding you." But his detective's eyes are saying, *I think there's something you aren't letting on.* "The facts are in the papers any way—the *LA Times.*" He flips some pages in the file, and stops at the one with the Latina's photo on the upper left. Not a mug shot, looks like something from the DMV. "Melina *Marla* Ramirez, daughter of cartel lord Dago Ramirez, a man you don't want to be within ten feet of unarmed."

"Detective, if you're here to nominate me to the upstanding citizen award, you're wasting your time." I stand up. "Like I said, the situation wasn't dangerous. Cujo was on a mild crack trip but he wasn't gonna shoot nobody. He never switched off his safety." Then I'm reminded that Cujo shot an officer in the ass in a training accident, I amend, "He shot anyone it'd be an accident."

"How do you know his safety was on?"

"I just know."

"Dago's dead." Grayson stares at me like he

expects a shudder. "He was found in his North Hollywood home with sixteen holes in him. According to his lackeys his inventory was wiped out. Cujo and Marla are suspects in a homicide. In their possession is over a hundred kilos of cocaine. You know how much that is?"

"Sure," I tell him. "It's a tenth of a ton."

To his partner Grayson remarks with a chuckle. "This guy knows his metric system." Then he leans forward and speaks to me all serious, "Does sixteen holes sound like an accident to you? I'm thinking he had his safety *off*, Mr. Chin. What do you think?"

Now this detective looks like a young Danny Glover, like when he played the cop in *Witness* but younger still, or maybe more like in *Escape from Alcatraz*. I'm meeting his eyes, the eyes of an investigator, pretty seasoned. The eyes that have probably seen it all in the ghettos of LA, in Watts and Compton and all round South Central. Or perhaps he's seen more somewhere else. I give him the benefit of the doubt and sit. "So you're saying the girl, Marla, shot and killed her own father?"

"Or Cujo. One of them did. The crime scene had the signs of a hostile takeover."

"Hostile takeover? Weren't they close?"

"Who and whom?"

"Marla and her dad."

"You must be joking."

I can't help but think about the pretty Latina, about how she made out with Cujo at the bank. Even if it was Cujo who killed her dad, she was making out with her father's killer. Now I'm asking myself what kind of daughter is that? *Were they close?*

"Doesn't make sense." I put her out of my mind and point out, "You said they cleaned Dago out. If they'd already scored big, why are they robbing banks?"

"You're asking me things that aren't in the papers." Grayson closes the files. "I'm not at liberty to volunteer that information."

"Marla said this isn't their first rodeo. How many bank jobs they pulled? That's in the papers, right?"

"It is, you should read it."

"How much money have they made off with so far, pulling bank jobs?"

"The *LA Times*, they're pretty thorough with those kinds of facts."

"What about the third guy? Who's he?"

He skips a beat. "I have no idea. And apparently, neither do you." My question seems to have erased his suspicion of me. "Look, I'm just saying you dodged a bullet today." Grayson stands up and studies my place of domicile, likely a detective habit. He surveys a one-eighty and just nods at random things, as if he approves. I have minimalist décor except around the mantelpiece, which is what he's facing when he stops. "Is this yours?" He turns to me impressed, but with a hint of skepticism. "A Purple Heart from the army? *You*?" A slight twitch in his eyes.

"It says my name there, doesn't it?"

"You were in Mekong Delta?" He recognizes the picture taken in Dong Tam's 9th Division base camp. "*You*?" he says in disbelief. "Unit, rank?"

I tell him.

"You don't say." He bobs his head some multiple times. "No wonder you're so calm and collected. Makes sense. I mean, Mekong and a Purple Heart? You've seen how serious shit go down, brother." A pause later he goes, "Wait, did you say Seventy-*fifth*? Holy mother of…" Now the guy's turning to me dragging his jaw, on the floor. "Man, what the fuck you doing *here*?"

I shrug and think, *What am I doing here?*

Damn, that's not a bad question.

****

The cops are in a hurry to get on with the chase, so after they get their story they leave, thanking me one last time for basically not losing my shit.

Cassandra, she decides to stay and have sex.

Cass likes to be on top so I just lay there and close my eyes, much like I've been doing for the past several months. The first time we did it I was intoxicated and woke up in her bedroom naked. Life is dull around here so the next time we did it was about two minutes later. Cass is not a bad looking female. Not remarkable, either. Just plain, like this town, like my job. I know all her moves, all her sounds, the moan she makes before climax, she's doing that now.

After we're done, she lies beside me and lights a cigarette. A drag later, she says, "I'm moving in with you, Chin."

I'm wondering if she's lost her mind as she expels more smoke from her lungs.

Smoke rises toward the ceiling, she asks me casually, "Tomorrow good for you?"

I just turn, staring at her.

"I had a gun pointed at me." Pulling the sheet to cover herself, she exhales. "I'm thirty-five this year. You know how old that is in Kentucky? My friends from high school are grandmas-to-be now. Pregnant at sixteen, their kids get knocked-up at sixteen. Do the math. I don't want to go on another year like this."

Between the sheets, she brings up her leg to scratch. The ash on her cigarette needs taking care of, but she pays no mind. "When I was looking into the muzzle of that gun, it was like that cliché—life flashing past and all. I've had all the fun. Berkley, Oakland, October '69… I had good times." Cigarette ash falls on the sheet and she remembers, "You wouldn't know, I guess. You weren't here."

I was in boot camp.

"Today, those criminals took you hostage and I thought I lost you." She rests the cigarette butt on the nightstand, flakes of ash falling onto the carpet. "I was so afraid. I don't want to lose you, you know, because…well, I'm in love with you, Chin." Now she has a green gleam in her eyes, a gleam from time to time I've found to be attractive. But then she says, "I've been with what—twenty, thirty guys? I lost count but I know it's not a lot. I don't know if I ever loved any of them, but with you, I know for sure."

I want to squeeze the bridge of my nose. It never quite does anything, the squeezing. It doesn't clear my mind, doesn't ease any pain, but it's a good indication to others, like a signal for them to shut the fuck up.

I squeeze the bridge of my nose.

"My folks are in town next week," she goes on. "They're road-trippin' all the way from Pike County, Kentucky. They'll stay at my place, and…they'll like you, Chin. Once they get over the fact that you're a…you know." She half-props herself, head resting on her palm and eyes casting down on me. "If they can't get over it, then to hell with them, okay?"

I want to tell Cass she can't have a life with me because I'm unable to provide her even the slightest prosperity. Moreover, a girl might knock on my door one day and say, "Hi Dad." Maybe she'd pop me too, like what Cujo and Marla did to drug lord Dago, put sixteen bullets in me before jacking my stash, that is, assuming I'd have a stash of some kind at all. I know Cass means well but Christ, moving in with a woman is the last thing on my mind.

Gazing up at her, I want to tell her she doesn't know me. Doesn't know about the daughter I may or may not have. Doesn't know about the letter I received. Letter asking me for money.

Cass thinks she knows me, but no.

"I know you, Chin." She's touching my face. "You're a good man. You're quiet but you got this thing, this reservoir of energy, I can tell. I-I feel so safe with you."

I say nothing.

"Will you say something?" Her hand reaches me down there, and she plays.

I can't tell her about the daughter I may or may not have. Can't broach the subject after concealing it for so long. Can't just bring it up after the woman decides to move in with me. Things like that either has to be revealed right off the bat, or you forfeit the chance to tell it at all.

"Chin, I need to tell you something now. I don't want to find out about it later and question my motive." What she's doing, is telling me something unpleasant right off the bat. "I'm two months behind on my rent." A pause later she goes, "Your house, didn't you try to sell it a while back? You took if off the market, right?"

The house is worthless. Not a single person was interested in purchasing it.

"And your car, you—" She suddenly realizes and goes, "Shit, I'm sorry your car's gone. Listen, I could pay for groceries, it's the least I could do. And we split the utility bills and the property tax…" She stops with a sigh. "Look, Chin, I understand why you tried to sell the house, I mean, the demotion was devastating for all of us." She keeps stroking me and comforts, "Don't worry, I'm gonna take care of you, okay? That's what people do when they're in love." She kisses my shoulder. "Now tell me, what are you thinking?"

"I'm thinking…" *You don't know me. Therefore, you're not in love with me.*

"What is it?"

I'm thinking the letter I got from 'Nam, on the backside of it a picture was attached, a picture of six girls ages seven to nine, sitting in a sweatshop with a sewing machine. A girl manually operates the thing and the others sew sneakers by hand. I don't even know which one of the girls is supposed to be mine. Which one of the girls is asking me for money, money she claims is long overdue. The picture cropped four inches wide, in black and white. The picture I placed in my wallet. I…

I smack my face. *Fuck.*

Cujo jacked my wallet, and with it, the picture of the daughter I may or may not have.

"Chin? You okay?"

My *only* picture of her. More importantly, I copied her return address on the back of the photograph. *I need to get it back.*

I close my eyes and think fast. In order to get it

back I obviously must find Cujo and Marla. Instinctually, I recognize the inconsistencies from Grayson's story. My military mind cranks. I can't help it. Not after having served two tours in 'Nam, on a job consisting of finding people who didn't want to be found.

Cujo and Marla possess over a hundred kilos of cocaine, and today isn't their first rodeo. Then where's their take? Where's the drugs? They came up all the way from Los Angeles. That's six-hundred miles away. They have no car, that's why they wanted to jack mine. So how did they get to Abisko? Shit, did they fly? Where'd they put their stuff? A tenth of a ton, what, in a locker somewhere? It doesn't make sense.

"Chin?" Cass is stroking me vigorously. "You're gonna tell me you just realized how much you love me, or what?"

"I…" Struggling to sit up, I'm hating myself for losing the only picture of the girl who may or may not be my daughter. "I-I need to ask you something, Cass."

She continues to jerk me off. "Shoot."

Propping my back against the headboard, I'm hating myself for not knowing which of the girls in the picture is supposed to be mine.

I need to find Cujo and I need my picture back.

So I ask Cass, "You know where I can get the *LA Times* around here?"

Chapter Three

I borrow Cass's car, a Ford sedan with no glass in the windows, and drive to the high school. This time of night, the public library's closed, but the library at the high school is open. I get there and kids are studying, pulling all nighters, little lamps lit at their desks. Some even brought pillows. I recognize Jimbo's kid, Huck, in the study group. He notices me and waves before coming over. "Mr. Chin, I heard what happened at the bank. Thank you for preventing people from getting shot, including my dad."

"No one was gonna get shot, Huck." I peek over him to his peers; kids' heads buried in books. "Shouldn't you be out partying?"

"Plenty of time for that in college." Huck swivels back to his friends and then to me. "SAT's next Monday. It's our ticket out of here. Our one chance, gotta make it count." He shrugs but full of purpose. "We're prepping for the test. What you doing here, Mr. Chin?"

Grayson asked, *What the fuck you doing...here?*

Thinking about Cass moving in with me tomorrow, not paying rent but paying for groceries. Cass, who vows to take care of me. And me, a man not taking care of his daughter but apparently in need of being taken care of. I survey the library; feeling shitty and feeling lost. I ask Huck, "Point me to the news rack?"

The kid leads me to it and then tells me where to find the archives. I retrieve the *LA Times* from the past week, plus a map of California, and situate myself far from the group of high schoolers.

Amidst the crime section's usual smorgasbord, I identify the three incidents involving Cujo and Marla, leading up to today's event. First incident: the shooting in North Hollywood. Dago Ramirez shot dead, his coke all gone, presumably jacked by the lovebirds.

Second incident: a bank in a town called Maxwell is hit three days later; a suspect matching Cujo's description was seen fleeing with a girl matching Marla's description in a stolen vehicle. They made off with north of four thousand dollars. Now, the state's Bureau of Investigation is on the case at the request of the Attorney General, tagging along with the LAPD so Grayson would have jurisdiction across the state.

Third incident: a bank in a town called Bend is robbed two days later—that's two days before today. Witness said the bank robber was intense but at the same time, said "please" and "thank you," had his manners. An empty car exploded on the other side of town which distracted the law enforcement. The robbers made off with just south of five thousand this time.

Two days later, they're here in Abisko.

I study the map of California. Los Angeles—Maxwell—Bend—Abisko, the towns are on a line—the Interstate 5 freeway connects them from south to north. Roughly three hundred miles from LA to Maxwell, from there on the towns are spread one hundred miles apart, just about evenly. At this rate, they should be near Eugene, Oregon in another day or two. Cujo and

Marla, they didn't fly, that's for sure. No airports in these towns. Maybe they drove, but where's their car? If the Chinese guy didn't have a stroke, were they going to flee on foot? More importantly, where's their *stuff*? And I don't just mean the cocaine. Marla had full makeup. Girl like her needs change of clothes. So where she put 'em?

I figure there's one other way the duo traveled to Abisko.

That means they're staying somewhere for the night.

"Daddy," a girl studying with Huck calls. Her father is here to pick her up. Time to go home.

Daddy. The girl wrote me in the letter, *I work hard I no get money, Daddy*. She wrote the word *Daddy* a total of seven times. Calling me her daddy. *Please send money, Daddy*.

I don't have her picture and I don't have her return address. Don't have any money to send her. Some father I am.

I fold the papers on my desk and return them to the news rack. Before turning to leave, a headline catches my eye: *Chinese coed found dead in dorm; possible drug overdose*.

Girls in 'Nam working in sweatshops, Chinese coed doing drugs up in American dorm—is growing up in one place really better than the other? The dated news injects me with a dose of melancholy. A Chinese student drug overdosed. What a crying shame.

Thinking about the responsibilities of being a father, I head to the bus depot.

****

The Greyhound's schedule is posted next to the

29

ticket counter, and above the schedule are two headshots, one of Cujo and one of Marla—copies of the same pictures from Grayson's file. *Wanted* is in bold red letters below their pictures, with the description *armed and dangerous* and instructions to call 911 if sighted. The posters obviously were put just moments ago, I figure, at least an hour after Grayson and Reese arrived to town. Otherwise the two would've been spotted right away stepping off the bus—a black guy thug looking with a Latina hot as hell.

I study the schedule.

A bus to Eugene left sixty-minutes ago. Chances are the cops are on it. Grayson and Reese must've notified CHP—California Highway Patrol—to set up check points all along the interstate and *wanted* posters at every Greyhound stop north of Abisko. They have to contain this before the criminals cross the state line, before the case goes federal, involving USMS, FBI, DEA and whatnot, a joint task force turning a little manhunt into a clusterfuck.

But if the cops knew what I knew, if they knew about the criminals' lack of *stuff*, they wouldn't bother going north. I check the schedule again, a bus *south*bound to Sacramento, with stops in Bend and Maxwell, left one hour and thirty minutes ago. Between Bend and Abisko, there's only one stop. A town called Plum Creek in the next county. I'll bet my ass I won't find any plums twenty miles alongside any creek in Plum Creek, but I'm sure as shit that I'll find Cujo and Marla, and my wallet.

I get in Cass's Ford, wait in line, and fill up the gas. I pay five bucks worth of unleaded—only got ten bucks on me. I stand there thinking about Cass's parents coming to town next week. Thinking about not having to worry about paying for groceries. Splitting the bills and the property tax. Would that save me enough money to raise a kid?

The answer to my own question brings a lump of emptiness to my chest.

I head to Plum Creek.

Chapter Four

For thirty miles I'm listening to the cassette Cass has in the deck. Listening to Pete Seeger and John Fogerty tell me I shouldn't be in 'Nam. When I pull into Plum Creek I turn on the radio, and it's playing pretty much the same things. The music isn't bad if I ignore the lyrics. Just one of the things I learned to cope with after the war. I park outside a diner and go in to use the can, then I ask the waitress if there's a motel or inn in town. The blonde girl frowns at me as she would an unfamiliar animal at the zoo. I figure I should buy something to get on her good side so I order a cup of joe to go, hand over three bucks and tell her to keep the change. When I ask her again, where's the motel, she still looks at me weird. Only three hundred miles from San Francisco, three hundred miles from the largest Chinatown in America, people still giving me the look. "Turn left up ahead," she finally tells me. "We have a Courtside Inn. You ought to know, they check IDs."

I find the Courtside Inn and drive past it, heading to the southernmost part of town, passing no plums and seeing no creek. I find the local Greyhound stop, which is the Shell Oil station with a sign twenty feet high. I enter the station to inspect the schedule. A bus left thirty minutes ago to destination: Sacramento, which means thirty minutes ago Cujo and Marla disembarked. I take one last look around the station, satisfied there aren't any *wanted* posters of the lovebirds. I was right—Grayson and Reese went *north* for the hunt.

I return to the Courtside Inn.

A handful of passenger vehicles are parked out front, with a dozen or so eighteen-wheelers filling the lot. A popular spot for truckers to stop and rest. The parking lot reeks of urine and cigarette smoke. I enter the inn's lobby and it smells worse. A teenager is behind the front desk, head buried. I peek over the counter and find him doing a test, a kitchen timer next to him, counting down. The kid's on a practice run for his SAT—his ticket out of town.

I clear my throat and he finally raises his head, annoyed. His practice session's interrupted. I flash him the receipt slip from the gas station. "Major Chin with the seventy-fifth MP. At twenty-two hundred hours, you had an African American male and a Hispanic female returning—"

"Room 108," the kid gives it up at once. He darts a glance at his kitchen timer before turning back to the problem at hand. I catch his scratch paper. $F(x) = x/2$.

"The United States Army appreciates your coopera—"

"Hey man, beat it." He resumes his attempt to find X.

Before I go off to find Cujo and Marla, I mess with the kid. "The answer's C."

There's only one hall, odd room numbers facing the street, even numbers facing the east parking lot. I get to 108 and the door to 109 is wide open, a trucker with a beard of Merlin is chilling by the door, tattoos from his forearm up to his neck, looking like an ex-con. He's drinking Budweiser out of a can, the TV on in the background. He scans me up and down, then smirks. "About time you showed up."

Don't know what he's talking about, so I ignore him.

"I asked for a lady whore"—he scratches his nut sack—"but I reckon you'll do."

Now I see what this is, so I respond to the guy, staring at the swastika tat by his throat, "Why don't you ask for a pig, so you won't dilute your inferior gene pool." I turn my back to him and knock on door 108, not hearing anything inside.

The trucker comes up behind me and swings me around as if I weigh nothing. "Let's go to my room and have some fun, what do you say? I had a long day, man. We can order some porno, or we can watch HBO. *Cable*, you heard of it? It's paid for. That's right, ten extra bucks I put down, I tell ya—"

"Listen dickwad, you're confusing me with someone who gives a fuck." I turn and keep knocking on 108.

"You can't turn your back on me." The trucker swings me back again and slams me against the door. "You stupid chink, who do you think you are?"

Strangely, I'm thinking about being a father. What if I was here with my daughter, and we ran into an asshole who insulted us? What would my daughter expect me to do? I think she'd want me to walk away. Be the bigger person. So I say to the trucker, "Listen, man, I'm just gonna walk away."

"You listen to *me*, I tasted boys like you in Lompoc." He takes a swig of his beer and he smacks his lips. Leaning in closer, his belly touches mine. "You little Asian punk ass chinks with your little tight assholes, I'll have you lick the hair off my ass crack, you hear? Ching chong cheeky-dee chink—"

Enough of this monkey shit so I knee him in his groin, then I kick his nut sack with the tip of my boot. My foot didn't even touch the ground for the one-two combo. Hitting below the belt is a bitch move but it's totally acceptable in life-or-death combat, or in situations involving lowlifes. I think my daughter would approve.

Now, the trucker dude's eyes are bulging, like he can't believe it, yet he still mutters, "Fuckin' chink." He drops his beer can on the motel carpet and hunches over. I wait for his head to lower a couple more degrees, wait for him to face me—for that perfect angle. Then I raise my right hand past my head, elbow forward, and ram it on the bridge of his nose. *Whack!* I feel the trucker dude's bone shatter upon impact.

It's called *Sok Sab*, or chopping elbow—a Muay Thai move I picked up from a fellow in Saigon. The trucker falls to the ground, hands over his nose and screaming in pain. I figure the guy's lucky I only cracked his nose. One time in 'Nam I saw a man *Sok Sab* a bastard and split his skull open. *Whack!* killed a man like that. Muay Thai sure don't fuck around.

"Ahh, my nose!"

My elbow feels like it bounced off of cardboard.

"Hey, quiet back there!" The trucker still screams and a voice from the lobby cuts above him, "Will you shut the fuck up!"

It's the teenager doing his SAT. His practice run is interrupted yet again and he sounds super stressed out. Now I feel sorry for the kid. I figure he should at least do his test in peace, same as Huck and his friends at the library in Abisko, making the most out of their chance to get out of town, so I proceed to drag the piece of trash back to his room.

At the same time, door 108 opens, finally. Cujo standing there in his underwear—a bright orange pair—looks like he's already calling it a night. He recognizes me and steps back, face distorted to a *what the hell?* expression, perfectly flabbergasted. The next second he's retreating, the way he's blinking fast tells me he's thinking about fleeing the inn.

"Put it out of your mind, Cujo. I found you and I will find you again. You fuck with the seventy-fifth, you fuck with the best, you know that shit. Now what I need you to do is to help me drag this Nazi piece of trash back to his room, and that's an order, soldier."

"Major? What the fuck?" Cujo's back to being flabbergasted because he's just noticed the man on the ground. The man's face is bloody; his hands switching from his nose to his crotch, unable to make up his mind as to which needs more tender loving care. Cujo steps across him and helps me drag out the trash, asking, "Why'd you kung fu his ass?"

"He called me chink."

"Shit, man, I thought it was your nickname."

"It is, but not the way he said it." After we dump the trash, we exit the room. I close the door, muffling his screams. "The way he said it wasn't meant as an identification, but as an insult."

"What's going on out here?" Marla appears in a bra and panties, black and black. I glance sideways at Cujo. *Lucky bastard.* She points at me and asks her man, "What's he doing here?"

"Miss Marla..." I step up to this monstrously good-looking creature. Instead of asking for my wallet back—the reason I'm here—the first thing out of my mouth is, "Did you shoot your dad?"

Chapter Five

In the seedy motel room, door closed and chained, I stand. The two are sitting. Cujo convinces me they're not armed. "I only got one gat, major. The Colt I stole from the army. They never asked me for it back. MPs busy rounding up grenades and landmines in the jungle, you know how it was. You saw that chink took my piece when he jacked us—my only piece. We're defenseless civilians, man. Like I said I'm sorry 'bout your car. But it wasn't my fault. Hell, not all of it."

"Relax." I heave a sigh. I figure the guy's telling the truth. If there was a gun between the two of them it'd be in my face by now. "I'm not here to harm you and I'm not here to turn you in. I just want my wallet back"—I glance at Marla—"and perhaps ask you some questions."

Cujo returns my wallet telling me he spent all of my money on bus tickets. I dismiss the deficit, satisfied the dainty picture is in the compartment where I left it—perfectly intact, and the return address remains legible. With mindful care, I tuck it away. Marla relates that my colleagues' wallets were in the money bag. Lost to the guy I believe to be Chinese.

The TV is on mute, a chair is in front of it, so I grab a seat opposite the two. Soon as I do, Marla rises and says she needs a robe. She turns around and I glance at the thong flossing her butt. A butt one could bury his face in and call it a sweet, sweet life. Seconds later she comes back decent from the bathroom, and sits with her legs crossed. She smells of cheap soap, but she smells fine.

I inquire, "So which one of you shot Dago, Marla's dad?"

They exchange frowns and Cujo says, "You talked to cops?"

"LAPD detective and a state agent, they're on your case. The detective came all the way up, must've been chasing your tails since Dago got shot. You hit Maxwell, Bend and then Abisko, they figured out the pattern and headed north toward Eugene."

"Well, how'd *you* find us?" Then he says, "Never mind, you was MP... *Shit*." As in, he knows he's done for. "Not just any MP unit. Drill sergeant told us on our first day, 'Make a mistake and the seventy-fifth will fuck you up and then your mama'." The guy's legs jitter. "I'm really sorry about your car, major. Listen, I'll boot you a new one if that's what you want."

"Forget about the car." And I ask again, "Which one of you shot DR?"

Marla springs up. "He was my father." She looks at me, her eyes ablaze.

"Forgive me, miss. But that doesn't answer my question."

"We didn't shoot him. None of us did." Her arms fold, and she looks nervous as she speaks fast, "I came home and found his body all shot up, just all shot up and messed up. Saw he lay there on the couch with his eyes open. Something—someone, took him by surprise. I didn't know what do to so I asked Cujo to come over. Then I don't know who called the cops, maybe the neighbor or somebody. We heard the sirens and Cujo said we had to bail. Now you listen to me—whatever your name is—he was my father, you get that? He raised me and maybe we weren't close, but he was my father and I loved him."

She loved him.

For a father's sake, I breathe a sigh of relief. Then I ask her, "Where's your gun?" just to make sure once again.

She tells me she doesn't have one. Only one gun between Cujo and her, and now it's gone.

I let my head bob for a bit and I'm looking at the picture behind the two, right above the headboard. A painting of palm trees by a sandy beach, scenery folks expect to see when they're in California. But around here, in reality, only a painting. "All right," my eyes move back to Marla, "I believe you."

"You do?" Cujo sounds surprised.

"Well, most of it." I look at the painting again, inhale, exhale, then back at Cujo. "I believe that the M1911 is all you got, and your weapon holds seven plus one. Assuming you had seven bullets in the mag and one in the chamber, that's eight total. But let's say you were furious and fired a second clip, that'd be eight plus seven, *fifteen* bullets in all, fifteen bullets at the *most*. How could you possibly put *sixteen* holes in the guy? You didn't do it." I shake my head. "You couldn't have."

Cujo's eyes are rolling in his sockets as he thinks it over. "Yes...yes! Ha-ha!" He jumps to his feet, clapping his hands. "What I tell you, Marla? The seventy-*fifth*. The man here just, uh, ex-ex..." he snaps his fingers, "what's the word? Ex-what? Help me out here."

I help him out. "Exonerate?"

"Yes, exonerated us!" Cujo basking in victory, looks like he's ready to call the cops and clear his name.

I turn to Marla. Thinking about the daughter I may or may not have, I say to her, "I believe you loved your father enough not to kill him."

She bites her lip and shifts her eyes away to keep in tears.

"Loved him enough not to kill him, but not enough not to *rob* him." My eyes move from the girl to Cujo. "Where's the money you got from selling his cocaine?"

"What—" Cujo's ass hits the mattress. "You know about the cocaine?"

"It's why you bailed the crime scene, isn't it? You took his cocaine."

"Shit, man, it wasn't my idea." Cujo shakes his head nonstop. "Marla told me where her old man stashed his drugs. Told me what it's worth on the street. The woman tempted me."

"If we left it there the cops would've taken it." Marla backslaps Cujo on his thigh. "But it was *you* who just *had* to boot a flashy BMW."

Rubbing his thigh, Cujo explains, "Coming around selling crack, your ride has to look legit."

"*You* in a BMW, in LA?"

"What you know, woman?"

Now the two are going into it. Marla saying they should've booted a Volvo or some low-key domestic. Cujo saying, *Negative, it had to be stick-shift and no front license plate*. Marla inquires, *Why, to throw off the cops*? No, *woman*, Cujo explaining, *it had to be that way or else it would affect the aerodynamic in a getaway or a drive-by, you dig?* Marla speaking Spanish, *Asshole, what we gotta do drive-by for?* Cujo shrugging, *dunno, it's what people do, in the hood.* Marla berates, *No wonder you were called New Thugs on the Block, LLC, might as well be called Virgins Looking to get Fucked, Inc.*

"Let me get this straight," I interject. "You two made off with a stash of cocaine, stole a nice BMW and drove down to South Central Los Angeles—a place known as the *hood*—intending to distribute, and lost the *car*?"

"Dr. Martin Luther King Boulevard, man, always some crime going down on MLK, yeah." Cujo licks his lips as if too much talking is making him dry. "Homeboys cruise down MLK, they either get popped or somebody grand theft auto their ride. In our case, a fine automobile filled with crack."

Looking at this poster boy for birth control, I wonder why the army discharged his dumbass prematurely, saving his life. Now he's doing more damage on home turf. I turn to Marla, wondering what she sees in him. "Let me guess," I take a stab, "the stash belongs to somebody, and that somebody is bad news. That somebody is on your tails unless you pay him back. That's why you're robbing banks?"

"Yeah, a cartel dude found us," Cujo admits. "Said we owed him thirty G's, yo. Said it's only a fraction of what it's worth. We had 'til the end of the month to pay up, or else it's hasta la vista for us. And now? Shit"—slapping his forehead—"now the cops are onto us. What we supposed do? Thirty grand…"

"Pay them back 'til the end of the month?" I recall

today's date. "Christ, that's next Monday. Today's *Friday*."

"We'd be halfway there if it weren't for that chink with the stroke." Cujo looks up at me, apologizing, "My bad, major, I mean no disrespect—"

"None taken." To Marla, "Can you tell me more about this man representing the cartel, the man who's making you pay?"

Cujo starts, "Man, I'm telling you—"

"Please," to Marla again, "I want to hear your take."

She uncrosses her legs and crosses them the other way. "Mexican," she tells me. "Short, stocky but good looking, drives a low-key Pontiac." A disdained glance at Cujo. "He's clean-shaven and nicely dressed—a *real* gangster." Another stab at Cujo. "He goes by the name Mad Dog."

"*Mad* Dog? Isn't that what Cujo means?"

"It is?" Cujo folds his arms. "Whatever, man, he ain't gonna find us. We a thousand miles from LA."

"Five hundred seventy miles. You seriously think he's not going to find you?"

"We've been dropping bread crumbs," Marla, well-aware of the deep-shit they're in, says. "Plus the bank jobs' been in the papers. He'll figure out where to look for us. Just like the cops. Just like you did." She looks at me.

I make eye contact with her and I can't help but feel sympathetic. "Why didn't you just hit one bank? Organize it well, hit it and quit it."

"That's what we was gonna do," Cujo says. "The first bank only had four thousand. That was it."

"You mean there was only four thousand in the

cash drawers. Why didn't you look in the vault?"

"*Vault*? What vault?"

So he doesn't know. Probably doesn't have a bank account. Probably never set foot inside a financial institution of any kind before he robbed one.

Thinking about the kids taking their SATs, making it count, I tell these two, "If I were you, I'd hit *one* bank and make it count."

"Yeah? How would you pull it off?"

"How should I know?" I stand up. "Marla, any idea who killed your father?"

She shakes her head.

"How about the cartel guy, Mad Dog, you think he's a suspect?"

"I thought about it, but then, why didn't he move the inventory?"

"How well did your father stash it?"

She thinks about it, a small glimmer of intelligence in her eyes. She's thinking about the possibilities, going back to the crime scene. Was the place trashed? Anything unusual about the air? How many people could've been there? "Maybe he looked for it but couldn't find it?" Adding, "It's a maybe."

A nod. "So where's the money from your previous robberies?"

She hesitates. "It's somewhere safe."

"Not here?"

She says nothing. Doesn't even blink. At which point Cujo reveals, "Even I don't know where she hid it. Afraid I was gonna spend it on dope."

"Cujo, you want some free advice? You should just let *her* rob the bank." Hearing the guy say, *yeah, uh-huh, what?* I go on, "And you shouldn't call her *woman* in a derogatory way."

"Derogatory? It's what she is. She a woman, ain't she?" He checks her out as if making sure.

"You may call her *woman* for identification purposes only. Someone asks you, 'Who's Marla?' You say, 'She's that woman with the fine ass.' *Woman* is used for ID-ing purpose, as well as *fine ass*. Nothing wrong with that. You say, 'Woman, know your fucking place,' that becomes a derogatory usage—an insult. And the same applies for me. You may say, 'Major Chin? He's that chink working at the bank.' And that's fine. You tell me to go back to where I come from, stupid chink, you and I will have a serious problem."

"Man, ain't nobody using no racial slurs against me 'less he from the hood, you feel me?"

"Cujo," a quick sigh and I tell him, "you'd do well to know that words are neutral by themselves. They're not harmful, they don't have feelings—slurs or not— they're just *words*. It's the person conveying the words and the way he or she says it that hurts us." I study him and I don't think he's listening. Instead he's trying to sneak a peek past me.

"Yo, is that the bank from today?"

I turn around and I'm staring at the TV. "Cujo, turn it up."

The volume increases and an anchorwoman sitting behind the desk is talking about today's holdup, a little picture of the bank cropped next to her head. She tells the time and place of the incident, nothing we don't already know, then she informs viewers, "According to the branch manager, the estimated loss is upwards of seven thousand dollars."

"Wait"—Cujo springs up—"*how* much?"

The camera cuts to an anchorman. "Luckily no one was hurt today."

The anchorwoman says, "Thank God."

"What the hell?" Cujo cusses at the TV. "Seven thousand, my *ass*." He throws the remote at the screen, missing it. "Those bags were *light*. There was two, three grand at *most*."

Cujo's right. I'm thinking, Ester must be counting the dye pack. Why would she do that? What is she up to?

The thug is cussing non-stop. Marla just shrugs. "What's it matter? We got hijacked and we ended up with *nada*. What's it matter how much they say we took?"

"Woman, will you shut your stupid mouth!"

To this I stand up and order, "You need to calm the fuck down, soldier."

Cujo's eyes cast downward. He says nothing.

"Marla's right. It doesn't matter how much they say you took. So put it out of your mind." I pick up the remote and turn off the TV. The room is quiet. And I'm wondering what the hell am I still doing here. I already have what I came here for, why do I linger? I turn to the door and I say nothing.

I just leave.

****

I walk past the lobby of the Courtside Inn, and the teenager preparing for his SAT at the front desk calls me, "Hey mister, wait up." As I'm wondering if the trucker made a complaint of some sort, the kid inquires, "How did you know the answer was C?"

That breaks my stride. Curious, I approach the front desk. "I got it right?"

46

"Well, no, actually"—he shows me his practice exam—"The answer's B, X equals twenty five point three."

Perplexed, I ask the kid, "What was your question again?"

"How did you know the answer was C? I mean, you took one glance at my test and said 'The answer's C.' You done the calculation."

I read his nametag, "*Dangerous.* Your name's Dangerous?"

"Middle name. Call me Shawn."

"Shouldn't it be *Danger,* a noun, and not an adjective?" Confused more than ever, I say to the kid, "You know what? Never mind, Shawn. I don't know what you want from me. I got it wrong."

"But"—he eyes me over—"you're Asian. You're supposed to be good at math. Please, mister, I *got* to do well on my SAT. You don't understand, I *cannot* spend the rest of my life in this miserable inn. Will you just explain this function to me?" He sounds so desperate.

I want to depart but then I remember Cass is in my home, in my bed, smoking cigarettes. Cass telling me she wants to spend the rest of her life with me, in Abisko, California. Wanting me to tell her that I love her. Telling me her parents will be in town next week, and they'll like me, once they get over the fact that I'm a...you know. *A what?* Shit.

I feel like I'm at a crossroad. I could settle down with Cass but if I don't, I should be out there providing for my daughter. Daughter or Cass, it's one way or the other. One thing's for sure though, I don't want to go home. Not tonight. I need time alone to contemplate some very important life decisions. So I turn around and to the kid I say, "You got a vacancy?"

He's taken aback as if the question were preposterous. Vacancy? As opposed to what—full? In Plum Creek Courtside Inn?

I figure if Abisko is halfway through its death rattle, Plum Creek must be on life support, hanging by a tiny thread. "Tell you what, Dangerous Shawn, I'll help you with that function problem and you give me a room for two dollars cash. I'll make the room before I leave. Maids and manager won't even know I was here." I'm thinking, I have the car so Cass will have to walk to work tomorrow morning. Tough.

The kid hands over a key card and I hand over two dollar bills. The kid asks, "Where you from, mister?" expecting somewhere exotic.

"I'm from Abisko," I reply, disappointing him.

"Oh, I'm taking the SAT there on Monday."

I sit beside him and study his practice exam, keeping my end of the bargain. F of X...looks pretty difficult. "Okay," I mutter, "So do five times nine here..."

And Shawn mutters his times table like a grade-shooler, "one-five five, two-five ten, three-five fifteen..." He gets to nine and writes it down. "Hey, don't judge. Sometimes the oldest trick in the book is what works. Now what do I do next? Square root it?"

We keep at it for a little while.

Then, sirens blare in the distance.

I tense up right away. *Shit*. The cops figured it out? I peek down the hall, Marla, Cujo... The sirens increase, then stop outside the motel. Blue and red lights flashing bright. My eyes are fixed at the front entrance. I expect to see a SWAT team burst through the door or hear a bullhorn order the suspects to come out with their hands behind their heads, or else get shot. However, there's no SWAT and no bullhorn, two paramedics in uniform rush inside and ask us at the front desk, "Room 109, which way?"

The kid points down the hall.

109? That's where the trucker with the broken nose lies. The bastard called for an ambulance?

"We should see what's going on." Shawn sighs as he closes his book and then withdraws a walkie-talkie from around his waist. Pressing a button, "We got a possible 641." To me, he explains, "Sex for one— Masturbation overdose. 109 just ordered porn."

Thought he got HBO.

"He got *Big Cock in Little Bangkok.* Hardcore stuff."

"Jesus Christ."

Shawn and I catch up to the paramedics. The kid shouts, "No, don't break the door, I got a master key." He unlocks the door and the paramedics rush in. Behind us, door to 108 opens and Cujo, once again standing there in his bright orange underwear, is peeking at the fuss, bewildered. "Major, you still here?" Peering across the corridor, he says, "Oh shit, that the trucker you kung fu'd, right?"

Now Shawn's gazing up at me like he's right, like saying, yeah you, funky Chinaman from funky Chinatown, you're good at math *and* you know kung fu. Kid thinks stereotyping is the way to go.

"It's Muay Thai." But what difference does it make?

The paramedics set the trucker on a stretcher. A *stretcher* for a broken nose, here, in the home of the brave. In 'Nam when your leg got blown off you just hopped on one foot until you got to safety. In California, your nose gets broken and you call in the medic to carry you out on a goddamn stretcher. No wonder the communists kicked our asses. Now, the trucker's coming out I hide in Cujo's room, hearing the guy yelling, "Where's that oriental cocksucker?"

The paramedics carry his heavy-ass away. I step to the hallway and Cujo nudges me. "See that, major? Now *there's* a man with good medical coverage."

Then something hits me. To the kid Shawn, I inquire, "When and where you say's the SAT?"

"Abisko," Shawn says. "It's next Monday."

"Tell me, Cujo..." I turn to the thug. "How'd you know to set a fire to distract the cops?"

"For real? It's one of the oldest tricks in the book. It works, don't it?"

"Oldest trick..." I mutter, and then I think, there may be a way to make it count...

Chapter Six

I rise at 0500 and check out after I make the bed and do the wash. I drive back to Abisko in Cass's Ford, praying the remaining fuel in the tank will be enough.

A head-on collision on the Interstate 5 delays my ETA. When I get to town the fuel indicator light comes on and the bank's already open. No money to replenish the gas. No time to change into my work attire. In three years I've never been late. I figure being punctual is more important than being dressed properly, so I head to work in my blue jeans and a shirt with three buttons and no collar.

Still, I'm ten minutes late. Everyone is at their stations when I arrive; Jim at his desk sharpening a pencil, Cass at her window, licking her thumb and counting money, an old lady customer is facing her, apparently making a cash deposit in dollar bills.

"Where were you last night?" Cass stops counting and asks me. "I called the high school library and people said you left. I almost called the cops again."

"Thought I could find the bank robbers so I gave it a shot." I move to my station and place the plaque with my name on the counter. "It got late, I stayed at a motel."

"Chin, I know you can take care of yourself, but do let me know next time, okay?" Then she asks as I returns her car key. "So you got your car back?"

"My car was taken by a different robber."

"Well, it's parked in the back."

"What"—a double take to make sure she isn't joking—"it is?"

"It was there when I showed up this morning. If it wasn't you then it must've been returned here sometime last night."

Sure it's mine? Curious, I exit the building and go around the back and there it is. Front row and center, and it appears to have gotten a wash. The key dangles from the door. I sit myself in and adjust the helm. The passenger seat is still red from the dye pack explosion, but the windshield and the dash have been cleaned, best as possible. Traces of pink still cling here and there, a softer shade of red.

I turn the ignition and let the engine rev, making sure it works. It does, and to my surprise, the tank's full. Guy jacks my car, returns it the next day with a full tank. Honestly, how can I complain? I pull the key and return to my station, asking Cass, "You see who dropped it off?"

"No, but couldn't have been the cops, right? Cop would've dropped it off at your place, and I was at your place all night. It's a mystery but I'm glad you got it back, because now you can help me move-in."

An old-timer enters and it's back to work as usual. The old-timer is one of our few regular customers, goes by Buzz, a WWII veteran who lost his hearing. He thinks I'm Vietnamese, a refugee from the war. The first time he talked to me he asked me *how are things back at home?* I told him I'm from here. He said it must be hard with the war and all. I told him I fought in the war. Then he asked me, which side?

My next customer is a granny by the name of June. June bug likes to come in and deposit her coins into her savings account, coins ranging in the amount of five bucks to fifty cents. One time she came in with a whopping ten dollars. And then, she'll come in the next day to withdraw what she deposited the day before. Cass says it's folks like June that keep the bank busy, so we still have jobs. I don't argue. I reckon she's right.

From inside the bank, I spot a sheriff's Grand Fury cruising by, and then there it is again after a few minutes, heading in the opposite direction. Sometime later, I see it again. The bank's being monitored, no doubt. But what for? I turn to Cass. "Sheriff thinks we're gonna get hit again?"

"They're tightening security details on us." She looks out to the door, watching the street, which is empty now.

"Just because we got robbed yesterday doesn't mean we're gonna get robbed again, today."

"Well…we did get robbed *twice* yesterday."

As the morning wears on, some customers visit us just to inquire about the robbery and how the losses will be covered. We assure these folks that their money is safe. No, the bank won't take it out on their customers. Never. The bank is covered by Federal Deposit Insurance Corporation, otherwise known as FDIC.

It's Saturday so we're closing at noon, which is only two minutes away. I see the cop car again and after it passes, the guy who pretended to have a stroke yesterday, enters.

How do I know it's him? He's the only other Asian I've ever seen in this town.

He doesn't look as old as he sounds, fifty-five at

most, hard lines on his face but his skin isn't sagging. He's wearing khakis today, grease spots here and there, resembles someone who works at a restaurant. He surveys the bank and just stands around. Not approaching us, not engaging anyone. Then he stares at me, and I keep eye contact. In this weird moment, wordless, two messages pass between us. From me to him: *I know you from yesterday.* From him to me: *I know you know.*

I become aware there are more eyes falling on me: Cass and Jim. I know what they're thinking, their small minds wondering, *Is the guy related to me?*

My hand touches the alarm button.

At the same time, Ester, the branch manager comes out of her hole and disrupts the trance. "Everyone, in my office, please, I have an urgent matter to—" Then she sees the Chinese dude standing there. "I'm sorry, I didn't know we still had a customer. How can we help you, sir?"

The guy gives Ester a wave, grinning at me. Then he turns and exits the building, all quiet, walking a perfect walk. The whole time, no words leave his mouth.

Ester directs her eyes to me. "Who's he?"

I watch the guy until he's lost to sight before I let go of the alarm button. Like everyone expects, I say, "My uncle?" but with a question mark. *Just who the hell is that guy?*

"Visiting from out of town? How nice." Not wasting a second, the boss lady beckons, "I don't have time, so c'mon everyone, there's an urgent matter we need to discuss."

As we hustle to the back office, Cass keeps

frowning at me. I avoid her eyes and put the stranger out of my mind for now.

In the branch manager's office, Cass and Jimbo sit opposite Ester. I stand against the wall because all the seats are taken.

Ester begins, "As you know, after yesterday's incident I'm required to file a claim with FDIC." She pauses as if for effect. Cass and Jim nod and she goes on, "I spent the entire morning tallying the losses and came to the conclusion that we've been robbed of six thousand seven hundred and thirty two dollars."

Jim nods in his chair, but Cass is shaking her head nonstop. I know what she's thinking: *That is* triple *the estimate.* I reckon Cujo robbed us of two to three grand. I know roughly how much was in my register, and Cass knows how much was in hers. How on earth did Ester come up with over six grand?

But I don't say anything, however, Cass turns from me to the boss and leans forward. "Are you out of your fucking mind, Ester? You think I don't know what you're doing?"

Ester sits back. "What am I doing, Cassandra?"

She scoffs, not even looking at her. "You're ripping off our *bank*."

"Technically, it's not just me, it's *us*, not ripping off *our* bank, but ripping off the FDIC."

"You're gonna *over*-report it by *four* thousand dollars and pocket the difference!"

Jim points out, "That's one thousand for the each of us, correct? It's an even split."

Ester nods twice.

And I'm thinking, *Goddamn you, Ester. One thousand the best you can do?*

To my delight, Jim asks her the same question that's on my mind. "Is that the most you can over-declare to the FDIC?"

Ester replies as if she rehearsed the answer to this exact question, "The vault was never opened, James. I can't declare more than what we lost outside the vault. What I'm doing is claiming our foreign currency reserve, which we just happen to keep outside. What I'm saying is that they robbed us of two thousand seven hundred, as well as four thousand worth of foreign currencies."

The loan officer closes his eyes and nods a couple of times. No doubt thinking the same thing I'm thinking. *One grand—shit, is it worth the risk?*

Finally, Jim opens his eyes. "I'll take it."

I'll take it too. One thousand isn't enough to raise a child but I'll take whatever I can. Better than nothing, that's for sure.

"*Jim*, don't"—Cass turns her whole body to face him—"this is like, I don't know, *embezzlement?* We'd lose our jobs and we'd do time!"

"No we won't. Stick to our story and no one has to know, which I'm guessing is why we're here." Jim loosens his tie. "Look, Cassandra, Huck is going to college next year, and his grades, you know, they aren't good enough for a scholarship. I'm already knee-deep in debts, and with the second mortgage...plus, we all got hit with a pay-cut a while back. I could use the help."

"This is an opportunity," presents Ester. "The economy the way it is..."

"No, I will *not*." Cass stomps her foot, absolutely determined.

Ester looks from Jim to her, not bothering to look at me. She heaves a long and heavy sigh. "Cassandra, I'm retiring, could be as early as next year. I'd like to recommend you to take my place as the manager of this branch."

Cass tilts her head, creasing her neck and her forehead. "You're bribing me?"

"Cassandra…" Jim pleads, "Ester and I, we have children. You don't know how that is, but when you're a parent you'd do anything for your child. If you won't do it for yourself, then do it for us, for Huck, please…"

To this Cass scoffs and gets up. "Do what you want, split it two-ways, just leave me and Chin out of it." Now she's speaking for me.

I wonder if I tell Cass I have a daughter, would she reconsider?

"If we do this, it has to be the four of us." Ester rises from her seat, hands on the table. "It has to be *unanimous*, or we don't do this at all."

"Good." Cass moves to the exit. "C'mon Chin, let's help me move."

"Wait." Jim grabs my wrist before I get to the door. "What's your opinion, Chin? You haven't said anything."

Cass turns to study me. The green gleam in her eyes is at its max. This girl who loves me and has said she'd take care of me. I have to change her mind.

But here is not the place.

So I'm looking at Cass as I tell Jim, "If it has to be *unanimous* and one of us already disapproved, then what does it matter what *I* say?"

Cass grabs, yanks and drags me out of the office, out of the building. Behind us, we hear Easter shouting,

"Just think about it! I have until Monday to contact FDIC. Just think about it, please!"

****

Saturday afternoon, I'm helping Cass move her stuff into my house. It's happening whether I like it or not. Her stuff's all packed in cardboard boxes. She tells me they're just her clothes and the essentials—hair styling products, marijuana paraphernalia, rock and roll records, etc. She's leaving behind her furniture and her kitchenware, for when her folks come to stay next week.

"Can you believe what Ester asked us to do?" She's carrying a box marked *feminine product* to her car. Jesus Christ, a box full. "To be complicit in a scam so full of holes, what was she *thinking*?"

I'm walking alongside her, carrying a box and trying not to wonder what's inside. I ask her kind of curious, "When did you pack? I thought you only decided to move in with me last night."

She ignores my question like she didn't hear it. "I mean, can you imagine what if the cops catch the robbers? What if they can't find the extra four thousand? What if the FDIC launches an investigation on *us*?"

Her car's already full so we stack the boxes in the trunk of mine. "It wouldn't matter." I figure now's a good time to persuade her for a change of heart. "Actually Cass, I thought about the details. If Ester worked out the same problems I have, the FDIC would be convinced enough not to question us."

"What problems?" She turns to me from the trunk of the car, a hand on her waist. "What details?"

"Details of the fiction." I try to close the trunk but

the boxes are too large for the lock to engage. "First, as Ester said, it has to be unanimous, and all four of us need to stick to our story to the grave." I give the hatch another push but it does no good. So I just leave it be. "Second, I know for a fact that a dye pack exploded." I point to the passenger seat where traces of red dye still remains. "That would make a large portion of the money unaccounted for. I mean, who's to say the robbers didn't just dump the tainted cash? Scattered it in the wind and onto the wasteland?"

"Listen to yourself"—now two hands are clutching at her waist—"you're saying it's a good idea, what they're proposing?"

"Honestly? It's not a *bad* idea. Not terrible." I think she might be coming around.

"I'm not gonna do it, Chin. Nothing to do with how well the plan works out or not. I'm not gonna do it because it's simply the wrong thing to do."

I reckon it isn't going to do any good to press her. Time's what it will take to change her mind, so I decide to let the matter rest till tomorrow.

After our cars are stuffed we drive to my house for the unloading. We unload her car first and she tells me I'm free to unpack for her, go through her stuff. We're living together now and she has nothing to hide. There are still miscellaneous items remaining at her place so she drives back to collect them on her own, leaving me at my fortress of solitude with my last minutes of bachelorhood freedom. I make several trips from my car to the house, and after my last trip I go to the mailbox to fetch the last deliveries of the week. Only two things in the box, an ad for tires, and a letter postmarked from Vietnam.

A letter I know to be from a girl who may or may not be my daughter.

As I'm walking back up my driveway, holding the letter unopened, a sense of dread overcomes me. At the same time, a Pontiac sedan enters the neighborhood and stops by where I stand, blocking the entrance of my driveway.

A short dude, Hispanic, emerges from the car. Sharply dressed, all black, with gator hide for boots. He approaches and stops six feet away. A scar is visible, from below his left ear to his upper lip. A gangster all right, the type who hustled on the street when he was young but nowadays calls the shots on deals at least five figures large. He flaps his jacket and reveals a shoulder holster and a black pistol grip—a Beretta M9, I peg.

His expression isn't one of a happy camper. He asks me, "Where's my fucking money?"

Chapter Seven

I'm standing in my driveway, the guy's car blocking the entrance, and he demands, "The money, go get it now. Don't waste my time."

The guy's short, and appears even shorter on the lower incline of the driveway, but there's nothing small about his voice. His demeanor and expression pack serious weight, not to mention the Beretta tucked under his arm.

"Those are some nice boots." I gesture with the envelope in my hand. "Louisiana gator or Florida?"

"Tabasco, Mexico," he conveys with an emphasis on the *M* in Mexico. "Now, the money," he demands, with that *M* sound again.

"I think you've made a *mi*stake." I put a hand in my pocket, just to relax. And the guy's hand goes inside his jacket.

Not pulling the gun, he just orders, "Hands where I can see them."

I do as he says, turning my empty pocket inside-out in the process so he knows I'm not packing heat. "Easy there," my palms facing out, "you're not gonna shoot an unarmed man, not right here, are you? Not in this quiet neighborhood. Not on this sunny day. You're in California, why don't you chill out and enjoy the weather?"

"Where are the palm trees?" He surveys the area

and then his eyes fix onto me. "This isn't California. Southern Oregon is more like it. They must've fucked it up when they drew the state line."

"The country line too, for that matter." Still trying to act relaxed, I shoot the shit after a steady exhale, "Say, Mad Dog, how's the weather in Mexico?"

"You know who I am, and you want to stand there and jerk me off? Talk about the weather in Mexico?" This time he pronounced it like *Meh-hee-co*.

"I told you, you made a mistake. Let me venture a guess what Cujo said: a Chinese guy ripped them off in Abisko?"

A nod. "Precisely."

"And there goes the extent of his story telling ability. Listen, Mad Dog, I'm not that Chinese guy. It wasn't me who ripped you off."

"There's only one chink in town. How do you think I found you? 'Where's the chink?' 'He lives that way.' Easy. No one said anything about a second chink."

"I think the *other* chink is just passing through."

"Please, there aren't chinks dumb enough to settle here. Crossing the Pacific for this shit? Emigrate from a third world toilet to a third world latrine? Look at this place, it looks fucking condemned." He pulls out his gun, and from his inner pocket he extracts a silencer, taking his sweet time. He examines the tube, using a sleeve to make it shine. Then he looks through it like it's a scope and blows a breath in—what is he, making sure it isn't blocked by anything? Like what, specks of dust?

Finally appearing satisfied, he attaches the silencer, making the 9mm into a BFG—a big fucking gun—its barrel length at least six cunt-hair long. He points it at my eye level, then at my feet.

He fires.

"Jesus Christ." I jump back. He missed my foot by a couple of inches. "The hell's the matter with you?"

He squeezes the trigger again. *Phut.* Delicate smoke rises two inches from my little toe. The bullet didn't ricochet, it went right in the sun-baked pavement. 9mm *si vis para bellum*, messing up my driveway, preparing for war. *Phut. Phut.* Two more shots. Now I just stand there refusing to dance like a monkey at the shootings. And the truth is, my reflex has given up. I'm unarmed and I can't dodge bullets. If he wants to kill me right here and right now, there's nothing I can do about it. Jumping around would only fuel his amusement.

So I stand at ease, and I'm thinking about the last thing I want to do before I die. In this particular moment, I'm pretty sure the last thing I want to do is read the contents of the letter in my hand. The letter from Vietnam. Then what am I waiting for? I break the seal and withdraw a piece of paper from the envelope, right in front of the gunman shooting at me, I read the letter.

"Hey you fucking chink," Mad Dog inquires. "What are you reading?"

"Something called none of your business." I don't bother to look at him.

The first word on the page is *Daddy*, in a familiar child's hand is written, *Ma canna work because mans say she too old. I work hard and hard and boss white man like me very long time. I too hungry to Ma sold me for ten thousand American dollars. I home is now factory to I work. Boss white man say I free in 15 year because I work hard and hard and I for food. All money I have use buy stamp to letter you daddy. I free in 15 years and I find you daddy. I miss you I love you daddy I no want home to now factory and work hard and hard. I tired daddy. I hungry. I no have home.* Name signed in Vietnamese.

"Jesus fucking Christ," I utter.

Phut. Mad Dog keeps shooting at my feet.

I've read the letter and now I don't want to die. I close my eyes. The daughter I may or may not have just got sold to a fucking child labor camp like a fucking slave. Ten thousand dollars for fifteen years of life. Now she doesn't have a fucking home. *Phut.*

"Will you fucking stop!"

Eyes still closed, I hear a car approach. I open my eyes feeling like I'm coming out of a trance. It's Cass's Ford, returning from her last trip to her former home. The motor stalls some as it nears, and she peeks out the window, soaking up the scene.

Mad Dog tucks his gun under his belt at the sound of the engine approaching, his back to the car. Cass halts her ride by the curb behind the Pontiac. She can't see the gun but she sees Mad Dog in his suit and she sees me standing there immobile like a statue, like I'm in a holdup. The guy in the suit, so out of place—a suit in New York, no one'd think twice; in LA or Miami, it depends; in Abisko? Not a chance. I catch Cass's eyes, her eyes just yards away, eyes asking, *friend or foe?* Foe, for sure. And she knows.

Right then and there, she sounds the horn and doesn't let up. A sharp, constant, perpetual ringing that wakes the entire neighborhood. Rabbits jump in the bushes and hide, birds flap their wings and take flight. Mad Dog looks like he wants to cover his ears so his head won't split. Saturday afternoon, folks are home. I see movement in some windows far across the street, then a neighbor comes out to inspect the blare. He shouts our way, "Chin! Everything okay?"

After a sigh of relief I compose myself. I wave at him and Cass ceases the alarm. All is quiet now but my ears are ringing. An everlasting sound hangs like feedback.

"Everything's fine, Bill," I dismiss. "The car malfunctioned, that's all."

"That Cassandra's car?" Neighbor Bill is now crossing the street, butting in. "Mind if I take a look?"

Mad Dog's hand is on his gun, about to pull it out, but not yet. I can tell by his expression, he's making a tactical decision, drawing up the pros and cons of wasting everyone right here and now. *Pop, pop, pop* would be all it takes. Five seconds of killing would buy him maybe ten minutes to search my house, plus Cass's car and mine. Ten minutes won't be enough, not with the boxes loaded in the cars. He must be a wanted man. He can't risk exposure. Not even in this town. Thinking about how he gave Cujo until Monday to come up with the cash, I'm inclined to believe he's a reasonable man. I mouth him my plea, "Not here, please."

Meanwhile, Cass climbs out of her car and greets Bill in the middle of the street, they begin to converse. "Cassandra, what's with the boxes?" "I'm moving in with Chin." "I thought you two were casual." "We're in love." "I'll tell Jen to bake you a pie." "I'm allergic." "To pies?" So it goes…small town small talk.

Now that the atmosphere is somewhat relaxed, I

move closer to Mad Dog and attempt to escort him to his Pontiac. At the same time, I introduce him to my fellow Abiskians, acting happy, "Guys, come meet my old war buddy before he leaves. The man's visiting from out of town."

Billy appears delighted. He comes right up, enthusiastic, hand extended from yards away. "I didn't catch your name."

With a straight face, the visitor says, "I'm Mad Dog."

"Whoa, I believe you." He shakes Mad Dog's hand, flashes that neighborly smile. "I was known as the Hot Dog 'cause I sold hot dogs at the little league games. Guess we got somethin' in common, huh?"

I amend, "Mad Dog was an MP."

"Man, that's badass, real badass. Speaking of which, Chin"—he nudges me—"good thing to have a veteran around during that robbery. Keeping everything cool and all. I think they're gonna nominate you for the upstanding citizen award."

Mad Dog's glaring at me, desperately wanting to pull the gun just so he can shut this guy up.

Billy goes on, "What's this I hear about *two separate gangs*? The newcomer took off with the dough, right? Man, what are the odds?" Small town, news travels. He nudges Mad Dog. "Chin tell you anything about it? You MPs got any ideas?"

Mad Dog's eyebrow gives off a subtle twitch, seems to make his scar move as well. He turns toward me and nods a little. Hand moves away from his waist area. He closes his eyes for two quick seconds, maybe thinking about the information Billy volunteered, maybe thinking I was telling the truth.

Cass hikes the driveway and joins us. "You dudes want to stand around, or help this damsel in boxes settle in?"

Mad Dog sighs, a hint of weariness in his exhale, possibly tired from the drive. He states, "I will leave," and walks to his car. Before he pulls the handle he jumps back. "*Dios mío*, is that a snake?"

We all turn to look at the ground he stands on. I catch a glimpse of a sidewinding tail that belongs to a serpent. In the following second it gets lost from view.

"It's pretty common around here," Billy informs him with a casual shrug. Then he backs away chuckling, "I'll go see about baking you something you aren't allergic to, Cassandra. Welcome to the neighborhood." To Mad Dog, who is shuddering as he gets inside the Pontiac, "Hey, it was nice meeting you, man."

The Pontiac's door slams, its engine yelps, and it coasts away groaning.

When everyone leaves, when it's just Cass and me on the driveway, watching Billy safely enter his home, I say to her, "He fired seven shots at me before your timely return. You saved my life."

"Jesus Christ." Her arms fold. "Who the hell *is* he?"

"Mad Dog."

"That part I heard. Think he belongs to the same canine pack with the guy who robbed the bank? Cujo, right?" Then she notices, "What's that in your hand?"

I tired daddy. I hungry. I no have home.

"It's junk mail." I pocket the letter, grab a box marked "Summer '69" from the trunk of her car and head for the house in an attempt to leave this madness behind.

"Chin." She catches up to me and glares. "Put down the box and tell me exactly what the hell is going on."

****

A sheriff's deputy shows up and instructs us to stay put. An hour or so later, detective Grayson and agent Reese are in my living room again, sitting in the same arrangement as the night before. Reese is in a pencil skirt showing bare legs, Grayson is still in those socks with holes, holes poked by his long toenails. He doesn't look as uncomfortable as last time but he smells kind of bad. Both cops look beat, black under their eyes darker than their skin. They haven't slept since they got the call about the robbery the afternoon before. Stayed up all night at the border to Oregon, the border where they screwed up the state line, or so Mad Dog believes.

"Are you so incompetent you can't locate your own asshole in a diarrhea?" Cass is on her third smoke, second pack. Her legs jitter. "How hard is it to find a Pontiac in this goddamn town?"

Grayson leans forward a bit. "The roads are sealed so we think he's laying low."

"Laying low? You're saying he's still in *Abisko*? Oh my God, that maniac was in our *driveway* and fired *seven* shots at my boyfriend!"

"*Our* driveway?" Reese tilts her head, expecting my explanation.

"I've moved in to take care of him." Cass gestures to the boxes in the living room, some are opened, some she decides should stay boxed up, like the one marked *romance novels*. Wiggling her butt on the couch, her butt close enough to rub with mine, she points out, "I

68

saved his life."

Saying it like that, her moving in with me doesn't sound like a bad idea.

"Ms. Roselyn, I'm sure your boyfriend handled the situation with grace. I mean, he had plenty of experience being shot at." The detective winks at me. "Am I right, major?"

Well, affirmative, hence the Purple Heart on display. Medal they give you for basically stepping into shit, fucking it up in combat, and letting yourself get wounded. Shit's nothing to brag about. I remember how it went, getting shot. I felt the pain and the warmth and I saw black, that's when I passed out. When I came to, a corpsman was asking me all kinds of questions about my girlfriend. "She a sweet young thing, I bet," guy said as he injected me with morphine. "Stay with me and you'll go home and fuck her brains out. You'd like that, yeah?" What he was doing was keeping me from passing out again, or else I could flat-line and go home in a body bag. But I told him, "I don't have a girlfriend." True at the time. Then the corpsman asked, "Family?" My reply: "They died." Patching me up, the guy said, "Christ sakes, MP, you want me to save your ass or what?"

That's how it went in 'Nam. I was shot just below my armor. Today I was only shot *at*. Yet I imagine what it would have been like if I was hit. How would I feel? And I think this time I'd feel different. I'd feel like I have some unfinished business. Girlfriend? *Well...check*. Family? *Well...shit*.

Ma sold me for ten thousand American dollars.
I free in 15 years and I find you, Daddy.

Grayson is now telling me about the fellow called

Mad Dog. He's a killer, plain and simple. Cartel life is his life and killing people is his business. He lists some of the crimes Mad Dog was involved with, making no jape about finding the facts in the *LA Times*. The interesting thing is, Mad Dog is just out of prison and on parole. Did time on some dubious gun charge, pleaded guilty to take a fall for Dago, his brother in arms, allegedly.

Reese adds, "He's also reputed as quite a racist."

The cops talk and all I'm trying to figure out is how I'm going to free the daughter I may or may not have.

Cass dumps her cigarette butt in a mug, a mug with the text *Employee of the Month*. Her mug or mine? I don't know. We were all employee of the month at some point. She lights another cigarette, fourth one from the second pack, and blows smoke to Grayson's face. "I think you should be out there, capturing this Mad Dog. Shouldn't have let him out of his cage in the first place."

"What we want to understand is, why was he *here* in the first place?"

Tired of the questions, tired of today, of working at the bank, of helping Cass move in, of getting shot at and of everything that's happened—*I tired. I hungry. I no have home*—I need these investigators to leave, just leave me to my peace. So I tell the two cops, "Here's what happened: Mad Dog killed Dago but didn't get his drug inventory. Cujo and Marla got it instead. However, Cujo and Marla *lost* the inventory and Mad Dog is making them pay or else he'll kill 'em, hence the bank robberies. And now, Mad Dog is in town to collect." A pause later I ask, "Get it?"

Grayson and Reese exchange glances and then, Grayson fishes out a notepad and starts writing things down. Reese inquires, "When you introduced Mad Dog to your neighbor, you said he was your old war buddy, in town for a visit?"

"Would you have preferred if I said, here is Mad Dog, a hitman for the cartel? What are you, nuts?"

"We'll look into what you said." Grayson finishes writing, rises and does the same routine as the last time, acting like he has to go but must survey the living room to make sure everything is in perfect order. He stops short at the window looking out to the driveway. "So you got your car back. What's that about?"

From Cass to Reese to Grayson, some eyes me curious and some are suspicious. I didn't talk about the hijacker because I felt a strange kinship when he spoke Chinese. But who am I kidding? I got a girl claiming to be my daughter and she needs my help. The feeling of kinship should be toward her, not some man who jacks my car. So I tell the cops about the Chinese guy.

When I finish, Cass mumbles under her breath, "I *knew* he wasn't your uncle."

Reese asks, "Why didn't you reveal his ethnicity to us last night?"

"I wasn't sure until I saw him again at the bank today."

"And you didn't think to report it to the police?"

"I was pretty busy getting shot at, so I'm reporting it to you now."

Grayson rubs his chin, eyes closed and thinking hard. After some time he mutters, "Chinese guy robs a bank...has a stroke...hmm..."

The room is quiet for half a minute.

When all of a sudden, "Hey Reese." Grayson practically drags her up from her seat. "I need you to call in a sketch artist from your office in Sacramento. Get me the best."

Agent Reese straightens her skirt. "You wanna tell me what's on your mind?"

"I got a hunch." Now he's resembling more of Danny Glover in *Witness* than in *Escape from Alcatraz*, looking like one competent detective. "If I'm right, then this thing just got a whole lot bigger."

And all I want to know is, *How much longer is this interview gonna take?*

Chapter Eight

The entire process took nearly six freaking hours, half of which was waiting for the sketch artist to arrive from the state capitol. After he reproduces the guy's likeness based on Cass and my input, Grayson stares at the sketch for a little while. "We must follow up on this, gonna have to check up on something back in Sacramento." He's slipping into his shoes when he says to me, "We'll meet again, Mr. Chin."

After the cops leave, finally, I contemplate the best course of action in regards to the bailout of the daughter I may or may not have.

The girl's mom sold her to the sweatshop factory for ten thousand dollars for fifteen years of labor. The previous letter I got from her was a month ago. Assuming the price for her did not change in a month, I should be able to bail her out of the sweatshop for the amount used to purchase her—ten thousand dollars. Now, that kind of money isn't exactly easy to come by. I tried selling the house and not one person showed any kind of interest. Applying for refinance would take too long to get approved or, declined. There's the FDIC scam Ester is cooking but the payoff is only one thousand per head. So where and how am I going to obtain ten thousand dollars?

Where and how?

I know, there's only one other way. The answer's

there.

I'm thinking about all of this, while Cass is grinding me hard, cowgirl style, reversed.

The where—bank.

The how—robbery.

I reckon robbing banks in small towns isn't as hard as in big cities; small staff, next to nothing security, a handful of cops on duty in the entire county. Cujo pulled it off, twice. Almost three times if it hadn't been for the outlandish Chinese guy.

Cass rides. "Chin, you're going limp."

I go limp, and I think I'm going to need some help if I want to pull this off. I need someone who can follow orders, someone I don't have to sell this to, someone who's willing to go for broke—someone in crime.

Cass turns around, with me in her—an around the world. She slaps my chest. "Hey, you need to focus."

I think about the daughter I may or may not have left behind…working in a sweatshop in Vietnam for the next fifteen years. If my folks were alive today, what would they say to me about what I have, or haven't done?

The woman on top of me grabs my hand and plasters it on her breast, she squeezes for me. Moaning, "Yeah, that's good."

I'm looking at Cass now and I pick out her flaws. Her thirty-five year old body is sagging, her skin wrinkled at the neck. A vein pops from her armpit to her nipple. She's clutching me between her thighs. Her waist isn't bad but her hips are getting pretty wide. Fat rubbing the scar I got from the bullet wound. I'm picking out her flaws, trying to convince myself that I should leave her. I'm here thinking, imagining what her aesthetic will be like ten years from now, if I were to stay with her. Just for me to keep it up she really needs to stop smoking. For our benefit I request, "Cass, you need to stop smoking."

And she moans, "Whatever you say." The sound she makes before climax, she's doing it now.

Right before she comes, hard pounding is heard.

On the door.

"What the fuck?" Her grinding slows and she frowns. "Who could it be? What time is it?"

I check the clock on the wall. It's past midnight.

The pounding continues on the door.

Cass shouts, "Whoever this is, go away!"

"Cassandra?" a voice calls.

"Beat it! We're having sex!"

"Cassandra? It's Mom…"

"And Dad."

Jesus Christ. Cass dismounts and pulls a sheet to her breasts. She looks more frightened about having her parents at the door than Mad Dog, a mad killer, in the driveway.

"I thought you said they're coming next week." I try to find my underwear, but I can't.

Cass shakes off the surprise, puts on my T-shirt and pulls on her panties. She orders, "You stay here," and darts out the door.

The living room light comes on and the front door opens. They're shouting "Surprise!" and continues to converse in country accent. Cass too, the country coming out of her. Cass is demanding to know what the hell they're doing here. They're only expected around next week. Her mom and pop say they wanted to drop off the homemade chicken, carried it all the way from the Bluegrass State, since it's authentic and it'd be a shame if it spoiled. And besides, hon, they explain, it's past midnight, technically, it *is* next week.

"You have to take off your shoes," Cass's voice, coarse from the sound she makes before climax. "This is my boyfriend's house. How on earth did you find it, anyhow?"

"We went to your place," an old man's voice—her dad is saying, "we knocked and called for a long time and woke the neighbors. They said we'd find you here. Why do we have to take off our shoes?"

At this point, I come out clothed, figure I should make an introduction. I have guests at *my* house, after all. Her folks see me. Her dad is smiling, nodding as he takes off his shoes; her mom's face turns purple, looks about to gag. She strides slowly to the kitchen and keeps her eyes on me as she places a large tray in tin-foil on the kitchen counter. After her hands are free, she covers her face, appalled like in that Munch painting *The Scream*. "Cassandra, you're sleeping, w-with...a-a *gook*?"

Gook means me.

Her daughter rolls her eyes. "Mom, please...whom I sleep with is none of your business."

"But *Cassandra*, to dishonor us like this." Now her mother looks to be in tears. "H-how could you?"

"If you don't approve how I live my life, then by all means, *leave*. You weren't invited to begin with."

"You unmitigated whore..."

"Mom, screw you."

To say "conflict is escalating" in a sit-rep (situation report) would be an understatement. Like that, the mother and daughter exchange insults, saying things I never thought I'd hear a mother say to a daughter, and vise versa; their voices so loud and incomprehensible, one would think they aren't speaking English. Then, one of them goes to the sink and grabs a dish, and drops it on the floor, shattering it. For whatever reason I cannot grasp.

I wonder if the daughter I may or may not have put up a fight with her mother upon learning she was getting sold to a child labor camp, breaking dishes and saying *f-you*.

The dad looks at me, apologetic, and just shrugs. I approach him whispering, "Should we stop 'em?"

"Best I leave my shoes on," he says to the shards on the ground. At the doorway, he hands me a pair of my slippers. "Tell me, how many rooms you got in this house?"

I wear the slippers. "Here, a bedroom and a den."

"Why don't we take refuge in the den." He points down the hall in a gesture that asks, *that way*? I confirm and he leads me to it, skipping over the glass shards in the kitchen. "You want to grab us a couple of beers?"

"I only keep bourbon in the house."

He lights up. "That's even better."

****

Hour 0100, Cass's dad and I are in my den drinking Blanton's, Kentucky straight, neat and sweet. The man is in the twilight of his fifties, benevolent countenance, has a snowy white beard and a potbelly the size of my head. Shouting is still going on outside the door. Old man Roselyn takes a swig of whisky and coughs a little, being the old timer he is. He starts by saying, "Thanks for bringing out the good stuff, uh"—

then he looks at me and realizes he doesn't know my name—"what do they call you?"

I figure my nickname wouldn't amuse him, so I rub my chin. "It's Chin."

"No, I saw your medals. You're a civilian now, but I'm a man who salutes the rank—which in your case is what?"

"Major."

"You're kidding." He studies me over. "I want evidence you've hit puberty, major."

"I enlisted after I finished college, had a head start," I explain with a swig of my own. "Plus, rank and medals came in fast in 'Nam. Grunts rose and got decorated every time shit happened. And shit happened aplenty there, every minute of every day."

He raises his glass to a toast. "*Semper fi.*"

I wasn't a marine, but whatever. "*Oo-rah.*"

"I apologize for my wife, major. She's a hillbilly through and through. You get that, right? Her father screwed his uncle's daughter, who I think is my wife's mother." Coughing, he takes a sip of Blanton's to keep it down. "Please don't blame her, it's not her fault."

Glass shatters outside the door. Then again.

The man looks at me sorry-eyed. "I hope your collection isn't valuable."

"It isn't."

"Good, I'll pay for it." The way he said it, it was a statement not to be disputed. Another swig and he tugs his beard, good natured. "You took a good look at my old lady there? See the massive pounds of flesh on her lower body? That's her ass. When I met her, she was a cheerleader, if you can believe it. Word to the wise, major—a good look at my wife would let you know what's in store for my daughter. All women become their mothers, you know? That's their tragedy."

"All men don't, that's *their* tragedy—Oscar Wilde."

"Who the hell's that?" He gives me a wink like he knows but doesn't want to admit it. I join him in another toast, and he says, "Frankly, if I knew my wife's mother could inflate endlessly, I'd think twice about marrying that family. Jesus, I'd probably marry Tabitha, the evangelist. She's insane but God bless her, at least her ass stayed where it is—where it should be."

"Sir—"

"Call me Larry, major. You outrank me by a mile." He's looking at my bookshelf, eyes squinting. "I know what you're gonna ask—ass or personality, right? Let me tell you, when you're old as me, you gain perspective. What perspective?" He clears his throat. "Speaking the truth, of course. Whether it's ass or personality, it doesn't matter. What matters is you need to speak your mind. Trust me, your life would be a whole lot easier. Hell, when you're old as me, you just don't give a shit."

From outside the door, the woman shouts, "Son of a whore!"

Cass rebuts, "You just called yourself a whore."

More glasses shatter.

"Boy, this fight is gonna dent my wallet." Larry heaves a sigh, smiling ruefully. "She's a ferocious one, isn't she?"

"You mean your daughter, or your wife?"

"Both, I suppose." He checks his wristwatch, squinting his eyes and looking drowsy. "It should be over soon."

"You must be tired from the trip." I point at where he's sitting. "It's a sofa-bed. You want to lie down?"

"I should be good for another ten minutes. By my calculation they'll be hugging by then. But if they're still at it, we'll have to intervene, make sure this doesn't burgeon into a homicide. Those shards lying around could be dangerous." That gets me worried and he detects it. "Relax. C'mon, pour me another." He thumbs at the Blanton's. "Don't be stingy, major."

Sure enough, about ten minutes later the living room quiets down. Larry and I exit the den and approach the battlefield, taking tiny steps. The women are standing in the kitchen, exhausted and with tears in their eyes. The ground looks like an earthquake hit a pottery barn. I move forward and *crunch*, I step on glass. Scanning the aftermath, I feel everything is my fault, even though I didn't do any physical damage. I mean, *I* was the subject of this conflict. So I tell everyone in the room, "This is all my fault."

"No," Cass's mom cries, shaking her head. "I'm sorry. I-I don't even know your name. I just came in your house and…oh my God. What has gotten in to me. Your kitchenware…"

Cass picks up a mug that seems to be intact. She examines it and puts it on the counter. Wiping her tears, she says, "I think this one can be salvaged." It's the mug with the text, *Employee of the Month.*

Right then, the women embrace just as Larry predicted. The dad nudges me, his eyes saying, *What'd I tell ya?* Cass's mom glances at me, sniveling. "So you're not Japanese, Vietnamese, or um, Korean, right? Good Lord, we've been at war with all those heathens." Then she surveys my domicile, eyes critical. "This is your place? I would've thought you'd know better. That vase over there and the arrangement of the sofa in respect to the windows, it's not very feng shui. It's all wrong."

Cass steps back and suggests, "Mom, why don't you take Dad to my place, we'll talk tomorrow. It's late, I'm exhausted and I need a smoke." Her arms are folded when she shoots a glance at me. "My last one, I swear."

"Cassandra." Her mother's voice is soft. She looks from me to Cass. "I need to ask you a favor. I need— your father and I—we need to ask you for some money. And…we need it now."

"*Money*? Is that why you're here? Is that why you decided to drive nonstop, *uninvited*, to ask me for *money*? Is that what this visit is all about?"

"C'mon, Cassandra, why do you sound like such an ingrate?"

"You want money from me? You owe me money for our dishes! Owe *us*!"

Her mother's clutching her waist, circumference round as the moon. "Honestly Cassandra, sometimes you can be a real bitch."

"Oh, I'm a bitch…"

And, there it goes again. World War III. Cass yells, her mother too. The daughter grabs the thing nearest to her, the mug, and smashes it onto the ground. "Employee of the Month," it's finally in pieces. Not to be outdone, the mother also seizes glassware—it's the tray she brought with her, a large tray covered with aluminum foil. It looks heavy and I'm thinking, well, hell, at least it's not mine. She raises it and then she hesitates.

"Wait!" Larry springs forward, hand in the air calling for cease fire, trotting on broken glass in his shoes, shredding bigger pieces into smaller ones. "Gimme *that*." He seizes the tray from his wife and returns to the den, beckoning me to follow. "Kentucky fried chicken, you ever tried it?"

In the den, he takes a bite.

Chapter Nine

I ask Larry what's it like to raise a girl.

According to Larry, one of the worst things about raising not one, but *two* daughters, is keeping a constant lookout for who they fuck.

When they're kids, still in their single digits, Larry says you got to keep an eye on your own damn relatives, 'cause you know one of them hillbillies is a possible pervert/molester son of a gun.

When the girls get to their teens, you give them obligatory sex ed, tell them to insist on contraceptive. Tell them, no rubber, no play. If the guy doesn't have one handy, make sure to take one from the bottom drawer of the sink. Larry keeps standard, large and XL. He educated the older daughter when she was fourteen. The younger one when she was thirteen.

Larry says he's prepared for parenthood because he lost his virginity at age fourteen—or was it fifteen—down by the river. He remembers his first lay. Don't we all? The girl wasn't much younger. How did her parents feel about their daughter getting dicked that young? Now he knows.

Larry is in a talkative mood.

When the girls hit high school, Larry emphasizes, the risk of pregnancy is at all-time high. He's drinking Blanton's and eating fried chicken when he relates to me that there are girls in Kentucky, girls who get pregnant and they think they're the Virgin Marry. It happens. They tell their parents they're pure and the growing belly is a divine intervention. Pregnancy confuses girls in bible country.

"Some folks feel compelled to send their girls to the nut house." Larry is chewing. "The parents ought to be the ones locked up, if you ask me." Larry telling me what's it like being a father, in the good ol' US of A.

I feel like taking notes.

And after high school, it's not just about the fornication any more; it's about committing crime, selling pot and growing weed on a farm. Larry knows this, because one time one of his daughters was arrested while she was fucking her dealer. She'd been helping him sell and grow to make a little cash on the side. Which daughter? I ask. He doesn't say.

Watching his daughters grow up beautiful—that's the best part of parenthood, according to Larry. It's worth all that fucking he had to look out for. Watching his wife get fat in the process, man, ain't so great, he says and coughs. "My daughters... they're my greatest joy and my worst enemies."

He says to me, "You know the absolute worst part about being a parent?"

To condemn your child to a sweatshop?
To never know your child at all?

"It's never having enough money." Larry is shaking his head as he speaks. "You'd think raising two girls in Kentucky would be cheap, but there's never enough. You think you could do better. You think, maybe if I sent them to a private school—to an all-girls institution or something fancy. Maybe if I had the means to pay for college..."

The second absolute worst thing about being a parent to two girls? According to Larry, it's to witness them not talking to each other for over ten years.

Why?

Ask Cassandra.

The place is quiet for a minute or two.

And the very worst part about being a parent, he says "worst" for the third time and stops.

"What is it?" I ask, curious.

"The absolute *worst* thing about being a father…is watching your daughter die. Knowing you can't save her, because you don't have enough money."

The old man drinks all of my Blanton's.

And he weeps.

****

When Cass's parents leave, I've already gotten the gist of the story from Larry, about why they need the money. And why they need the money is because their daughter—Cass's sister, needs an operation and needs it fast. It's one of those situations where a large portion of the money must be put upfront, because the family lives in a house with wheels and the hospital doesn't think a payment plan is feasible.

I say to Cass, "I didn't know you have a sister."

It's three in the morning now and we're in bed, between the sheets. The kitchen left the way it is, neither of us up for cleaning. Neither of us is up for sleeping, either.

"Chin, there's something I need to tell you." She smokes the cigarette which she promises for the third time will be her last. "Now that we're living together, I should tell you. It wouldn't be fair if you were to find out down the line. It's embarrassing, and well, shit, here it goes"—she takes a breath—"I was engaged once upon a time."

I'm not sure why I should take this as a shocking discovery, but I guess I should. So I let several heartbeats pass before I say, "Okay."

"He was about your age then, had this dirt bike he showed off with pride, had the coolest look about him, the way he took off his helmet and his hair gleamed. I was young and naïve. He used to take me for rides."

"On his dirt bike, or on you?"

"Well, bike first." She chuckles dryly. "Then it was on me, and then it was my darling sister. That bastard. I found out after our engagement. You know what he said when I confronted him? He got puppy-eyed and said, 'Well, my philosophy is, it's not cheating if it was in her ass.' Her ass means darling sister's." She takes a pause. "You wanted to know why I'm not talking to my sister. Guess who she married?"

"Jesus Christ."

"Christ wasn't available," gusty smoke she blows, "darling cum-bucket married the cheating bastard. I bet he's not doing a damn thing about her bills. I wish I could say, 'Serves her right,' but...shit. She's my sibling, and she needs my help."

I just nod.

"Chin, I've been thinking..."

I know what she's been thinking.

"My poor, poor Dad, he shouldn't have to go through this, at least not go through it with my mom. That woman says the most atrocious things. You heard her, and you saw my dad. He looked so frail. You know he's a veteran, same as you?"

"A marine."

"I want to help them."

"You have the money?"

She chews her lip. "No, but, what Ester was proposing today…" She studies my reaction, attentive to my eyes. "Us, over-claiming with the FDIC…it has to be unanimous." She shifts her body toward me. "Listen, I know this is a lot to ask of you. I know under ordinary circumstances you'd say no, but consider what's happening now. If you love me…"

I look at her. An honest woman turned into a crook, doing what she has to do for the people she loves.

"Chin," she says. "You know I'd do the same for you, in a heartbeat."

I recall what she said last night. *'Cause that's what people do when they're in love.*

"You don't have to commit to an answer right away. I just want you to think about it. Ester said we have until Monday, right? Please, just think it over till then."

I think it over now. What do I have to lose?

"Just think about it, okay?"

Thinking about Cass having a change of heart, about willing to commit a crime to save her kin, I can't help but feel sympathetic, at the same time peculiarly drawn to her.

"Cass"—I stroke her hair—"I really appreciate you for telling me about your previous engagement. In fact, I admire that about you."

Her forehead creases. "You admire…my previous engagement?"

"No and that doesn't matter. I mean to say I admire the fact that you're a straight shooter." Probably inherited the quality from her dad, it makes sense. "I could never feel like you're concealing things from me, and it makes you really easy to talk to—"

"Don't"—her eyes blinking fast—"now you're making me wish I told you that a long time ago."

"No, don't think like that." I'm wondering if I should tell her, that I may or may not have a daughter, be straight with her for once. "Cass, there's something I want to tell you too."

"What is it?"

"I…" *I…can't.*

"Yes?"

Now I feel like I have to confess something, just to reciprocate her honesty.

Gulping, "I was in 'Nam."

"Yes, I know."

"And well, shit…something happened."

"What, Chin?"

A laborious sigh. "You know what I did in the army?"

"Military Police, that's what MP means, right? I don't know what that entails, exactly. I mean, you never talk about it."

"One time I was tasked to bring in three deserters." Now I'm talking about being an MP instead of what I really want to say. Although, talking about 'Nam is just as burdensome.

"Deserters?"

"Yes. Deserters are bad for the army. They could be captured by the enemy, could be tortured, made to divulge tactics, formations, things essential to our military success, and of course, they could be killed."

Cass nods, unsure. "Okay…"

I tell her a story, "I knew one of the deserters. He was two years my junior in college. The school was gonna drop him 'cause he was unable to pay tuition. Then ROTC stepped in, said they'd take care of his bills if he did two tours for Uncle Sam, which Tanner agreed to. Tanner—the guy I knew, went AWOL with two Italian boys from Brooklyn, boys were eighteen years old, drafted out of New York and sent to die. So I found them, found them hiding downstream deep in enemy territory. Tanner gave up but the Italian boys resisted and were gonna put up a firefight, and then I told them they were facing court martial in the states, which actually delighted them to no end. Everyone willingly turned over their weapons, glad to be in custody. They thought they were going home."

"So you saved them."

"Before I could take them to the disciplinary center, their CO made me release them back to his command, right back into action. The guy was short on men, wasn't gonna send three able-bodied boys home just because they wandered into the woods to take a dump. He said to the them, 'You run off again, I'll personally see your asses locked up in Ft. Leavenworth.' Guess what happened?"

"They ran off again."

"The Italians did. Can you blame them? Leavenworth doesn't sound half bad compared to Suoi Chau Pha or Phuoc Long, does it? They ran away again just so they could go to Leavenworth. When I found them the second time, it was too late. Their bodies...they were already...they were...Jesus."

Silence for a spell.

"What about Tanner? Did he go A-wall again?"

"A-W-O-L. No..." I shake my head. "He got blown up by a grenade."

"Oh God, Chin." Cass brushes my hair with her fingers. "It's not your fault, you know?"

"Sometimes I think that Tanner would still be alive had he had the money for tuition. He wasn't made to be a soldier. He just wanted to graduate." I heave a sigh. "Sorry Cass, I don't know what's gotten into me."

"Don't be sorry. But...I don't get it, why did you want to tell me this?"

That story wasn't what I wanted to tell her. What I wanted to tell her was about the daughter I may or may not have left behind.

What I wanted to say was, I have to free her, even if she isn't mine.

What I wanted to say was, I need to go back...to Vietnam.

The things we do for our flesh and blood, I say to Cass, "I'm in."

"In what?"

"The FDIC scam, Cass, it's unanimous. Take my share of the money and help your sister get better."

She leans in closer and for a second there it seems as if she wants to kiss me, but she doesn't. "Chin...I'll pay you back, okay?"

"No, don't." I sit up. I don't want her to pay me back. Don't think I'm going to be around for that long. "Instead of paying me back, Cass, I want you to do something else for me."

She's sitting as well now. "Anything, Chin. Just tell me what you want me to do."

I have no specific task I want her to do. All I know is the basic principle that seems to work out pretty well for the army—follow orders. So I instruct vaguely, "When I ask you to do something you wouldn't approve of, I want you to consent, no questions asked."

She considers that for a long moment. "Okay...but I draw the line at *if it's in the ass, it's not cheating.*"

"Please, Cass." I look at her. "*I* get fucked in the ass, I'd call that rape."

Chapter Ten

Dear daughter I may or may not have, whose name I do not know,

You and I met not long after you were born. I looked into your eyes and you looked into mine. You may or may not be my daughter, but as this moment, it doesn't matter. I don't know what you look like now, I'm sorry to say, I don't know which one is you from the picture you sent. I don't know how to say your name because I can't read Vietnamese. I don't know anything about you at all, but I do know your mother, and she is beautiful.

As you may have heard, the country where I'm from, America, disagreed about something with the country you call home, Vietnam. I was sent there to fight just so we can all be on the same page, essentially, about how we live our lives. I know it sounds outrageous, but that's what happened. Many men and women died because of this, it was terrible, and I wish it would never happen again. But it was because of this conflict I had the chance to meet your mother.

She was working in Saigon at the time. Her job was to release the pressure for men who came from America, one hour at a time. You may not understand exactly what she did, but all you have to know is that, she made many men incredibly happy. She made my life worth living in a time when hope was lost. Your mother, she is remarkable.

I stop writing and read it over. All this talk about her mother, I'm not sure if I'm making sense. But the important thing now is to get my thoughts on paper. I'll revise it if I have the time, and if not then, it's worth having the mental exercise.

Cass is sleeping in the other room. I keep writing.

I remember when it was just the two of us, your mother and I, we talked about how one day, I'd take her to America, and she said she would like that very much. I wasn't serious, and I don't think she was, either. It was part of her job, to make the men happy, to say what men wanted to hear.

The last time I saw her was the first time I saw you. I remember that day well, it was raining. Your mother said you are mine, and I can see how she sees it that way. You have black hair, black eyes and brows. You don't look like the people from America, and although I'm from America, I happen to look like you.

I suppose you'll want to know the reason why I left. There are many reasons, to be honest. I can go on and on about how I did not believe you are my daughter, how I was selfish, how I felt my youth was taken away from me because of the conflict, how I had my own plans about how I'd live my life, and how I just did not want to take responsibility, whatsoever. But the truth is, my dear girl, none of those things would've mattered much, if I had money.

I didn't have money then, and I don't have money now. You know something funny? Your mother made more than me at the time, and I was putting my life on the line for the country I call home. And the fact is, I'm not doing any better now. I'm sorry I was unable to send you money, even when you asked for it. I feel ashamed and I am so sorry. I don't want you to blame your mother for what's happening with your life, because the fault lies solely with me.

I'm sure you've heard people say that America is the land of opportunities, but that really depends on where you are on this land, which time period you're talking about, and which cards you were dealt. Or, if you choose to have your cards dealt for you, rather than dealing them for yourself. I've been living a rather passive life, content of having cards dealt for me, but all that is about to change.

Because I want you to have the freedom to pursue your dreams, I do, whether it's in Vietnam, or here, in America. I want there to be no limit, no boundaries for your achievements. I want you to grow up to be whoever you want to be. It's what my parents said to me and now, I'm relating it to you. I want to provide you with the means, the means to achieve your dreams.

But first, I must free you from your present predicament, as soon as possible.

I'm bringing you home.

Love, Dad

(may or may not be biological, but whatever)
P.S. Don't hate me.

It's almost morning now. No point in going back to bed. In the den, I read the letter, and tuck it away in a copy of *Great Expectations*, but then I switch it to Donald E. Westlake's *Bank Shot*. A much appropriate choice, I think. I leave a note for Cass on the fridge, *I'm heading out.*

I go off to find Cujo.

Need to talk to him in regards to matters of a heist.

Chapter Eleven

I arrive in Plum Creek at 0605. Dangerous Shawn is just about wrapping up his shift at the Courtside Inn. He recognizes me and relates at once that I'm wanted by the local police. "The trucker they carried out on a stretcher the other day"—he shakes his head—"you're not gonna believe this, he's pressing charges for aggravated assault."

"Tell that Nazi bitch to kiss my ass."

"Isn't that what he wanted to do in the first place?"

I leave Shawn and get to room 108 and knock. I hear some commotion behind the door, footsteps shuffle then stop, like people getting into formation. A moment later, Cujo opens the door to a crack. "Major?" Peeking through it, he whispers, "Permission to speak freely, yeah? Okay then, the fuck you doing here?" His voice sounds nasally.

"Is this a bad time, Cujo?" The first thing that comes to mind is that the guy's having sex.

His eyes roll to his right side and then he nods, not to me. His eyeballs are bloodshot. He finally opens the door wide to let me in. The guy's all dressed, in the same clothes he was in Friday afternoon. He arches his back, and then, "*Escheew-ee!*" inviting me in with one hell of a sneeze. "You showered this morning? I'm allergic, man."

"To shower?"

"To shampoo." He rubs his bald head.

Coming into the room, I wipe off his spittle and I don't see Marla.

Next thing I know, there's a six-shooter pressed against the left side of my face.

By natural reflex, I raise my hands in surrender. Slowly, I turn my eyes to observe the gunman, expecting to see Mad Dog. But I see a short dude, as short as Mad Dog but younger and dressed in a suit and a pair of gator boots, must've stepped out from the same clothing store for career criminals under five foot five. The difference are his shirt's purple and isn't buttoned all the way; his chest hair showing. Latin persuasion, definitely.

"How do you do," I say to the gunman. To Cujo, "Who's the FNG?" Army for fucking new guy.

The gunman observes the courtesy, as well, "I'm doing great, thank you, how 'bout yourself?" Immigrant accent with a touch of Texas mixed in there, if you can believe it. To Cujo, he orders, "Close the door." Once the door shuts he steps in front of me, gun still held at my eyelevel, fingertip caressing the trigger.

"Yo, this is the guy I was telling you about." Cujo's off to the side explaining to the FNG, "This is the *other* chink, *not* the one who jacked my take. This is the ex-MP, man, *this* chink is on *our* side." To me, "Shit, major, I didn't mean to call you chink, word rolls right off my tongue, you know how it is."

The gunman scans me up and down, and then releases the hammer on the six-shooter and lowers the piece. He introduces himself, "I'm Rabies, what's your name?"

"Jesus...were you bitten by Cujo, or Mad Dog?"

"Your name is Jesus?" He says it like, *Hey-Zeus*.

I shake my head. "Where's Marla?"

"He grabbed her, man." Cujo's ass freefalls onto the mattress. "Mad Dog grabbed her and took all the money we robbed. Then he put his crony dude, Rabies, on me to make sure I keep robbing banks and pay him off. If I don't do it, he'll kill her, and he'll let this psychopath here shoot my ass too. This guy is trailing me, man, twenty-four-seven around the clock. I can't take a shit without him sniffing."

"Twenty-four-seven?" Looking at the single bed in the room, I ask, "You boys sleeping together?"

Cujo reveals, "It hasn't come to that yet. Thank God."

"Where's Marla?" I ask Rabies. "Seriously, you expect this joker"—I gesture to Cujo—"to pull off bank jobs? He got lucky the first two, three times, and you think he's hot shit? There's a statewide manhunt for him right this moment. You want him to rob banks? He needs his partner. He needs Marla."

Rabies says coolly, "He gets me."

I study him up and down. Guy doesn't stand too far off the ground. "What's your credentials?"

"I have six kills, so far." Peering down at Cujo, he smacks his lips. "Looking forward to lucky number seven."

"Oh my God." Cujo's face is buried in his hands, he mumbles, "Mama had me get rabies vaccination shot when I was a kid. Now I'm gonna get shot *by* Rabies. This is fucked up, man."

"No one's gonna get shot." I look from Cujo to Rabies. "We need a bank robber, not a professional hitman. No one is going to get hurt, not bank employees, not Marla, not us."

"That's what I been telling Rabies." Cujo jumps up from the mattress and goes to the desk. He opens the drawers and extracts a bunch of loose napkins. "Come look at this, major. I got a plan on how to do this with no guns."

I join Cujo, but Rabies isn't moving. He probably knows the plan already. I pick up a napkin from the desk, napkin you get from fast food joints, and see handwritten notes that look like they were either scrawled by a kid with dyslexia, or by a handicapped chicken. In gangster prose is written, *Hello, my name is Cujo, and I am going to ROB your bank. Please put all them bills in the bag, and not the dyke pack...* I toss the napkin aside and tell the illiterate thug, "It's called a *dye* pack, not *dyke* pack."

"Yeah, man"—he wipes his mouth—"I'm keeping it real."

"Keeping what real? You know what, never mind." I read another paragraph of his gangster prose, "*I am heavy armed and outta my mind. Do as I say or I will waste you, motherfucker, and everyone in this room. You try calling 911, fool, I will have you feel the wrath of my menace.*" It's obvious from the cryptic cursive that he doesn't know how to spell *wrath* or *menace*. A Vietnamese girl writes better than this. And it's, "*Heavily* armed," I correct. "You ought to omit the adverb altogether."

"Yeah, that'll scare 'em." He grins. "Make sure they don't call the *po*lice."

"A mental institution is what they'll call." I turn to Rabies. "You approve this shit?"

"It's not my job to approve or disapprove." He

shrugs. "My job is to make sure he robs banks."

"And succeed, right? Look, in all honesty, it's not a terrible plan." I say this not to discourage Cujo. Judging from his handwriting, I can tell the guy's desperate. "The problem with his plan is, he can't pay off your boss in one score. How much does he owe him?"

"A little over twenty thousand. His previous robberies paid off nearly thirty percent of his debt. Mad Dog is impressed."

"But that was then. Now is different," I explain to Rabies. "The borders are sealed, so that limits his activities to California only. All banks in this state are already on high alert, probably doesn't keep that much cash in the drawer any more; CHP too, they're patrolling up and down the interstates. Cujo can't get too far without drawing the cop's attention." Rabies is yawning and I say to him, "Listen, I know you're just doing what you're told, and you couldn't give two shits about him getting caught. But, you do want to get *paid*. That's why you're in *crime*, aren't you? For the money, right?"

"*Hey-Zeus*, I like to kill."

"When it *pays*. Otherwise you'd be on a rampage like a rabid dog." I pause and admit to a guy called Rabies, "Not a great analogy."

He thinks it over. "So you got yourself a plan?"

"With contingencies. I have it all worked out." Then I spread out a fresh napkin and ask Cujo for a pen. I start to sketch the blueprint of my workplace. "Pacific Southwest, that's where I work. I know, it sounds like an airline." Drawing, I explain, "The beautiful thing about the plan is you'll have *me*, an inside man."

"Wait, wait"—Rabies lifts a palm—"you're gonna

take part in the robbery?"

"*Heist*." I stop drawing and cock my head at Rabies. "Of course I'm gonna be a part of it. And so are you. I thought that much was clear."

"C'mon, Rabies, let him help," Cujo chimes in. "He was in the seventy-fifth MP, you have any idea what that means? One time they ran through an enemy minefield long as three miles. Six mines went off and blew two dozen souls to kingdom come, two dozen on the *enemies'* side. Man, seven-five walked out with zero casualties, like *God* was on their side."

"That was before my time, but"—I admit nonetheless—"sure sounds like a miracle."

Cujo pats me on the shoulder. "You guys are legends, major."

"I don't give a shit," Rabies says to me. "There's something important we gotta settle first, hoss. If we can't come to a conclusion we're satisfied with, then there's no point in involving you. No point in your plan."

I ask him, "Settle what?"

"Well…" He looks from Cujo to me. "Settle how we gonna split the money."

Right then, three knocks on the door.

The three of us turn our heads, holding breath.

"County sheriff! Open up!"

We turn from the door to look at each other, our eyes revealing we're all thinking the same thing, *Now we're fucked.*

Chapter Twelve

"*Shit*, cops," Cujo whispers. He has the good sense not to shout. He leaps toward the window and attempts to lift it so he can skip right out. Before he cracks it open, "*Escheew-ee!*"

Rabies cocks his gun and stands against the wall adjacent to the door. He says casually to Cujo, "God bless you," holding out the gun with his arm straight. He cocks the hammer ready to kill anyone who crosses the threshold. He inhales, and...doesn't exhale.

Shit. Cops find me here with Rabies and Cujo, I'll be SOL—shit out of luck. I place no faith in these two assholes to keeping their mouth shut for me. No honor among thieves. I'd be charged with aiding and abetting, obstruction of justice, attempted robbery—armed. Worse, if Rabies shoots a cop, I'll be an accessory to murder.

I'll rot in the state pen while the daughter I may or may not have rots in a child labor camp, in Vietnam.

Knock knock knock. "We know you're in there. C'mon, open up. Let's go!"

"*Wait*," I whisper to Cujo and Rabies, the former already has one leg out the window, the latter maintains killing mode. "Be quiet and listen..."

We listen. No one's breathing.

Silence for ten rapid heartbeats.

And then a voice I recognize. "Sir, I didn't call the

cops. Some guests must've recognized you in the lobby and made the call. I mean, we don't have a lot of oriental persons here."

The voice belongs to Dangerous Shawn. Now Cujo and Rabies are throwing me a *what the fuck* look. The cops are here, not for *them*. But for *me*.

"Goddamn, I almost shit my pants." Cujo adjusts his belt. "In fact..." He rushes to the bathroom and doesn't close the door.

I order Rabies, "Go with him and stay in the bathroom unless I tell you to come out. I'm gonna take care of this."

Trotting his way to the bathroom, Rabies shakes his head and complains, "I don't get paid enough for this shit."

When the two criminals are out of sight, I take a breath before I unfasten the chain and ease open the door. Outside, Dangerous Shawn stands in front of two deputies of the law. I slip out and leave the door ajar just a bit, to convince the deputies I got nothing to hide.

In the hallway, I look left and right; about half a dozen doors are open. Heavy ass trucker dudes with beards and tattoos stand about, some smoking joints, some scratching their crotches, all are enjoying the impending show. One of the cops, a guy in his early twenties, announces to the hallway, "Everyone go back to your rooms, please." Some folks mumble to themselves. No one complies.

I remark to the cops and Shawn, "I thought this was an inn, didn't know it was a headquarters for the Aryan Brotherhood."

The older sheriff's deputy is wearing a cowboy hat, which he removes in an apologetic manner, revealing a patch of gray hair with strands of blond. The man cuts the bullshit and gets right to it. "Just tell us, sir, was it self-defense?"

Seeing a straight shooter, I don't attempt to act dumb. I know exactly what he's talking about. He wants to know if I acted in self-defense in regards to the trucker whose nose I broke. I step back and let the deputy take a good look at me—let him decide whether or not I'm the type to actively cause trouble—before I say, "Yes, it was self-defense."

"You did bust his nose," the younger guy states. "He's pretty messed up."

"I'm not sorry for what I did."

The young deputy scans me over pretty curious. Probably wondering, how did a guy like me mess up a big dude like that? He tilts his head back and casts his eyes down at me, he asks, "You used a weapon?"

"I used my elbow."

"Elbow?" Surprised, he requests, "Show me how."

"Okay..." So I mime while I convey the instructions. "You want your elbow to come down in a chopping motion in close range. *Whack*—like that. It's effective in breaking your opponent's guard and their stability. If you aim at the forehead or temple, it could be fatal."

"No shit," the young cop mimes after me.

"Is this right?" Dangerous Shawn, too, is whacking his arm in the air.

"If your opponent doesn't go down you could double tap." I slap my elbow twice with the other hand. *Slap slap*. "Or if he's too far you can do a downward jumping attack. This way you can put your whole body weight into it."

The young cop asks his partner, "Why don't they include this in the training program?"

His partner, the old timer, just nods and flashes me a wry smile. "Sir, I'm sorry but I still have to take you in. Please come with us willingly or—"

"Now wait a minute here." I lift my hands in surrender and out of their reach. *Shit*, I just confessed to assault and battery. They could lock me up in a cell until I get arraigned, which would demolish my plans for the heist. The only practical option is to try and talk my way out of this jam. To the older cop, I take a stab, "You have children, deputy?" Seeing a nod I let on quick, "I got a daughter. The trucker was threatening my daughter's welfare, saying all kinds of racist filth. I wasn't defending just myself, I was defending my family. You're a family man, what would you have done in that situation?"

Before the older cop replies, Dangerous Shawn, the kid I tutored backs me up. "It's true, deputies. I mean look around, this place might as well be a halfway house."

The young cop is staring at my shoes when he says, "Sir, you served?"

I nod. Not really surprised but I ask nonetheless, "How'd you tell?"

"Your posture and demeanor plus, your boots are a dead giveaway." Then he raises his head to me. "My brother served in 'Nam. He had a pair that was identical."

I follow this up by revealing my unit, rank, and where I've been. Telling them about the Purple Heart the army gave me after I got shot. When I'm finished, both cops look impressed. Then the young cop whispers something in the older cop's ear.

The older deputy asks, "Are you armed, mister?"

"Negative. Should I be?"

"No." After a long and thoughtful pause, he says, "I know you must feel you're a long way from Chinatown, but next time someone threatens you or your family, please call 911 and you let us handle it, okay? This time, we're gonna let you off with a warning." He puts on his hat and shrugs to his partner. "All right then, let's do our protect and serve somewhere needed."

The young cop salutes. "Thank you for your service to this country."

Like that, the sheriff's dispatch is responded to and the deputies leave. At the same time I breathe a huge mental sigh of relief. But as they pass the observers in the hall, one of the truckers objects, "What, that's it? You ain't gonna arrest him? He assaulted a fellow brother!"

The cops ignore him and the guy keeps shouting his objections. Next thing I know, more people are gathered in the corridor. Seven in the morning and everyone's getting their wakeup call. I see some brown faces and a couple of black ones. This is California, after all. But I don't see any Asiatic faces. Not in Plum Creek, Courtside Inn.

The trucker who was shouting blocks the cops in their paths and demands, "I want to know why you ain't arresting that rice beaner, deputies."

"I don't see a rice beaner. In fact, I don't know what that is," admits the cop with the hat. One of his hands is on his waist, fingertips on the nightstick. "Now step aside or we're gonna have a problem, sir."

"Man, this is bullshit. I saw him whack Leroy with some kind of karate chink shit."

The cop turns back to me and winks, like he's letting me know he's on my side. Then to the trucker, "When did you see the assault?"

"Two nights ago. I saw it with my own eyes." The trucker points at his own eyes, which happen to be located very close together.

"Where did you see it?"

"What you mean where? Right here in this hall."

"Where were you standing, exactly?"

"I was staying like six doors down, laying it over from a round trip to Nevada."

"Why were you standing outside your door?"

"I was standing by the door, waiting for my call girl like everyone else."

"You mean you called for a prostitute?"

"A fine hooker she was," he says, smacking his lips.

"You're admitting solicitation, to a deputy of the sheriff?"

"So? You're saying that like it's a crime."

"It is a crime, last time I checked."

"What? Wait…where am I again?"

"This is California, dumbass." The cop shakes his head. "You think you're in Vegas?"

The trucker scratches his nut sack. "I'm in America and I know my rights. Shit, I pay my taxes."

"And I'm not wasting tax payer dollars for some asshole who got what he deserved. Now, if you want to keep your job and make that delivery to Nevada, where you could pay for a hooker legally, then I highly suggest you move aside, *now*." The cop basically pushes him out of the way.

The law just leaves the scene and the scene isn't getting any more peaceful. Now the trucker is marching toward me, saying, "Why don't you come to my room, Chinaman? I'll give you a lesson on our saviors Jesus Christ and Adolf Hitler."

"Gee thanks, but no, thank you."

"What are you, afraid? Don't you want to learn? You'd like a good, free, American style education, right?" Sounds like he's making a pitch, but what he's really doing is making a threat. "Don't you want to know what our saviors say 'bout the likes of you? I'll tell you, man, the teachings of Christ and Adolf."

"I think I rather drop my nuts in a meat grinder."

"I'm surprised you got nuts at all."

The cops are out of sight and I'm a little confused. Should I call 911 now? Or after this trucker gives me beat down?

The big dude's about four feet away when Dangerous Shawn interjects to me, "Sir, I think you better check out through the rear window."

"108 checking out." I figure escape is the better part of valor, so I thank Shawn for presenting me with a way out of this mess and retreat to the room immediately. I lock the door and chain it up. Then I knock on the bathroom door and command, "Wrap it up in there Cujo, we gotta bounce." Rabies coughs and Cujo sneezes, then the toilet flushes. I remind, "Don't forget to wipe your ass and wash your hands."

I leave some loose change on the nightstand. While Cujo stashes a roll of toilet paper in his hoodie pouch, Rabies steals a wire hanger from the closet and wedges it under his belt.

A moment later, the three of us hurdle out the window.

In the parking lot of the Courtside Inn, the cops are just departing in their cruiser. They swerve out of the lot and pick up speed until lost to sight. I propose to Rabies and Cujo to meet at an establishment that serves breakfast, a place where we can discuss the heist. Heading to my car I realize Rabies is just standing there, sizing up the vehicles in the lot. At last he hooks a pair of gold-rimmed sunglasses onto his face, looking gangster.

"Can't remember where you parked your car?" Cujo sneers at his captor.

"I want to steal a new one that's going to bring me luck."

Christ, guy comes to town and has to steal a car. Behind his shades, his eyes scan from left to right, finger pointing from one car to another, like doing an *eeny meeny miny moe*. Then he approaches a cream-colored Chrysler Fifth Avenue that's at least ten years old and bends over to inspect its tires. Finally, he lays his hand on the roof and pats. "This one...I like it a lot."

"This piece of shit?" Cujo also examines. "I thought you wanted to steal a *new* one. You see the paint job here? It's flaking."

"He's right." I approach the criminals. "Must have at least two hundred thousand on the meter." I gesture to a car from this decade. "Why don't you commandeer that one?"

"It has to be this one," Rabies insists.

The three of us in the motel lot talk over which auto to grand theft.

"Pick any car, any car but this." I point out, "It's got an Alabama plate. Can't be seen driving around California in a stolen vehicle with an Alabama plate. You'll stick out like a wart on a nice looking cunt."

"*Hey-Zeus*, you need to look closely." Rabies extracts the wire hanger from under his belt and hands it over to Cujo, instructing his captive to do the dirty work. "You notice what it actually *says* on the plate?"

The plate has three rows of text, all etched in and unadulterated, from the department of motor vehicles. Looks to be standard: the top says *Alabama*; the middle is the license plate number; on the bottom is written, *God Bless America*. I conduct a quick survey of the cars around me. No other cars have a third line on their plates. I suppose, only in Alabama.

"God bless America, *Hey-Zeus*. Tell me you don't find that glorious." The Mexican gangster adjusts his belt. "I'm taking this car."

Chapter Thirteen

Cujo, Rabies, and myself, America's minorities, are gathered in Plum Creek's roadside diner scheming about getting paid big in the land of the free, exercising our rights set forth in the constitution of the United States, specifically in regard to the pursuit of happiness, to our American Dreams.

God bless America.

Cujo, African-American, is wearing his standard thug uniform—a black hoodie. He lays his head low, not wanting to be seen. Rabies—Mexican—is chewing gum, making a mole on his face move up and down. His choice of cover is the pair of gold-rimmed Raybans, even though the diner is dimly lit. And me, Chinese-American, ex-military with a Purple Heart, looking like I fought for the other side in 'Nam. I suppose we're all doing our best to act inconspicuous, but man, it isn't working. The waitress hesitates to approach our table, and when she does she appears quite amused. She takes a good look at us, up close, probably trying to peg which one of the Village People each of us is supposed to represent, probably thinking we're a second tier cover band, in town to do the *YMCA*.

After the waitress leaves to get our orders in, we huddle up and start to chatter in whispers. I realize how ridiculous this is, plus Cujo didn't brush his teeth, so I lean back and speak at a casual volume, "First of all, no one gets hurt. Anyone gets so much as a bruise I'm at liberty to call off the heist. Second, as Rabies said, we have to settle the split." I turn to the cartel man. "Can you please take off your sunglasses? You look like you're either a criminal or fucking blind."

He complies and asks, "So, how much are we talking about here?"

Looking straight into his brown eyes, I tell him, "One hundred thousand, give or take."

His eyes light up. "There's that much in the cash drawers?"

The waitress returns to pour our coffee, I wait till she's done and out of earshot, then I continue in a lower voice, "We're after the vault, people. We're not talking chump change here. I work at the bank so I know, roughly one hundred grand cash money in the vault. Minus the twenty or so Cujo owes Mad Dog, that's eighty grand, for the take."

"You said no one gets hurt?" Rabies frowns. "How we gonna get the vault open if we don't break some legs? What we gonna do, spread terror with our *words*? How's that different from what Cujo scratched on those napkins?"

"I'll convince the manager and she will open the vault willingly. *Trust* me." Because Ester, Jim, and Cass are already robbing the bank. Open the vault for them also opens up a *bigger* score with the FDIC.

"Eighty grand..." Rabies sits back in his chair, tilts his head to the ceiling, then closes his eyes. When he opens them he's looking at me. "I'm a reasonable man, *Hey-Zeus*. Forty for each of us, okay? We split fifty/fifty."

"How'd you come up with that?" Cujo leans forward, arms folded on the table. "Y'all split it two ways there ain't nothing left for *me*. You're saying I get nothing? Nada?"

"You get to pay off Mad Dog and *live*," Rabies states with a cold-ass stare.

Cujo appears to be appreciative but still goes on saying, "C'mon fellas, throw a dog a bone. At least something-*somethin'*, how 'bout ten grand? C'mon dawg."

"Okay, ten," I volunteer. "You can have ten out of my share."

"For reals? Hey wait, major, I think I spoke too soon. How about twenty? C'mon now."

"Only if I have more to spare." I look over to Rabies. "We cool?"

Rabies is nodding and frowning at the same time. "Why are you doing this?"

"You mean split my take?"

"No, I mean, *this*"—he taps the table with his index finger—"*helping* us."

I'm doing this for the daughter I may or may not have...

Not wanting to appear vulnerable, I produce a scoff. "Why do you care?"

"I need to know you can be trusted."

"I didn't turn you over to the cops at the inn, did I? You don't have to trust me, but know this—you need me as much as I need you. And I'm not helping *you*, I'm helping *myself*."

Eyes squinting, he says, "You do know that if you cross me, you will die."

I shrug. "Of course."

He thinks about it over coffee and nods several more times. "So when do we do it?"

"Tomorrow afternoon."

"That's too soon."

I tired daddy. I hungry. I no have home.

Not soon enough.

"Listen to me," I lower my voice. "The bank caters mostly to small businesses around town. Friday is when people make the deposits, and Monday is the slowest day. Tomorrow also happens to be the last day of the month. First of the month, armored truck comes in and moves the large bills. Moreover, I know for a fact that some other shit's going down on Monday, which I'm hoping is gonna keep the cops busy. So, in conclusion, if you want a big score, it *has* to be tomorrow." *It has to be.* "We got one shot at it, and it's all part of the plan I've worked out."

"What exactly is the plan?"

"I got one plan and two contingencies. The latter are to succeed the former in case shit goes sideways. And trust me, as much as I'd like to execute this like clockwork, shit *will* go sideways. I speak from experience..." I stop talking as I look up.

The waitress is approaching with three dishes of cheeseburgers. She sets them down and asks us out of the blue, "You boys from San Francisco?"

The three of us tilt our heads at her, our expressions saying, *What makes you say that?*

"My cousin ran away from home, he was your type of guys, you know, always pretty queer even when we were kids. Don't get me wrong, he was my best friend and I love him. He ran away and he's working in San Francisco in a dance company, maybe you've heard of him? Goes by the stage name Rodimus Prime. No? Oh all right. You boys enjoy your food."

I glance over at Rabies, and he looks like he's ready to shoot her in the back.

Cujo shakes his head and informs us, "Rodimus Prime, that's the robot who stepped in for Optimus Prime as the leader of the Autobots. Rodimus was one lousy leader."

I take a deep breath and clear my thoughts. I say to the pair, "You ready to hear about the plan or what?"

Taking a bite out of his burger, Cujo hums, "Umm-huh."

Rabies cools down somewhat. "Just fucking tell us already."

I start off by saying, "There's a fable that should be known universally. But since we're such a multicultural bunch, I feel compelled to make sure." A pause. "Raise your hand if you never heard the story about the boy who cried wolf."

Part Two

Eric Qiao

Chapter Fourteen

Monday. Day of the robbery. I rise early. Cass is still sleeping on what used to be my bed; now it's our bed. As I watch her sleep in peace, I try to imagine spending the rest of my life with her, sleeping together, waking up together, working together, dining together, and sleeping together again, repeating the same things in the same small town, until we die, or one of us dies. A life without meaningful endeavors, a death of a tired, old, and unfulfilled pill.

It cannot work, especially not with a little girl in 'Nam, who may or may not be my daughter.

I shit, shave, and get dressed for work, quietly. Pants, shirt, and socks, I wear my tie and pin my nametag, thinking of the various what-ifs. What if Cass figures out the heist? Doesn't matter. I'm leaving her and I'm leaving this place. But what if someone gets hurt? What if Cujo or Rabies goes off script? No, I'll be there and no one will get hurt. The plan's solid, and I've led men into more daring missions. I take a moment to decide which shoes to wear. Running shoes or dress shoes? I figure I ought to go to work just like any other day. I wear my dress shoes.

Looking in the mirror now, I acknowledge the facts. Today will be my last day in town. Last day of being an upstanding American. Last day with Cass. I nod at myself. *10-4, over and out.*

Once ready, I take a look around the place of my domicile, the house my parents left me, a house they bought to fulfill the dream of their parents. I don't intend to stay. I go to the mantelpiece and pocket my Purple Heart.

I get in my car and leave without Cass. Whenever she stayed over we always went to work our separate ways. I figure today ought to be no less different.

Some unusual traffic on the road which is just as expected. It takes five minutes more than usual to drive to the bank. I wish in that prolonged journey I'd think of an alternative to procure ten thousand dollars. But I couldn't think of any.

I park at the rear lot of the bank facing the backdoor. No assigned spot for me but I've parked in the same spot for three years. I gaze upon the brick and mortar, the flat roof and tinted windows, the place where I spent three years of my life. I close my eyes and run the plan one more time. I think of the possible scenarios, of the chances of shit going sideways, and I lose the track of time. Then, I hear a car pull up next to mine.

It's Cass. She too, has dressed for work. Now she's drawing circles in the air with her index finger, miming for me to roll down the glass barrier between us. The green gleam in her eyes is faint at the moment.

"Why didn't you wake me, cowboy?" she says, her elbow sticking out of the window. "Remember you used to make me breakfast whenever I stayed over? Now that I've moved in, you abandon me." She brushes her hair back, doesn't look too upset.

"We're out of milk."

"Think you're gonna find milk in there?" Her head

gestures to our workplace. "Cookies, yeah. But milk?"

Acting calm, I shrug. "What's milk without cookies, right?"

From less than six feet away, she requests, "Can I come over?" And she does before I reply. Getting in my car, she points out, "You forgot to turn off your headlights."

I switch off the lights and say nothing.

"I don't blame you for leaving without me." She gazes at the bank building as well. "Because believe me, I know how you feel right now."

I turn to her. "You do?"

"Of course." Her words come out with a big exhale. "I have a conscience too, you know? Last night, I had nightmares. I dreamed how you got caught with foreign currencies—just you. They took you away in the middle of the night in handcuffs." She rubs her face and shakes her head, as if shaking off the horrors of her nightmare. "I'd rather it be me than you."

"You mean that?"

"You have to ask?" She adjusts the seat a couple of inches back, then her head hits the headrest. "But it was only a dream. In reality, it's all of us getting caught. We're in this together. That's why it has to be unanimous, right?" She looks into my eyes. "I'm sorry you have to do this because of me. I know it's putting you through a lot. You're a honest man, Chin, and now…"

Now…two more cars pull into the lot.

It's Ester and Jim.

It's only forty past seven in the morning, and all the employees of the bank are gathered. Jim parks next to Cass and climbs out miming a tip of the hat in the air.

Ester parks at the only reserved spot in the lot. Perk of being a manager, although the lot is never full. "Everyone's early." Getting out of the car with a cup of coffee, she remarks, "I'll take this as a good sign."

"Maybe they've turned us in." Jim treads lightly.

Ester waits for the three of us to approach, and says to Cass, "Did you? Turn us in?"

"It crossed my mind." She stops at six feet away.

"And?"

"And...nothing," Cass replies, not looking at the boss. In a little voice she says, "I just want what's mine."

Jim blows out a sigh of relief. Ester too, but only a small one. "Good. What about you, Chin?" She now turns upon me with a critical stare. "You're the wildcard now, as you haven't voiced your opinion at all. You with us, or are you here to turn us in?"

I'm here to rob the bank.

Taking a good look at the three of them, I just say, "Ester, you still have those cookies in your office?"

* * * *

In large cities such as San Francisco or LA, banks don't stock foreign currencies. They have to request them days in advance. Request them from banks in nowhereville. Our bank keeps Swedish kronas, Deutschemarks, Japanese yen, very unpopular currencies, which means the reserve is well stocked enough to cover our little scam. Ester knows this because she oversees the reserve. She knows exactly how much is in there.

Cass points out the various risks in such a scam, talking about the what ifs. What if this? What if that? Why would the robbers take the foreign currencies in the first place?

In her office, Ester assures her, "That's for the robbers to answer. The important thing is, we stick to our story, and no one will ask these questions to begin with."

"It's a risk," Jimbo acknowledges. "But a risk I'm willing—willing and ready to take."

Sticking a cigarette in her mouth and not lighting it, Cass mumbles in agreement, "Whatever."

Then they all turn to me. "Chin?"

Cass is looking at me with those eyes, eyes saying, *If you change your mind, I'd be with you.*

I don't change my mind. "I'm onboard, but"— given the opportunity, I instill the idea in their heads, paving the way for the heist I'm about to pull—"I think the scam would work so much *better*, so much *simpler*, if the robbers made us open the vault."

"Well, unfortunately they didn't steal from the vault. So this is the way it has to be." The boss lady then observes the clock on the wall, twenty minutes till the bank's open. She claps her hands and stands. Her chair squeaks as her ass leaves the cushion. "Well boys and girls, pleasure doing business with you all."

Cass and Jimbo leave the room. Before I do I grab a cookie from the desk. One for the road. I make for my station, taking a deep breath. The hours are counting down.

It's American crime time.

Chapter Fifteen

As soon as the bank's open for business, I know something's wrong.

A police cruiser passes by every fifteen minutes or so just like on Saturday. This isn't a patrol. This is *surveillance*.

Not a single customer in the first hour. The traffic outside is busier than usual, as expected. But the police cruiser has driven past four times already, which is unexpected.

Keeping an eye out, I strike up a meaningless conversation with Cass, just as I would on a normal day, "So, what're your parents up to?"

She's doodling something on a pad, killing time. Not looking up from her doodles, she replies, "They're gonna try to use my library card for some books. They weren't impressed by my romance novels."

Remembering how Larry quoted Oscar Wilde, I figure we have similar taste. "I got plenty of books in the den, Cass. They're welcome to them."

"Great, I'll call now and let them know." She goes off to use the only phone, which is on Jim's desk.

Before she finishes the call, a siren wails.

Weewoo weewoo.

The cruiser—the same one doing the surveillance on the bank—screeches to a halt in a matter of seconds. Two wheels crash on the sidewalk, the front bumper less than a foot from the entrance of the bank. The deputy in the car, I recognize him now. Deputy Morris, the guy Cass was seeing on and off when she first moved to Abisko. Maybe he's running surveillance because he wants to keep Cass safe after last week's robbery. Maybe he still has feelings for her. Or maybe he's just a creep and he's stalking her.

Morris rolls down the window and kicks the car door all the way open. Then he kneels behind the door, like he's using it as a shield. He draws his weapon, pointing it straight at the bank's door. He's speaking to his shoulder radio when Cass, Jim, and I burst out of the building.

"The hell you pointing that gun at us for, Morris?" Cass trots forward, leading us.

"Cassandra...good, you're not hurt." Still pointing the gun in our direction, he commands, "Get down, quickly."

"Get down?" Cass turns a one-eighty, left to right and back again, flabbergasted. "Christ, Morris, you been drinking? On the *job* no less?"

It takes Morris a good five seconds to grasp the peace and serenity inside the bank as well as all around us. Slowly, he rises from behind the car door and lowers the gun. He's wearing a maroon colored uniform, standard in this neck of the woods, but it makes him look like he's with Parks and Recreation rather than with the County Sheriff. "I'm sober, Cassandra." His eyes scan us and the bank. "You folks not robbed?"

"We *were* robbed, three days ago." Cass is clutching her waist. "Little late for you to show up guns blazing, don't you think?"

Morris blows out a gust of relief and speaks to his shoulder radio, "Stand down. False alarm. Over."

Jim comes up from behind Cass. "Deputy, what made you think we were being robbed?"

There's more radio activity going on and Morris ignores it. He shrugs to us. "I just got the dispatch. They probably thought the alarm was tripped somehow."

I step up as well. "Why would they think that?"

He looks at me, a glimpse of contempt in his gaze. He replies, "I don't know," and holsters his weapon.

The scene is causing traffic to slow. Folks peer at us from their cars wondering what the hell's going on, why is the police cruiser parked on the curb, in front of a bank? Its siren lights flashing red and blue.

"We're getting some traffic in town today," I remark and ask Morris, "They move the date of the county fair or something?" as if I'm oblivious to what's going on.

"It's SAT day," he says, indifferent. "It's our turn to host."

"Host?"

"As testing center." My colleague Jim nudges me and relates, "Huck's there right now giving all he's got. Haven't you heard, Chin?" He lowers his voice to a whisper. "The Russians might finally hit us. This might be *it*."

Might be what?

"The schools have to rotate," Morris explains the SAT. "We're hosting six high schools from three counties. Testing administrators too, all the way from Sacramento. It'll be one hell of a day." He straightens his uniform and gets inside his car, not wanting to waste any more time.

"The sheriff's short handed then?"

"Got a CHP unit helping us out, facilitating traffic on and off the freeway." Morris slams the door and fastens his belt.

Before he rolls up the window, I ask, "You're overseeing this turf then?"

He doesn't hear me and mumbles some jargon to his shoulder radio.

"When's the testing over?"

Engine starts and he says, "Look, you mind? I gotta get going." To Cass, "It's good seeing you, Cassandra. You look good. And...be safe, yeah?" He backs off the curb and the car rocks so hard his head hits the roof. Old Plymouth Grand Fury, a hand-me-down from a bigger department. Suspension worn. Fury ain't so grand.

I'm thinking, *See you soon, Morris.*

The three of us watch the car get lost to sight, Jim saying, "I wonder why they think the alarm was triggered."

"Yeah, I wonder why." I scratch my head. "Jim, you said the Russians might hit us? What does that have to do with anything?"

"The *draft*, Chin. They're saying Reagan might bring it back. Draft boys outta school and send them off to fight communists all over the world. Cuba, Nicaragua, USSR... SAT's now a matter of life and death. Christ Almighty, what's the world coming to?"

"Chin?" Cass looks up at me with worrisome eyes. "Can I talk to you for a second?"

At the same time, our regular client, Buzz, crosses the street shouting at us, "Comrades, how are you gonna safeguard the future of this institution if you just stand around all day?"

"Buzz, buddy," Jim calls. "What do you need?"

"Speak up, son." Buzz points at his hearing aid. "I swear I fart louder than you talk."

I tell Cass, "Later, okay?"

She nods her consent as we return to the bank to help buzz.

The weariness in her eyes isn't going away.

****

In the second hour, I see the Grand Fury cruise by twice—two fewer times than the previous hour. The traffic dies down. Test starts in the morning, probably already commenced. I remember the draft during 'Nam. Not in school or don't have the grades? Report to Uncle Sam and be shipped off to some godforsaken corner of the world, go on mandatory suicide missions fighting for who knows what.

It's ten past eleven o'clock.

The traffic is light yet it takes Morris exactly thirty-two seconds longer than the last time to respond to the tripped alarm. The differences are: the car is parked neatly by the curb, not on the sidewalk; the siren isn't blaring, although the lights are on; and he doesn't cower behind the door. He's standing straight, peering over at us.

Cass, Jim, and myself exit the building again. Our hands spread and our necks stick forward, the universal sign of *what the hell?*

Morris keeps his eyes on us as he tilts his neck to speak to his shoulder radio. "False alarm, again. Over and out."

"I think you're a wonderful man, Morris. But"—

Jim rubs his chin—"where were you when we needed you—last week?"

"At the fire," Morris replies. "You know, the one that could've devoured your house?"

Cass crosses her arms and they bring up her breasts. "Don't you think it's a bit redundant, for one bank to be robbed in such close intervals?"

"I know you don't want to see me, Cassandra. But I got the call, what do you want me to do?"

"That's so unbelievable." I place my hand on Cass's shoulder, an affectionate, protective gesture. Like I'm protecting her from another robbery, or her from him—her ex-bf. I ask the guy, "The silent alarm was triggered, again?"

"Looks like it." He surveys me then Cass.

Cass is leaning in closer to me, the left side of her face resting snugly on my shoulder. She uncrosses her arms and places her hand on my waist. We're in a sideways-hug.

Morris looks away from this subtle public display of affection as he ducks inside his cruiser and suggests to us before closing the door, "You ought to check that alarm of yours, make sure it's working right, Cassandra." He does a quick nod at the lady in my arm and then starts the car.

We return to the bank and Ester is out of her office—a rare occurrence. She inquires, "Is everything okay?"

Getting back to his desk, Jim casually informs her, "Seems like our alarm has gone haywire."

About this alarm—it's a telephone line is all it is. The line only goes one way and it's to the sheriff's. There are three panic buttons under the counters. Cass has one, I have one, and a third is at the counter on my right—a counter unattended. Doesn't matter which button is pressed, once it's triggered, it places a silent, distress signal to the sheriff's department's dispatch. Last Friday, when Cujo and Marla were robbing us, I pressed the button for the very first time.

And in thirty minutes, I'm about to press it again— my third time today.

Chapter Sixteen

I press the panic button, triggering the silent alarm. I cry wolf, for the third time.

There's a full minute delay compared to the first time he responded. Morris lazily parks the Grand Fury across the street and trots over with his hands in his pockets. He enters the bank saying, "Seriously, guys, I don't have time for this. The gas station is out of gas, if you believe their luck. There are two accidents off the ramp and the traffic light's acting funny. We have to get everything sorted out before the second wave hits."

I come out from behind the counter, hand in hand with Cass. "Second wave?"

He sees us rubbing skin and he looks to Jim in annoyance. "Yeah, two rounds of testing today. One in the morning and one in the afternoon. Our goal is to make sure the out of town folks leave so there's adequate room for parking."

"Sorry to take up your time, but we didn't trigger the alarm and we're obviously not getting robbed." Jim shrugs innocently.

Morris does a three-sixty by the entrance. The counters are on the right side of him, three stations, two tellers on duty. Jim's desk is on the left, a moderately sized flattop with two file cabinets underneath. Directly opposite him is the vault, an imposing steel door with a wheel that looks like it could belong on a very large ship. The vault is shut. Ten feet left of the vault is the passage leading to the back office and to the back exit. Morris turns to Cass. "Show me the panic button."

At this point Cass lets go of my hand and leads him to her station. They duck and find the red button hidden underneath the counter, the button the size of a quarter. I watch as Morris studies the little modern ingenuity, eyes marveling at it. Finally, he presses it.

I count the seconds.

Seven, eight, nine…

His radio comes on. A woman's voice, "211S, again. Over."

"Please ignore it. Over." He releases his radio, and to Cass he says, "Well, it's working." The guy is still kneeling and Cass is leaning forward, bent 80 degrees at the waist, her blouse hanging down and showing two-thirds of her bra, which is demanding Morris' attention at the moment. I stand casually two stations away and slip my fingers under the counter. I find the button, press it and make my way around, counting the seconds.

Seven, eight, nine, ten…

I'm standing on the other side when Morris' radio pings him again, "211S, what the hell's going on?"

He stops leering at Cass's bra and stands up. He finds me opposite him, my hands flat on the counter. I act like I've been standing there for a while.

Morris is staring at me when he responds to the radio, "Ignore it. Over."

Cass rises. Adjusting her blouse, she points out the obvious, "It's broken."

"I don't think the button's been used since they built this place"—I drum the counter with my fingers—

"until last Friday, of course. When we were being robbed, I pressed the thing pretty vigorously. I mean, you guys weren't showing up. I'm afraid I pressed it too hard or too many times and broke it or something."

"Well..." He sighs and looks around, appearing kind of hopeless. "You gotta get this thing fixed."

"We'll call the phone company."

"Think they'll fix it before the weekend?"

"Wouldn't that be a miracle."

To Cass, with some kind of self-deprecating charm, he shrugs. "Well then."

"Well then what?" Cass frowns at him. "You're gonna bust in here every time the alarm goes off on its own?"

"I wouldn't mind, normally," he speaks in a low voice. "Come in here and see you, in that blouse."

"Morris, please stop." Her face is somewhat blushed, and she casts a glance over to me.

"Fine, Cassandra, I won't." He puts up his hands. "You folks have yourselves a good day."

Poor Deputy Morris, realizing he's no one's friend at the bank, leaves the establishment he's trying to protect. He crosses the street and gets inside his car, then closes the door kind of slow. I observe his every movement. He's talking on his radio now, staring back at us. Then, he inserts the key and starts the engine. I wait for him to shift the gear, however, he doesn't do it.

His face is turned toward us, just watching, gazing. Motionless. Like a predator studying its prey right before the hunt. He's doing something that doesn't pertain to any version of the story—the story of the boy who cried wolf.

He sits there and he's not leaving.

Chapter Seventeen

Two minutes till noon. One customer graces us with his presence just to inquire about his account balance, and then the mailman comes in to drop off a dozen advertisements, ads from local businesses. Apparently, the tire shop is still having the buy-two-tires-get-two-free special. Little text on the bottom that says, While Supplies Last.

Deputy Morris has been sitting opposite the bank for nearly an hour. The "boy who cried wolf" master plan has backfired. Instead of not showing up here at all, a cop is on us like reeking body odor. What if he lingers here all day? For nearly an hour I've been thinking if I ought to start another fire just to get rid of the guy.

The clock strikes twelve.

Noontime should be especially busy but not today. SAT day's got everyone's panties in a wad. Parents waiting for their kids, living vicariously through the testees, as if they too, have a shot of getting out of town.

It's lunchtime and Morris doesn't even look hungry. He just sits there like a hawk staring at the bank's entrance. As I'm wondering if I should go out and talk to him, find out more about this unorthodox surveillance he's conducting, an old couple enters the bank.

It's the Roselyns.

"Mom, Dad?" Cass makes her way around the counter. "Please don't tell me you're here to embarrass me. Last time you visited my workplace you made me sing happy birthday." To me she explains, "I waited tables."

"Embarrass you? Nonsense, Cassandra." Larry Roselyn looks to be in a good mood. "We're here to open a bank account."

"You must be joking."

"That obvious, huh?" Larry winks at me. "So this is where you work."

Cass introduces Jim and everyone waves, smiling and observing courtesy. Then Larry says to me, "Major, we went to your place to checkout some books but then it's the darnedest thing, we got to your place and realized we can't get in."

So I fish my keys out of my pocket and I try to detach the house key from the chain.

As I'm doing so, Cass's mom, Mrs. Roselyn talks, "We went to the general store and, I'm sorry, but the china selection is so disappointing. After we return to Pike County we'll ship you a set. How does that sound?"

I won't be here, so, "Sounds great."

I toss the key over the counter and she drops it, saying, "Oops." She bends to pick it up, reaching, her stomach fat preventing her from bending too low. Now she's bending her knees one degree at a time. Larry checks out his wife's massive ass, smirking at me. The whole thing seems to happen in slow motion.

"You two must be hungry." The woman heaves as she finally returns to her upright position, pocketing the key. "We don't know what to eat around here so we were wondering if you care to show us the local delicacies."

So the mother and daughter discuss this matter. "What do you want to eat?" "Well, what's good?" "Mexican?" "I eat American." Jim chimes in, "You guys should try the pizza place."

At the same time, Larry approaches my counter and whispers hush-hush, "Hey major, remember what I went on about perspective and all, about speaking your mind? That's just an old man rambling. You get that right? I've been thinking and I believe it was a mistake to speak to you like that."

I nod a couple of times, not sure what this is about.

His eyes dart around like making sure no one is listening, and he resumes, "You know, major, a good woman is really all you need in this life." Reaching across the counter, he double pats me on the shoulder. "If you have a good woman who loves you unconditionally—even if her ass could collapse your lung if she accidentally fell on you—you'll realize her ass is the most beautiful in the world. Think about it, son."

I ponder a bit. "Appreciate the wisdom, Larry."

"Ah well," he says, speaking in his casual volume now, "just wanted that off my chest is all."

A good woman who loves you unconditionally?

With him in front of me blocking me from view, I press the button under the counter. Got to keep on crying wolf. I trot from behind the counter, joining Larry and gang. Acting carefree. Expecting a response.

Seven, eight, nine, ten...

The phone on Jim's desk rings.

The loan officer picks it up and a moment later he says, "Yes, deputy, we're being robbed."

Everyone turns to look at him.

"I'm just joking, Amanda. Ha ha. No-no, we're not being robbed. Tell the sheriff the alarm's acting faulty. Yes... Yes, not being robbed, that was a joke...bad taste, I know. We'll definitely get that fixed. Yeah... Thanks for checking on us." He hangs up.

Deputy Morris also enters the bank to check. He nods as he acknowledges our wellbeing, then he approaches Cass and asks in a voice so soft, I may just vomit, "Miss Cassandra, tell me, are you okay?"

Cass's mom, a hand cupped around her mouth, whispers in her daughter's ear so loud everyone hears. "Cassandra, who is this nice and handsome young man?"

Morris clears his throat and introduces himself, asking for the mother's hand to shake. "You must be Mrs. Roselyn."

Mrs. Roselyn's face is full of surprise. "How on earth did you know I'm her mother?"

"The resemblance is uncanny, ma'am."

Larry nudges me, his eyes are saying, *You believe this shit?*

"Your daughter and I used to date," Morris lets on. "I've actually heard a lot about you, Mrs. Roselyn." He turns to Larry, bowing a little. "And you must be Mr. Roselyn."

"Must be," Larry says. "You want a cookie?"

"Used to date?" Cass's mom looks from me to Morris. Her preference apparent, Morris, white and pale, is the type of guy she wants for a son-in-law. "Well, what happened between the two of you? Did my daughter hurt you? Did she—"

"Mom, *stop* it," Cass beseeches through her teeth. "I'm with Chin now, okay? Have you decided yet what you want to eat?"

Morris rocks up to his toes, acting cute. "I happen to know a great Mexican restaurant, Mrs. Roselyn."

"Oh, that sounds positively wonderful."

Even Jim's cringing.

Right then, I know exactly what I must do to get these people out of here. These people including Morris. *Especially* Morris.

"How about this…" I step up speaking three words at a time, "Cass and Morris…why don't you…take the Roselyns…to eat lunch."

Cass' mom's hands clap together and hold close to her body, getting in that standard cheerleader position. She appears more than delighted at the proposal. And so does Morris. Larry, on the other hand, is utterly flabbergasted. Cass glares at me like I've lost my mind.

I grab Cass's arm and yank her aside. I whisper, "I can't go to lunch with you guys. I need to cover the counter."

"Okay but," she's *not* whispering, "I think my parents and I—the three of us—can manage just fine."

"No," I command, "you *have* to take Morris."

"Listen, Chin," now she's whispering, "I wanted to talk to you about this earlier. Morris and me, we're done, okay? I made that perfectly clear to him last week. He told me he understood. So don't you worry about him."

I'm frowning when I say, "Last week?"

She has that *oh snap* look on her face, like she said more than she was meant to. "Well, yeah," she utters, "I told him I was moving in with you."

"Was this before or after Friday's robbery?"

"What does it matter?" She rubs her forehead. "I'm done with him, and that's that. Frankly, I don't know what you're trying to pull here. Why do you want me to have lunch with him?"

"That's not the only thing I want you to do. I want you to tell him at lunch in front of your parents that you don't want to see him, not even from across the street 'cause he's cramping your style, mine too. If he says he's here to watch the bank, tell him it's bullshit and that he's harassing you."

"Harassing me? Yet we're having lunch with my parents?"

"Yes, and use my break hour. I'm not hungry today."

"Chin, you want to tell me what's on your mind?"

I keep quiet and she's studying me up close.

"Well?" she asks again.

So I play my trump card. "You recall that night when you agreed to do what I ask of you, even if you disapprove? Remember what I said, no questions asked, right?"

"Shit." She grimaces, worried. "Is this about anal sex?"

"What—God no. I'm just saying, do what I asked you. Please, use my break hour, I'll cover for you."

She's wrinkling her entire face, eyes looking like they want to protest. But in the end, she nods twice. "I did make that promise. But I can't guarantee he won't come back to stakeout the bank."

"In that case, keep him at bay for as long as possible." A pause later I recommend, "At least two hours."

"*Two* hours? What am I supposed to say to him for two whole hours?"

"I think your mother will have plenty to say."

She blows out a windy sigh and then she cups my face with her palm. "I love you, Chin. I'd do anything for you."

A woman who loves you unconditionally?

When we return to join the Roselyns, Cass's mom is rubbing her stomach looking eager to have some tacos. Morris insists everyone rides in his police car and the woman appears rather pleased by this. Larry shuffles and dawdles after his wife. Finally, they all leave.

I check the time, *two hours, starting now*.

I press the alarm button again and count to ten. Nothing. Fifteen seconds, the phone on Jim's desk isn't ringing. Twenty seconds, no wailing sirens, no response. The boy who cried wolf is about to get eaten, just as planned, *at last*. I proceed to exit the building saying to Jim I need a bathroom break. Jim, taking out a homemade sandwich says to me, "Could've asked me to join Cass for lunch, Chin."

"I need you to cover for me, Jim. Thanks, I'll be back in five."

I sprint across the street, come around a corner and start to run. I dart past the salon, the bakery and the deli attached to it, all of these establishments have telephones I could use but also people that will wonder why the hell I went out of the way to use theirs. So I make haste all the way to the public library, to a place that has a payphone. I'm gunning at 20 mph in my slip-on dress shoes, toes blistering, sweat pouring across my forehead. I've been in better shape.

Old folks are coming and going at the library entrance, I look around and act normal. Just making a call is all. A quarter is in the slot. The economy is in the shit-can but folks around here still paying it forward. Standing at ease, I use the coin and dial, three rings and I'm checking the time. On the fourth ring it's picked up.

"Rabies…" I take a deep but short breath so I don't sound like I ran a marathon. A second later, my lips are touching the mouthpiece as I whisper, "Phase one is complete. Initiate phase two in ten."

"Negative," Rabies says. "Not in ten. Our boy Cujo's not gonna make it."

"Why?" My heart skips a beat but quickly recovers. "Give me a sit-rep ASAP."

"Here's your sit-rep, *Hey-Zeus*. In ten minutes, I'm gonna shoot Cujo in the head."

Chapter Eighteen

I'm on the library's payphone, hearing Cujo explaining his situation, "Major, I'm supposed to speak to Marla. Mad Dog says she's okay but I think he's lying, man. He won't let me talk to her, not a word. How am I supposed to know she's all right? Maybe he's killed her... God, what am I to do if he's killed her? What do I have to live for? Everything I'm doing is for her. I ain't robbing no bank, sticking my neck out if she's already dead. If Mad Dog wants to kill me 'cause I ain't doing it, then so be it. He'd be doing me a favor, letting me join my woman on the other side."

Rabies takes over the phone. "*Hey-Zeus*, we can still rob the bank. We don't need Cujo. Just let me dispose of his body first. Give me sixty minutes." His tone is hushed. "We split the money two ways. It's a better deal, yeah? What do you say?"

"I say you don't have to *kill* him." My voice may have been a couple decibels over the acceptable volume for a library, so I go on in a loud whisper, kissing the mouthpiece, "Have you ever robbed a bank? No. Neither have I. Guess what, Cujo has, not once, not twice, *three* times. Plus this heist is a three-man operation. We need him, Rabies. Can't you let him live?"

"Orders are orders, I'm afraid. I'm a cartel man first. A bank robber second."

"But"—I let out an uncomprehending scoff—"but you want to rob a bank behind your boss's back, pocketing the take."

"So?" He sounds baffled. "I don't have to get permission to take a shit, do I? This is a free country. I have impunity to exercise my own prerogative."

I rub my temples. "What's Mad Dog *thinking*? If Cujo's dead, he's not getting paid, either."

"That's a good question, *Hey-Zeus*. You should ask Mad Dog."

I mutter a curse under my breath as I check the time. An eighth of the two-hour window has already passed.

"I can find us another man for the job." Rabies requests, "How 'bout we do this some other time? I promise you I'll find a more suitable replacement."

I tired daddy. I hungry. I no have home.

My daughter is doing slave labor and every minute is taking a toll on me. I beseech Rabies, "There won't be a next fucking time. I told you, we only have one shot at this." Then I ask him to put Cujo on the phone and a second later, I'm saying, "Cujo, if you speak to Marla, then everything is a-go, right?"

"Affirmative, major. I just wanna hear her voice."

"So where are they hiding?"

"How should I know?"

"How do you reach him?"

"Don't know. He reaches us."

"Put Rabies on." More seconds are wasted as I repeat the same questions to Rabies. The conclusion is, Rabies is just as ignorant about Mad Dog and Marla's whereabouts as Cujo. "When's the last time he called?"

"Over two hours ago," Rabies says.

"When are you supposed to execute Cujo?"

"At thirty past noon—in five minutes."

"Why wait two hours since you got the order?"

"So he can have lunch and die with a full stomach. It's a matter of professional courtesy."

"Has he eaten?"

"No." There's a sigh. "I bought a hot dog from the vending machine, but he refuses to eat it."

From the background, Cujo saying, "Man, the hot dog is cold! *Hot* dog, asshole. I ain't gonna go out eating no cold dog. Don't got any mustard to chow it down with. This is some bullshit."

Rabies' solution: "I'm gonna have to shove it down his throat."

Cujo's little voice in the back, "Man, ain't nobody shoving no wiener down my throat."

My mind cranks for a split second and I say, "Rabies, delay the execution. Have him eat something warm at least. Give me one hour and I'll have Mad Dog call you back. Cujo will speak to Marla on the phone, and we'll go on as planned. Only it'll have to be on the double."

Persuading, I go on, "Think about it, Rabies. Phase one is complete. The plan's solid. You know it."

The line is quiet for a spell.

"You have forty minutes."

"You know what? *Thirty*." I shorten the time limit myself. "Thirty minutes, and that's till one o'clock. If Mad Dog doesn't call with Marla, shoot Cujo in the head."

I hang up the phone.

I close my eyes and think. *Where's Mad Dog?*

When my eyes are open, I'm back at being an MP.

Chapter Nineteen

So where's Mad Dog?

I review the facts, and the facts are:

MD drives a Pontiac.

The cops haven't found the Pontiac.

A BOLO is out for MD and said Pontiac.

After MD shot at me in my driveway, he traveled to Plum Creek and took Marla hostage.

Two hours ago, MD used a telephone to call Rabies.

The facts.

Deserters, AWOL and fugitives alike, I've found them, up and down in the jungle, in caves and huts, mountains and rivers. I was good at my job. And what the job entails is to think like your subject. Become him.

Become Mad Dog.

So the first question is, if *I* were a wanted man, how would I travel south unseen from Abisko to Plum Creek?

I wouldn't want to risk taking the bus. Cops aren't going to leave the road south wide open for a cartel man *from* the south. I wouldn't hitchhike; I'm a Mexican gangster in Hicksville, chances of getting picked up by a Good Samaritan are slim to none, getting picked up by a redneck trucker is more likely but in that case I'd worry more about my personal safety. No, I wouldn't hitchhike. Would I steal a car and abandon my Pontiac? It's a better move, but if I did, the cops would've found my Pontiac by now. In conclusion, the only way to get to Plum Creek—the only rational way, as according to the facts presented—would be to drive in my own car. Since the roads are blocked, I wouldn't be able to drive *on* the road. I'd drive *off-road*.

And the next question becomes, how do I get to Plum Creek *off-road*?

It's easy to get lost driving off-road. I'd have no sense of direction. I'd think I'm driving a straight line when in fact I'm thirty degrees off from where I started. In the jungle, you learn to identify a tangent line first to avoid going around in circles. Without a compass, the best way to establish a path is to consult the sun. The daily arc of the sun is at an angle relative to your tangent plane, and it moves along on the arc at about fifteen degrees per hour. Depending on the time of day, it may move more or less. It's a pain in the ass to do the calculations, so all of us in the unit would give up on the math instantly if there were a—say—stream nearby. We'd just use the stream as the tangent.

Now, I'm Mad Dog and I'm traveling off-road in my car and I don't know how to do the trigonometry thing with the sun. So what's my tangent? What is my stream?

The answer is plain and simple.

It's the railroad.

Back when locomotives were a popular form of transportation, you could take the train from here all the way to Illinois with a short five to ten-minute stop in Abisko and Plum Creek. The towns are connected. The rail line is defunct now. If I were Mad Dog, I'd travel in my car, A to PC, along the railroad.

Final question: Where am I now?

Answer: At a service station or an emergency stop between towns, just off the tracks, with access to a service phone.

I check the time, thinking, *wasted 45 seconds.*

I run toward the bank to pickup my car. I'm speeding 35 mph on foot. For some reason I'm thinking of what Larry said, *All you need in this life is a woman who loves you unconditionally.* I'm losing track of my internal clock.

Cujo's life counting down.

The window for the heist closing fast.

****

I swerve the car out of the lot and race past the bank, not stopping at the stop sign, heading toward the railroad to find Mad Dog and Marla. Jim won't be happy. I was due back in five minutes, and now I won't be back for another forty. Cass is gone so it's just him holding the fort.

I arrive at the traffic light before the track, at the place where the Chinese guy took off with my car, and I turn left, heading south toward Plum Creek, off-road.

The land is flat, goes far as eyes can see. The sky is blue and the ground is gray, grass dried from lack of rain. As soon as I'm parallel to the rails, I know mine's not the only car to have recently traveled on this desert plain. The signs are there, tire marks, weeds bent and broken. I step on the gas and bring the car up to seventy-five. The steering wheel shakes to a rumble as I'm wasting rubber. The clock reads 12:42. I have less than twenty minutes to find Mad Dog and convince him to let Marla talk to Cujo. I bring the car up to eighty.

Beside the rails and the timber tracks, I drive and think about the reason I'm in this town. Abisko, this is where my grandparents settled. They came to this country with their parents, on ships with sails, dreamed of a better life. In China, they dipped their fingers in red ink and pressed their fingerprints on a piece of parchment with words they didn't understand. They thought it was the ticket for the free boat ride to San Francisco, a town nowadays known in Chinese as the *Old Gold Mountain*. Instead, they were signing their lives away. They docked in the Bay Area along with the rest of the immigrants and were taken to somewhere in Nevada, which I bet was just as empty then as it is today. Want to go back to San Francisco? Want to dig gold in the *Old Gold Mountain*? Got to lay down the rails first, folks. From the land beneath your feet all the way to the ocean. Then you'll be in San Francisco. Got to do it 'cause your fingerprints say you will.

My great-grandparents died on the journey. My grandparents met on the journey. When they finally got to San Francisco, overcoming ridges and hills, valleys and mountains, the gold was all but dug. They were cheated. Cheated out of their life of liberty and pursuit of happiness. Cheated by this land of opportunity.

The car hugs the rails and I'm thinking the rails are the legacy of my ancestors. The rails are abandoned and obsolete.

My parents bought the house in Abisko because it's what *their* parents wanted in the dwindling twilight of their mortality. They wanted a place close to the railroad so they could watch the train go by, watch their life's work, watch their accomplishment, their contribution to America. So they could die knowing, their lives were not for nothing.

And now here I am, witnessing what they can't.

The railroad, their sole purpose, is now just my tangent on this journey.

I follow the rails. I follow the tangent.

Twelve minutes left.

****

The tire marks split up ahead. Two sets of trails. I figure one set must be from going south and the other from coming back north, and I'm right. Not far from where the trails split, there's a structure built from red bricks. This is the service station, and it looks like part of an antique toy train set. Higher than one story but lower than two. On top there' a clock about the size of a pizza, which to my surprise, is telling the correct time. The Pontiac is parked no more than twenty feet behind the structure. There's nothing else here other than nature.

Looks like goddamn Kansas.

Four minutes left according to the pizza clock.

The Pontiac, it's rocking.

I drive directly toward the building and use it to conceal my approach. Stop and park the car fifty yards away and run toward it.

Three minutes left.

The car is rocking up and down, harder and harder.

Ten yards in I see a service phone just outside the building. Bell Pacific must've never bothered to disconnect the line. Or maybe…maybe it has something to do with the clock being accurate as well. I push my curiosity to the back of my mind.

The car still rocks and I use the phone to call

Rabies first to make sure he hasn't shot Cujo yet. Also to delay my approach in hopes the car will stop rocking.

It's two minutes till deadline when Rabies is on the line. I ask, "Where's Cujo?"

"On the can." Rabies scoffs. "The man spends half of his life on the shitter."

Good, he hasn't shot him. "But I thought you wanted him to die with a full stomach."

"He was gonna drop a deuce in his pants. I don't want to deal with that kind of aftermath."

"Tell him to hold the phone for Marla. After she's done talking to him, initiate phase two, asap. I should be back at the bank the same time you arrive. You see me in there you wait for my cue."

"Wait—" Rabies says. "You gonna tell Mad Dog about the heist? 'Cause you know if you do, you risk the *split*."

I assure him, "I won't."

The phone's hanging off the cord and I turn to the Pontiac. The damn thing is still rocking. I can hear the suspension. It's dry.

With legs squatted I approach the vehicle. Thirty steps later, my back is against the trunk of the car. The car rocks up and down my spine.

The rear windows are tinted so I crawl my way to the front. My head pops up, my eyes above the hood, and I peek through the windshield. The front seats are unoccupied. Piles of clothes on the seats. Mad Dog's shoulder holster included. I don't see the gun. It must be buried under the clothes.

Now, the backseat is where the action is. There, Mad Dog's bare brown ass is in the air, humping the individual beneath him. Steady speed, thrust powerful enough to ram the car a good six inches downward. His head is down, buried between the seat and the woman. I hear some Spanish coming out of him, the language of *el passion*. I make sure the woman under him, the individual whose vagina's getting pounded, is in fact Marla, and that her arms are around the guy, legs too, hugging him closer and not pushing him away. Everybody's consensual, that's for sure. Though I must admit, this is some surprise.

I take a deep breath as I grab a rock from the ground. I see two options here, one is peaceful and the other is hostile. I don't have time to be nice, not if I want the heist to go as planned. I may have found these two in time to save Cujo's life but the hour is still counting down for the heist. So I choose the latter option. With the rock in my hand I smash the window on the side of Mad Dog's ass.

The glass shatters and I rise. I reach in the front seat and fumble through the pile of clothes, pants, panties, weapon holster and no bra, no steel either. *Where's the gun?*

At the same time, hysteria breaks out in the backseat. Mad Dog springs up and hits his head on the ceiling lamp and it knocks his head back down into Marla's. She's screaming. Screaming in Spanish. My Spanish doesn't go far past *como esta* but I'm sure nothing elegant is coming out of her mouth. Passionate though, yeah definitely.

The car still rocks but it's caused from an entirely different type of motion.

Then, it seems like from somewhere between her legs, Mad Dog retrieves his Beretta M9. He's going to shoot me and this time he won't miss, no question about it. You don't interrupt a cartel dude having sex by smashing his car window and live to tell the tale. I can't escape now so I freeze and think fast, only words are going to save me from getting shot. So before his weapon finds the target—my head—I blurt out the first thing that comes to mind, "Your boy Rabies is overstepping you!"

"You got some *cajones,* you fucking chink." The gun's pointed at my head through the broken window. The man glances sideways at the shards in the front seat. "Before I kill you, answer me, why did you smash up my car?"

Obviously the window was a mistake. As I'm wondering if the peaceful approach would've gone any better, Marla props herself up and demands, "Shoot him!"

This is disastrous. Supposed to catch these two off guard and now I'm the one about to get shot instead. The clock is ticking and I try my plea, "Marla, please, you need to tell Cujo you're okay." Naked, she looks more than okay.

"Cujo's dead." Mad Dog opens the car door with one hand, the other holds the gun. He backs out the backseat and studies the damage on the passenger window. "You know what, chink? This is the very first automobile I bought in America. I love this car. It's a symbol of my achievement, you understand that? I had it parked in a storage unit when I was in prison, where I thought about this car more than I did any *puta.* You have to explain this, chink. Why did you have to smash my window?" His voice is cold but profoundly perplexed. His trigger-happy finger where it belongs.

"*Perdóname, amigo.*" I lift my hands in surrender

and I recite my high school level *español*, *"No sé en qué estaba pensando." Don't know what I was thinking, man.*

He comes into full view, naked, with dick diminishing. The cartel man declares, "I'm gonna kill you for your senseless act of destruction upon my beloved personal property."

"Well, if you're gonna put it that way, why don't we call it even." My palms are facing him and I think fast. "You did shoot up my driveway. The house was my parents' and the driveway was paved by my grandparents—paved by hand. It was their first house in this country and it was a symbol of their American Dream. It contains the memories of their blood and sweat. You've dishonored their hard work by putting seven bullets in it."

He looks at his own hand and he remarks, sounding impressed, "Paved by bare hands?"

"They laid the railroad too." I dart a sideways glance at the tracks. "By hand."

He thinks it over. From the tiny nod his head just produced, I believe he's reluctantly agreed that we're even as far as destruction of personal property is concerned. Now he asks, "How did you find me?"

"I was a soldier and my job was to find people." I duly answer his question first, then I reveal, "Cujo is still alive. Marla needs to talk to him so he'll be assured that she's okay. Only then will he agree to rob the bank and pay you back for what's owed. Think about it, Mr. Mad Dog, you don't have to kill him and everybody wins." I chin toward the service station, at the phone hanging off the cord. "The line is already connected."

"If Cujo is still alive, then Rabies disobeyed my

order." His forehead creases with curiosity. "Why do *you* need the nigger boy alive, chink?"

I skip a beat. "His name is Cujo, and I'm gonna help him pull off a bank heist."

Which is news to him.

After a long and thoughtful pause he mutters to himself, "You work there... so you'd be a man on the inside..."

I break his train of thought by asking, "Why didn't you just have Marla speak to him, put him at ease?"

"She didn't want to talk to him." He cranks his head over to Marla in the car. She's buttoning up a shirt, covering her knockout figure. "Now, tell me, is Rabies involved in this heist you speak of?"

"Have Marla talk to Cujo first. He just needs to hear her voice."

"How much money are we talking about here?"

"Like I said, Marla needs to do her part first." He raises his gun by two inches, and I amend at once, "One hundred thousand dollars."

"A three-way split?"

I keep quiet. Tilt my head toward the phone hanging off the cord.

The thing about criminals is, they're curious to learn about a score. It's part of the job description. *Criminal*—responsible for finding out schemes others are cooking, and decide whether or not to partake or takeover the payouts. So the bona-fide criminal turns to Marla and commands, "Go to the phone and let him hear your voice." The girl speaks some Spanish in protest and Mad Dog bellows, "Do as I say. *Inmediatamente!*"

She struts to the service station, dressed now only

in her panties and a shirt half buttoned. Her ass looks as sensational as ever. A moment later she picks up the mouthpiece and appears to be talking.

"Now, tell me everything."

Standing there with the gun pointed at me, looking at the service station clock ticking down, I do the only practical thing I can.

I tell Mad Dog about the heist.

Chapter Twenty

I've never talked so fast in my life. I have no idea if I'm making sense, but when I'm finished divulging the plan to Mad Dog he lowers his Berretta. A good sign. I lower my hands as well, from the surrendering position to beside my pockets.

"Rabies, that fucking usurper." Mad Dog mutters some *español*. "He must know plotting behind my back has deadly consequences."

So yes, I sell out Rabies. The guy means nothing to me. I only need him in play to keep the heist alive. But now that Mad Dog knows what's going on, the plan is just as endangered. With the *split* being the most endangered part of all.

"I need ten thousand dollars, and that's all I want," I say, being up front with Mad Dog about it. "How the rest of the money is split is none of my business." Afraid of Mad Dog overtaking the entire pie, I make a sensible suggestion to the guy so he'll stay out of the heist. "You already know about the plot so it's *not* behind your back any more, it's right in front of you. Knowing what you know gives you an opportunity to plot behind *his* back. Rip Rabies off *after* he's got the money. Think about it, this way you don't even have to get your hands dirty." *This way you stay the fuck out of our way.*

He ponders and meanwhile Marla finishes her

conversation on the phone, returns and joins us. Just moments ago the woman told Mad Dog to shoot me, yet I still find her insanely attractive.

Mad Dog and Marla communicate in their mothers' tongue. I pick up the words I understand and string them together in order to get a general sense of what's going on. I gather that she's talked to Cujo, told him she's okay and not to worry. *The heist, it's a go.*

She tells Mad Dog that she also spoke to Rabies, and now she's relating that part of the exchange, and this is where her Spanish loses me. After a minute or two, which seems like forever, Mad Dog translates, "Rabies doesn't know that I'm aware of the heist." Adding, "Even if he does, he wouldn't very much give a damn." To Marla he asks something like, *Is there anything else?*

"*Si.*" She nods and asks, "Who the hell's *Hey-Zeus?*"

"Marla." I look at her, at this fine specimen of God's creation, and I can't help but say, "You do realize you were being penetrated by your father's killer."

She stands her ground and corrects me, "I was thoroughly *fucked*, but not by my father's killer."

Now Mad Dog takes two steps forward. "What makes you think I killed Dago?"

"You're saying you didn't do it?" I turn to him, looking at the Berretta in his hand.

"I went to prison for him. Why would I kill him if I went to prison for him?"

It makes sense precisely because he went to prison for him. The logic is there. Moreover, his M9 holds at least fifteen in the mag, and with one in the chamber, the math adds up. I don't want to get in a he-said-she-said argument, not right now, so I just back away and request, "Can I go now?"

He's contemplating.

I tell him, "You want to rip off Rabies after the heist, then you want heist to go as planned. That means you want me to go right fucking now."

He does that flickering thing with his hand on his face, like in the Godfather, and commands after a beat, "Go."

I step away saying, "Sorry about your car window."

In my ride, I start the engine and make a u-turn. From the rearview mirror I can see dust rise, drowning Marla and Mad Dog behind me. I drive maybe thirty yards and their figures appear smaller. I haven't picked up speed yet when I hear a noise, and the car vibrates from front to back. Next, I notice the passenger seat is sinking lower and lower. *What the hell?* The car's losing pressure like a punctured basketball. The wheels get out of alignment and then, *klunk!*

My tire's out.

****

Off-road wears the tires mighty fast. It happens. Should've taken advantage of the tire shop's buy-two-get-two special. But there's not a second to waste on complaining or cursing at my luck. I exit the car and pop the trunk, composed and ready to deal with the matter at hand. Whiners don't belong in the army, certainly not in any MP unit. I retrieve the wheel jack and the spare from the trunk's compartment. Before I get down to it, Mad Dog's Pontiac pulls up beside me.

"What you gonna do," he asks through the broken

window, "change a tire *now*?"

I glance over at him—him in the driver seat, Marla in the back, putting panty-hose on legs so long they never seem to end. My eyes cast down at his wheels. The Pontiac's rubbers are secured on chrome rims, decked out. I say nothing.

"I always get the best tires, rotate them every three thousand miles," he states the facts, looking little sly. "Don't want them to crap out on you at a crucial moment, like say, during a bank job." Shards of broken glass sparkle on the passenger seat, his head cranes to the back and says, "Sit next to Marla unless you want to cut your ass sitting in the front."

"You're taking me to the heist?"

Guy shrugs. "We're going in the same direction anyway."

"Mr. Mad Dog, no offense, but you aren't allowed to participate."

"And you aren't allowed to give me orders, chink. Look"—finger taps steering wheel—"I admit, your plan's good. I just want to make sure it gets done right, that's all."

"Your car's flagged," I point out. "You can't be seen in town."

"At no thanks to you. Well, how 'bout I drop you off by the edge of town?" Seeing I'm still hesitant, he says, "You know if one tire goes out the rest are soon to follow, right? Unless you have three spares in the trunk, it's better if I take you to Abisko."

I think it over and I think he's right, so I squeeze in next to Marla. "*Gracias*."

The girl scoots toward the door, away from me.

It'll take at least twenty minutes to get to Abisko at

the rate he's driving. Mad Dog makes the small talk. "Say, chink." He peers at the rearview mirror and we engage eye contact for a brief second. "We cool if I call you chink, right?"

Marla chimes in, "That's his name. It's on his nametag."

From the rearview, his blinks bemused. "That's a first. I wish niggers would do the same. Just christen their kids Nigger, it'd be so much easier."

I recall what agent Reese said, *guy's reputed as quite a racist.*

The racist dude clears his throat. "Well you know I go by Mad Dog. But my mother calls me Roberto." He says his name like *Row-bear-toe.*

"Your last name wouldn't happen to be Banks, would it?" I joke, "Row-*bear*-toe is Robert. Last name Banks would make you—"

"Rob Banks." He gets it and lets out a quiet chuckle. "Ironic thing is I'm not even allowed to take part in your bank robbery. No, my friend. My surname is Ramirez."

"Good Christ." I look from Marla to the rearview mirror. "You guys related?"

"No, and I resent that." Marla stares out the window, watching the tracks pass us by. "Ramirez is a common name where we're from. Isn't Chink common where you're from?"

In the backseat with her, I state, "I'm from here—from America."

"The girl at your bank—"

"Not *my* bank."

"—she knows what you about to do?" Marla turns from the window to me. "She likes you, I can tell. The way her eyes followed you as you left the bank with us, it was like she wanted to come with you but knew that she couldn't."

"Is this the woman who kept honking at me in your driveway?" Mad Dog says. "Good thing she made the noise, you know. Otherwise I would've killed you. Wouldn't have thought twice about it."

The vehicle rocks and sways on the desert plain.

"Does she know you're gonna rob the bank?" Marla asks again.

I shake my head no. "This has nothing to do with her."

"You don't feel the same way about her, do you?"

"You feel the same way about Cujo?"

She pauses a beat. "Let me ask you this: if she knew what you're about to do, would she be repulsed, or would she be by your side?"

Confused by the question and mystified as to why she's asking, I frown and admit, "How would I know?"

"*I* think she'd be by your side. Provided you tell her the reason for what you have to do."

The reason for what I have to do.

I tired, Daddy. I hungry. I no have home.

I free in fifteen years and I find you, Daddy.

"What if I can't tell her the reason? What if it's not what I'm about to *do* but the *reason* why I'm doing it that would repulse her?"

"You're thinking too much, chink," Marla says. "When a man thinks too much he acts womanly." Then she looks into my eyes for the first time. "I bet *she* isn't afraid to speak the truth. Even if the truth would repulse you."

"Miss Marla." I shift my ass to an angle so I'm

facing her as I speak. "Is this about you and Cujo? Something happen between the two of you? I mean"—I cast a sideways glance at *Row-bear-toe*, the man who just boned her—"Obviously something happened. But you're trying to redirect that emotional disappointment, or whatever it is toward *me* and Cass. That's not cool."

"Right, I remember." She grins. "That's what Cujo called her—Cassie Rose. Cute."

"*Peredone*," Mad Dog interjects. "What is it that you couldn't tell her, Mr. Chink?"

"Jesus fucking Christ." In vain and blasphemy, I plead, "Give me a break, will you?"

"Yeah, why can't you tell her?" Marla persists. "She's a big girl. She should be able to handle your secret."

"It's something kinky, yeah?" Mad Dog ventures a guess, "Something you like done with butthole? Something like that, yes?"

"Or maybe he's homosexual." Marla shrugs. "I get the feeling all Asians are queers. The two are practically synonymous."

"This isn't happening." I squeeze the bridge of my nose. "I should've just changed my goddamn tire."

Mad Dog turns all the way back, facing me and not the path ahead, "C'mon, Mr. Chink, you can tell me. Nothing wrong with a little butt play, right, Marla?"

"I think it's more than that." Marla squints at me. "I think it's something dark."

"You mean like S&M?" Guy says this flashing me a knowing wink.

"No. I don't think so," Marla says.

"Or you mean something involving candles?"

"Man"—I look at the cartel—"please stop."

They don't stop. They're having too much of a good time.

"Or maybe it's some kind of role play."

"Too embarrassed to ask her to play your sister?"

I point out, "What does any of this have to do with me robbing a bank?"

They don't hear me. They just keep going.

"Or maybe he likes young girls, Lolita."

"I'm thinking it's little boys—"

"All right, that's enough." I'd rather switch places with John McCain in the POW camp in 'Nam than be here, in the car with these two assholes. I can't take it any more so I reveal my secret, "I have a daughter, okay? She may or may not be mine, but that's what I can't tell Cass. I'm robbing the bank so I can bail the girl out of her life, in..." I blow out a helpless sigh. "In a Vietnamese sweatshop." I tell them about the letters I received.

The car's quiet for some time.

"Vietnam?" Marla's taken aback now. "You don't know for sure the girl's yours, and she's asking you for money? How do you know you're not being scammed?"

To this doubt Mad Dog replies, "Because woman, if it was a scam it'd be a threat more urgent. Threaten to rape the girl or cut her up or something drastic. Slaving in a sweatshop? What kind of mellow-ass shit is that? Trust me, Mr. Chink, I know this. I'm cartel." He keeps his eyes on the road, or the off-road, and he says, "But yeah, *por favor*, don't tell your girl your secret."

Cartel guy giving me relationship advice, on the way to heist a bank.

"What's *wrong* with you, *Row-bear-toe?*" Marla

berates Mad Dog in a string of *español*, then she says different, "No, Chink, you tell Cassie Rose. She'll understand. Trust *me*, okay?"

Mad Dog says, "Why should he trust you?"

"Because I'm a woman," she says.

Chapter Twenty-One

They let me out by the outskirts of town. I exit the car and I'm hit by a tumbleweed big as a wrecking ball. I check the time: 1330. Cujo and Rabies should have arrived in town as well, provided they departed immediately after the call and hit no traffic on the freeway. Cass will return in less than thirty minutes, that is if she hasn't already returned. The bank job, in and out, if everything goes as planned, will take ten minutes at most, plus five minutes for the getaway, that's fifteen minutes total. *Cass, please keep Morris at bay.*

I estimate it's a twenty minute walk to the bank from where I stand. Ten minutes if I run like the wind, which is impossible in these shoes. Five on a bike, if I happen to find one lying around. Options one to three are all unforeseeable. So I turn back to the car still parked there and tell Mad Dog through the broken window, "I need the car to get me closer to the bank."

"The car's flagged, you said so yourself."

"You can wait here and either let me or Marla take the car." I quickly go around to his side and open the door. "They're looking for a gangster in a Pontiac, not a beautiful woman or an Asian sucker."

"But—"

"I don't have time to discuss this. Every second counts." I motion for him to step out.

163

He instructs Marla in Spanish as he unfastens his seatbelt and gives up the wheel. I can tell he really wants the heist to go as planned because he readily surrenders his beloved vehicle. Marla hustles to the helm.

I climb in the back and slam the door. I tell her, "Go left then straight." Must avoid the school district.

She's shifting the gear when Mad Dog asks me, "Anything else I can help you with?" sounding somewhat sarcastic about it.

"Matter of fact, yeah. You see cops, distract them."

"How do I do that?"

"Just be yourself."

Marla takes us off and for forty seconds we don't converse in the car as we pass the residential area and enter the town center. After sixty seconds Marla remarks that the town looks busier than she remembered.

At second sixty-five I suddenly shout, "Wait—slow down, slow down!"

A Grand Fury dashes past the intersection two blocks ahead. Heading toward the location of the bank, going at least 45 mph. Could it be Cass? Returning from her lunch with deputy Morris? What's the hurry? I check the time, *it's too soon*. But then again, she's been gone for an hour and a half. What if she's had enough of his company? If so, the only thing I can wish for now is that she'll convinced Morris not to stakeout the bank.

"Drop me off after the next block." My hand is already on the door handle.

Marla stops the car as I directed and before I close the door, she tells me, "I was just doing what I had to do."

I step away from the car and look down on her through the windshield. "Cujo's putting his life on the line for you. Don't you know? He's a guy who…" I find myself gulping.

"Who what?"

"A guy who…loves you unconditionally."

Feeling strange as I say those words, I slam the car door and put the Latina out of my mind. Approaching the bank from the rear I find Cass's Ford is parked in the lot. Cass's car doesn't have any windows. I reach in and pull the lever by the seat, disengaging the trunk. From within I retrieve the lug wrench and make to the rear exit of the building. I use the wrench to bar the handle. No one's escaping out of the back door.

Seconds later, I approach the front.

****

The first thing I do is make a three-sixty to survey the scene. No Grand Fury parked outside. Nothing out of the ordinary. No cars on the road. No pedestrians milling about. Nothing suspicious that I can see. So the Grand Fury from earlier must've been passing through. It was going pretty fast so maybe it was responding to a dispatch. Some vehicle collision or domestic violence, whatever it is I hope it takes forever to get resolved. I draw a deep breath and hold it in. I enter the lobby.

"That was some dump you took," Jim remarks from my station as soon as the door swings closed behind me. Coming around the counter he points to the clock on the wall. "You were gone nearly an hour."

"Thanks for covering for me." We pass each other and I pat him on the shoulder. "Was the place busy?"

"Yeah, that'll be the day." He takes a good look at me and asks, "Chin, you okay? You look like my wife

165

after she was in labor."

I rub my stomach. "A major dump can do that to a guy." At my station, my eyes dart from the clock to the door, to the spot across the street where deputy Morris was parked this morning. I expect to see Rabies' car there any second.

While I wait for them, I go over the signals. In the military there are various visual cues. Fist in the air means attention. Fist in the air while pulling your elbow downward is for moving out. Palm facing outward is stop. Palm inward and beckoning is advance. But I can't very well apply cues in front of my colleague. So what I told Rabies is, if I drink water, that means green light. If I cough, that means yellow. If I turn my back on them, abort.

Jim is at his desk with his feet up, he relates to me scratching his ass, "Sheriff's department called again."

"What?" *What the fuck?* I'm staring at him when I ask, "When was this?"

"Soon after you left," he says with a yawn. "They asked the same thing, 'Is the place being robbed?' For a second I thought they were on to us."

"On to us?"

"Yeah, you know, what with Ester's FDIC scheme. But no, they were calling about a physical robbery, like a holdup."

"But no one triggered the alarm." In my mind, it's, *But no one was* here *to trigger the alarm.*

"They know the alarm's malfunctioned. Except"— he takes his legs off the desk—"they said this time someone *called* them about a robbery."

"Who called?" *Who the fuck?* "When was this again?"

"Minutes after you left to take that dump."

Right away, that eliminates Mad Dog and Marla. They thought Cujo was the only one pulling the bank job, and they were going to kill him.

Jim says, "Must be some kind of prank call. Kids these days…"

I'm thinking, could it have been Rabies? He was going to kill Cujo but he also insisted we manage the operation ourselves. He wanted the green light. It couldn't have been him.

Then who?

I continue to think, could it have been Cujo? Rabies was watching him therefore he couldn't possibly have gotten to a phone. Even if he did, why would he report the bank robbery? Wouldn't he tell the police to save him from an execution instead? It doesn't make sense. It couldn't have been Cujo. No. definitely not.

Again, who?

Cujo, Marla, Mad Dog, Rabies…

I'm thinking, No one else knows about this…

A car pulls up to the spot, the spot across the street, with the direct line of vision to my station. The car is the Chrysler Fifth Avenue.

Two men climb out. A Mexican in shades standing upright with shoulders back, and a black guy in a hoodie, hunched over street thug style.

I'd hope for better men but this is what I got. And they're here.

At the same time, a person steps in front of the entrance of the bank, blocking my view of Rabies and Cujo. She opens the door and comes right in, saying to me, "You won't believe what just happened."

It's Cass.

She has returned. And...Deputy Morris?

I cover my mouth and bend over, dramatic as can be. My abdominal muscles tense and my throat is ready to bark up a lung.

I fucking cough.

****

If Cass failed to persuade deputy Morris to give up the stakeout, if the guy's back on watch, then the heist is down in the toilet for sure. There is absolutely no conceivable way to rob a bank with a cop across the street, monitoring every movement inside the joint. He sees there's a robbery he'll call for back up, and all the cops facilitating the SAT will be redirected here in a matter of minutes, shutting down the block. We'd be caved in. Cujo and Rabies would either surrender or attempt to shoot their way out. Either scenario would be catastrophic for me. My partners-in-crime would rat me out in the former and people could get seriously hurt in the latter. Casualties and my own incarceration aside, I'd get no goddamn *money* for my poor, poor daughter.

I'm still coughing as I peek to the outside and see Rabies nudge Cujo. They both stop advancing. They nod at each other, acknowledging the signal. Rabies is expressionless, and Cujo appears mildly disappointed. They return to the stolen vehicle and get in. Rabies rolls down the window facing me.

Drinking water means green light. Coughing means yellow. I stop coughing and Cass asks me, "Chin, you want some water?"

I make sure I'm facing the entrance, facing Rabies and Cujo when I say, "I'm fine. Some saliva went down the wrong pipe is all. How was lunch?"

"You won't believe what happened, Chin." She

heaves and turns around. "Jim, you need to hear this too."

Trying hard to suppress the urgency in my tone, I ask Cass, "Where is Morris?"

She informs me, "There's been an incident."

"There was an incident here too." Jim joins us. "While you were gone, Chin took a dump that lasted nearly an hour."

Cass, in no mood to talk about one's dump, starts, "Soon after we got to the restaurant, Morris' radio came on. Some kid assaulted a testing administrator at the high school. Apparently the time was up and the kid wasn't finished with his test. When told pencils down, the kid got furious and wouldn't let go of his answer sheet. An administrator tried to take it and the kid attacked him, breaking his nose."

"Jesus Christ."

"The administrator retaliated and other kids joined in and caused a riot. Kids must've been under tremendous pressure, with folks talking about the draft and all. When I left the scene, at least five people were arrested."

Jim follows up quickly, "Who's the nose buster?"

"Some kid from a neighboring town. Plum Creek, I think."

"Was Huck involved?"

"Don't think so, although some kids might have to take the test again."

Curious, I ask, "How did the kid break the guy's nose?"

"I heard he used his elbow." Cass rubs her arm. "It was bad. I saw them carry the victim out on a stretcher."

"Elbow?" A pause later I mime *Sok Sab*. "You mean like this?" Elbow *whack* in the air.

"How would I know?" She frowns. "I didn't see it happen. When we got there the riot was just dying down."

"So you didn't eat lunch? And where are your parents?"

"We had to *walk* back all the way from the high school." She's not happy. "My folks went to your place. They still want to check out some books."

"And Morris?"

"He took some people in to the sheriff's station."

So he's not coming back any time soon. Five arrests in one day, that's got to be a county record. Taking statements, talking to witnesses, filing papers and trying to convince whoever's hurt to drop the charges. The department's understaffed and there's still an afternoon session to facilitate. Morris definitely won't come back.

For the hell of it, I trigger the silent alarm and count to ten. Nothing. Not even a phone call from the sheriff's.

Finally, a goddamn break.

I clear my throat and I say to Cass, "I think I'll have some water, after all."

Chapter Twenty-Two

One forty-five in the afternoon, three hours before closing, the bank gets robbed.

I know this, because I'm the conductor of this orchestra. Cass and Jim, they know it as well, as soon as two men of minor ethnicity enter the bank. Can't accuse them of profiling because it isn't hard to figure this out. Rabies, the Mexican gangster, doesn't bother to take off his shades. He's dressed in a new suit, looking badass with the blue steel in his hand, making no attempt to conceal the weapon, or the purpose of his visit. Cujo is wearing a mask that looks like his underwear but with two cutouts for eyes, black skin contrasts with the orange fabric, resembling a ridiculous clown.

The clown approaches the counter with a little bounce in his steps. He winks at me and turns to Cass, pretending to read her nametag. "Well, well, Cassie Rose, aren't you a baby doll? See my friend there?" His friend means Rabies. "See what's in his hand? Yeah, you know what we here for, you feel me?"

Cass darts a glance at me and then her vision casts downward. My hand is under the counter pretending to trigger the alarm. Her hand isn't, because she knows it's a lost cause.

No one shows up for the boy who cried wolf.

"You're Anton *Cujo* Samuels," Cass is telling this

thug with his underwear on his head. "You don't have to wear that mask. There are pictures of you plastered all over town."

"Shit, dunno what you talkin' 'bout, girl." Guy coughs out a nervous chuckle. "I ain't no Cujo Samuels. I'm the Notorious BRG—bank robbin' gangsta."

Cass, very composed, goes on, "You were conceived in Watts, twenty-nine years of age, arrested twenty times in the past nine years. Dishonorably discharged by the army, and you were with the New Thugs on the Block, LLC. You robbed us last Friday."

"What is you, some kind of psychic?" He turns to me for answers and quickly fixes his eyes back to Cass. "How'd you know it was me?"

"Other than the fact that you're wearing the same clothes with the same snot at the same spot? You called me Cassie Rose." Cass tips her nametag forward. "No one ever calls me that."

"What the fuck?" Cujo strips off his underwear and reveals his face. His face displays wholehearted disbelief. "Hold on now, let me get this straight. Your name's *Cassandra Roselyn*, ain't nobody called you *Cassie Rose*? Girl, where'd you grow up? What planet you from?" He swings his body back to Rabies. "This is bullshit, dude. I wasted this undie for nothin'."

Rabies is just standing there, with his gun, not lifting it to point at anyone. His face expressionless, body motionless. The guy is idle. This is not how one should participate in a bank robbery. One really needs to be active about it and not be a goddamn statue. Say some scary shit and wield the gun some. C'mon, man.

"Yo, Rabies, what's up with you?" Cujo notices it

as well. "You remind me of a kid with stage freight at the talent show."

Rabies has a deadpan stare.

"If you ain't gonna use that gun, then hand it over, *amigo*."

Cujo reaches for the weapon and Rabies jerks back. He lifts the gun and points it at his partner.

Cujo surrenders and backs away. "All right, fine. You get to play with the toy but why don't you point it at that dude over there?" That dude over there means Jimbo.

So Rabies cranes ninety degrees and points the gun at Jim. Jim looks like he wants to wet his pants but is doing his best to hold it in.

Cujo does all the talking. "So there's the vault, that's one big mofo, for sure. How come I didn't notice it last time?" He's asking me. "What's the mumbo combo for this jumbo door?"

"We don't know," Cass replies, her voice calm, not scared one-bit of the self-proclaimed Notorious BRG. "You're never gonna get in there."

"We'll see 'bout that, Cassie Rose." To me, he relays what I taught him, "You, Chink, go fetch the manager, that fat lady. Yeah, I remember her. Tell her to crack the vault open or else my *hombre* there'll pop a bullet in the white boy. And you"—he orders Cass— "go guard the entrance. Tell anyone who approaches that the bank's under maintenance and will be closed for the day. If you run, you'll have white boy's blood on your conscience."

I back away, and before I head to Ester's office I put my hand on Cass's shoulder and give it an affectionate squeeze. "Everything will be all right."

She throws me a look like she knows exactly what the hell's going on. Then she heads for the entrance doing as told.

I put her expression out of my mind as I enter Ester's office without knocking. Just barge in and catch the boss lady crunching cookies and licking the delicacy off her fingers, completely oblivious of what the hell's going on. She looks at me startled. "Chin, what a coincidence, I was just gonna call for you." She points to a large square envelope on her desk. "This is the official claim to the FDIC. We missed the mailman so I need you to drop this off at the post office before they close, make sure to expedite it."

"Ester, forget about the claim." I make myself sound urgent by stammering, "W-we're being robbed, a-*again*."

She shifts her body weight forward, taking forever. "What, right now?"

"*Yes*, right fucking *now*."

Her head turns to the door. Her eyes move in their sockets as she thinks fast. Finally, she pushes up on her armrest in order to lift her ass and suggests, "Let's slip out the back."

I let her migrate to the rear exit and pull on the handle. The door doesn't budge, the lug wrench I took from Cass's car is wedged in place. Now that she realizes her fat ass isn't *slipping* anywhere, I cup her shoulders and shake her. "You need to open the vault for these criminals, asap, or else Jim's getting a bullet to the head!" She doesn't seem to grasp the horror so I continue, "These people, they're out of their minds! They said"—quoting Cujo's gangster prose—"they said they'll have us feel the wrath of their menace!"

"Oh my God, what does that even mean?" She shudders. "This can't be happening again. Y-you trigger the alarm?"

"The alarm's broken and the cops aren't coming, Ester." I look into her eyes and I plead, "We *need* you, Boss. We need you *now*."

After my words fall, I let my eyes wander to the envelope on the desk. Her eyes follow. We both stare at it for a spell. The claim to the FDIC. The vault wasn't opened last time so her scheme could only go so far. But now…they're demanding for the vault to be opened. Open the vault and we'll be reimbursed. We *all* will.

Halleluiah!

I pick up the envelope and shred it to pieces, ending her previous scheme for good and I present her a scheme that's new and improved. "Forget about the last robbery, Ester. Swapping the foreign currency? Please, it's a *terrible* idea. Where the hell you gonna exchange Japanese yen for dollars without people getting suspicious?" I toss the shreds in the air and they fall like snowflakes. "If you open the vault—"

"The *vault*?" She waves away the flakes. "But, what if they rob us blind…"

I understand her apprehension. If they rob us blind, there won't be anything left for her to skim. Say there's a million dollars in the vault, and they take the whole million, she couldn't very well claim 1.2 million to the FDIC and pocket the 0.2 difference. But if they only rob a portion, she could claim they took all, and pocket a huge chunk for herself.

I assure her, "They won't take everything, Ester."

"They won't?" She nods a little but then her eyes

are blinking fast, blinking unsure. "How do you know they won't take everything?"

"Because of their demand. They said, 'open the vault and take out one hundred thousand.' That's all they want."

"One hundred thousand? That's rather specific."

"Yes, because, you know what I think? I think they're in debt and need to pay it off. They're only doing what's necessary to survive in this world—just like me and you, Ester. Just like every one of us."

I let her absorb the information.

"One hundred thousand?" She says the number again. "That's roughly what we have in box 56, right?"

Box 56 is the large bills box.

Ester deliberates. "If we just open that box and let them take what's inside—one hundred thousand..." Her face flashes a subtle radiance. "It does sound rather reasonable, doesn't it?"

It sure does to me.

I stand up straight and I look her in the eyes. "Ester, what are you gonna do?"

"Well...shit." A deep breath later she slaps her meaty thighs. "Let's open the vault."

Chapter Twenty-Three

When Ester and I come out from the back, Cass is arguing with someone by the entrance of the bank. I know they're arguing because their body language is all frantic, heads shaking, bodies turning left and right, arms flailing, clutch then fold. From where I stand I can't hear them, but Jim can. I know because he's looking at me with eyes saying something like, *You're in some shit, man*. The door swings open and now they're inside. Rabies turns the gun on them, and the newcomer doesn't even bother to notice him. She just marches directly toward me and yells, "You! When were you going to tell her?"

It's Cass's mom.

"Yo, lady." Cujo steps in front of her. "I'm sorry but the bank's closed for periodic maintenance." He says what I taught him to say.

She ignores him and keeps yelling, "Were you *ever* going to tell her? You know what you are? You're a liar! *You*"—her fat finger directed at me—"you're a mendacious gook!"

"Whoa, ma'am." Cujo, the guy robbing the bank intermediates, "You need to calm down, okay?"

Cass is peering at me with those green eyes, emeralds a shade lighter than usual, lightened by the mist across their surface. "Chin, is this true?" Her voice sounds so crestfallen.

"Cassandra, I told you," her mother is telling her, "he's no good for you. I mean, look at him, what do you see?" She's staring at me and so is everyone else. *What do you see?* "I'll tell you what you see. You see a *gook*."

"Now hold on a second." Cujo lifts a hand. "Ma'am, I don't believe you're using that word for ID-ing purposes. And besides"—he scans me up and down—"the word gook is not the right, um, the right no-um"—he snaps his fingers—"no-no, what you call it, the right no-um…"

I help him out, "Nomenclature?"

"Yeah, that's it, that's it." He snaps two more times. "Yeah, the word *gook* isn't the right no-men's-clitter. Don't be using it on him 'cause he ain't a gook. He a Chinaman so it's chink, you get it?"

Now the woman from Pike County, Kentucky is glancing sideways at Cujo, whispering into Cass's ear, "*Who's that colored fellow?*"

"Ma'am, please. I prefer to be ID'd as an African-American." The bank robber exchanges his views on minority nomenclature with the mom of a bank employee, during a holdup.

"*Ahem.*" Rabies, the man with the gun, makes a sound so no one forgets about him.

"See the guy over there?" Cujo gestures their attention to the gunman. "That's a Mexican, or you may identify him as a Latino, or a Hispanic, or simply as *a brown dude with a gun pointed at my motherfucking face*."

Cass's mom whispers to her daughter again, "Why's the well-dressed plumber pointing a gun at us?"

"Yes, I forgot to mention," Cass casually replies,

but with an obvious melancholy undertone, "we're being held up, Mother."

"What, right now?" The mother grasps the scene and realizes, *yes, right now.* "What the heck, Cassandra, how'd you let something like this slip your mind?" Reluctantly, she raises her hands. Moving her body behind her daughter, she speaks to the robbers in a little voice, "Please don't hurt us."

Now Cass is asking me what she asked before, "So is it true you have a secret daughter tucked away somewhere?" Her voice is shaking.

"Holy shit, man." Cujo tilts his head at me, bending at the knees. "You have a *secret* daughter?"

Dumbfounded, I frown at the dude and I say nothing.

"She's your squeeze, right?" Cujo thumbs at Cass. "Marla figured as much. Man, you kept that from your girl?" His hand is on his forehead. "Tucked away? Your *daughter*? I'm telling you, dude, that is messed up."

"Not tucked away, as she puts it." I feel like I have to explain myself here, and not just to Cass but to everyone. Jim and Ester, my coworkers, are hearing all this and they're looking at me with their heads tilted as if trying to make sense of some bizarre animal's behavior at the zoo. Even Rabies has lowered his gun a good three inches, intrigued by my domestic situation.

"It's true!" Cass's mom, cowering behind her daughter, accuses. "He has a daughter with a whore. He wrote a letter to her and hid it in a book! He *abandoned* her!"

"Abandoned her where?" Cujo asks.

"In Vietnam!" the mother shouts. "It was in a letter he hid in a book!"

"Goodness, major." Cujo rubs his eyebrows. "You paying alimony?"

The bank's employees and my girlfriend's mom, together with the bank robbers, are talking about the daughter I may or may not have, like a scene from a Spanish soap, but during a holdup.

Rabies has his gun lowered to 45 degrees now, disappointed at me shaking his head, as if to say, *how could you do that, man, your own daughter.*

Cass is trembling when she asks me for the third time, "Chin, is this all true?" There's a single teardrop at the corner of her eye, about to fall. "Tell me it isn't true."

My head gives off a subtle nod, but I quickly amend, "She may or may not be mine."

"That's just typical," her mom comments from behind her.

"Don't say it like that, man," Cujo offers me his wisdom. "Take it from me—a guy with three daddies— you don't want to deny responsibility, man."

Cass takes a step forward. "Why didn't you tell me?"

"Tell you?" I skip two beats. "How?"

"Just come out and say it. Say, 'I screwed a prostitute in Vietnam and she had a kid, the kid may or may not be mine.' That's it. It'd take you less than five seconds to come out and *say* it!" She wipes off the single tear but another drop quickly replaces it.

"Yeah, dude," Cujo concurs. "It was 'Nam, man. Nothin' to be ashamed of."

I want to say to him and to everyone else: What the fuck you think I'm doing here? I'm robbing the place so I can pay for my daughter. But I keep quiet. Peering past Cujo, I find Jim. The guy shrugs at me like he's saying, *Yeah, should've told her.* I then turn to Rabies for some kind of dissent from the rest, but he eyeballs me like he wants to point the gun at me instead. I feel like a preacher who can't get a single amen in a goddamn church.

"Why didn't you tell me?" Cass takes three steps forward. She gets around Cujo and stands in front of me. "Why didn't you just tell me?" She pounds on my chest, light and then harder and fiercer. "Why didn't you tell me, if you love me?" Her hands switch between hitting me and wiping tears.

Cass and I, bank employees in a domestic dispute at our workplace, during a holdup.

"All right, break it off now, break it off." Cujo intervenes and a couple of swings land on his chest. To me, "Man, you better apologize, quickly."

"Okay, Cass." I say, "I'm sorry."

I don't think anyone's heard me. Cujo wrestles Cass out of my orbit. He grasps her wrists so she cannot attack, meanwhile her mother shouts with her hands in surrender, "Let go of my daughter!"

Thinking about what Larry said, about perspective and how one should just say what's on his mind, I cut above the chaos, "I don't love you, Cass. Okay? I-I *can't* love you."

Suddenly, everything stops, like I've hit the pause button on the VCR.

"I can't...not with my daughter... I-I don't think—"

"You don't love me?" Her green eyes drown in tears. "How-how could you say that? I-I've moved *in* with you."

"To save on rent," I mutter my defense.

"I was gonna pay your property tax. The house isn't even mine!"

"You offered to *split* the tax."

"I let you fuck me."

"You've let lots of people."

"You met my parents."

"They met *me*."

"You bastard."

"Call me Chink."

"That's not how I think of you."

I decide to say nothing, and silence fills the room.

No one is moving.

Until next to me, Ester raises her hand in the air, slowly, like a kid in the back of the classroom with a question she's been dying to ask.

Cujo notices and calls on her like he's the teacher, "Yeah, lady. What's your name?"

Ester puts her hand down and steps forward. "Ester Fields. I'm the manager here." She introduces herself like it's a question, like she's unsure of her position and who she is.

Now that's she's stepped closer to him, Cujo scans her left and right. Then his eyes switch between Ester and Cass's mom, like he's noticing the similarities between the two—Caucasian, female, same age group, similar hair and clothes, same weight class and body type. Cujo's done his scanning and asks the ladies, "You two related?"

The women make eye contact briefly and break at the same time. "No."

"You ladies pregnant?"

"No," the pair says. "Why do you ask?"

"Never mind." To the manager, "So what's up, Ester? What's your question?"

"Listen, mister," Ester says, matter-of-factly losing patience, "since I stepped out of my office, everything that's happened has been interesting to say the least. But"—she points to the vault—"you assholes gonna rob a bank or what?"

Chapter Twenty-Four

Presently, everyone gets their shit together. The bank robbers are back to robbing the bank, Cujo saying scary gangster shit and Rabies holding his weapon up high, finger on the trigger. The bank employees are back to being compliant or scared as they should be. Cass's mother puts her fury behind her for now, and is just waiting for this holdup to be over with.

Ester's fat ass is facing the audience, her hands turning the wheel on the giant vault. Jim is at his desk, not looking like there's any chance he'll play hero. He's no doubt thought of the same scam that we have. Rip off the FDIC a big fucking time.

Ester finishes turning the wheel and pulls the vault open. The thing opens slow and heavy like it's a gateway to an ancient palace. I can smell the odor of money coming at me from yards away. Smell I can taste.

"One hundred thousand." Ester opens up the vault all the way. "Chin, come in and help me count."

I enter the vault with Cujo and Ester, Rabies stays out keeping the gun on the rest. The vault has three walls of safe deposit boxes. Two thirds of the boxes are empty. Folks around town have nothing valuable to rent a box for. Pay twenty bucks a month for what, a brooch their grandma left? So most of the occupied boxes belong to the bank. Box 56 has the hundred and fifties.

57 has the twenties and tens. 58 the rest.

Ester with the keys tells the bank robber, "The contents in box 56 should suffice."

"What about these other boxes?" Cujo turns left to right, seeing hundreds of boxes. "Why don't you open all of these and I'll decide what ought to suffice."

"I can't," Ester admits the truth. "Most of these boxes are for lease and the leaser has the key. I can only open the boxes that belong to the bank. Like I said, box 56 has the hundred dollar bills plus the fifties, and it should suffice."

Cujo finds Box 56 on the left side of the wall and inquires, "Well, which box got the twenties?" When Ester hesitates he demands, "Answer me!"

"It-it's the box next to it. B-box 57."

"Well, you're gonna have to open that too, lady. We're taking the twenties as well."

"What you see inside the vault, *esé*?" Rabies asking, Mexican accent with a touch of Texas.

Ester opens box 56 and box 57.

"I ain't no wizard, but I'm seeing like, I don't know, a quarter million, maybe?" He takes a brick of hundreds from the box and sniffs it. "*Eschew-ee!*" he mutters to himself. "Damn allergies."

"Wait—but you said you only need one hundred thousand." Ester's eyes are getting bigger, leaving their sockets. "That's why I agreed to open the vault." She sounds nervous and regretful at the same time.

"I didn't know there was gonna be like a quarter million here. C'mon, lady, you can't allow me to see that kind of money and expect me to take less than half. What kind of criminal would I be?" To his partner, he shouts, "Yo, Rabies, you with me?"

Rabies utters some Spanish to himself and then moves so he can get a better look inside. He catches a glimpse and his eyes pop. "Take it all, Cujo."

Truth be told, I expected this.

No need for me and Ester to count so we exit the vault, providing Cujo adequate clearance to do his thing. I watch him from the threshold.

"Now this is what I'm talking about." Cujo awes at the cash money before his eyes. "Oh my God, will you look at this. I'm *rich*, bitch!" He grabs a money brick and steps out of the vault, showing Ben Franklin's smirking face to Rabies. "You know what I'm gonna do with this? First I'm gonna get high, then I'm getting myself medi-care, yo. That's what I'm gonna do. I'm gonna get the best kind, full coverage, you know. HMO, shit, 401(K), endowments, accidental death insurance—all them motherfucking shits white folks has. And something nice for Marla, too."

I suggest, "You might want to think about going back to school. Get a GED."

"Man, fuck that. Thug for life, you dig?" His hand makes the number four at his chest, like a sign saying, *Thug4Life*. "Fuck welfare. Fuck food stamps. Fuck everyone's mama and all ya'll motherfuckers. I'm keeping it real." He pockets the ten G's and returns to the vault to stuff another ten in his pocket. With two pockets full, he orders Ester, "Bitch, get me a bag, please. Yeah, thanks in advance."

Ester's looking from Cass to me. "Where would I get a bag?"

"We don't have bags." Cass shrugs as Cujo appears again with a brick in each hand. "You took the bags last time. We haven't had a chance to get more bags."

"*What?*" He drops a brick. "You telling me you ain't got no bags?"

"Where's your own bag?"

"I didn't think to bring one."

"You're robbing us and you expect us to provide you with the bags, like it's default? You expect a hand job while you're at it?"

"*Daughter*, the filthy things coming out of your mouth." Her mother's face distorts with disgust. "Breathe in Jesus"—she inhales deep—"See what you've become, Cassandra? Living with a gook and not attending church?"

"Ma'am, once again, that ain't the correct no-men's-clitter." Cujo's tucking the two bricks around his belt.

"Sure you don't want to go back to school?" I ask him.

He says nothing, but flashes me a snarling look as he heads inside the vault once again. When he comes out, his belt is gone and there are six bricks tucked under his waistband. He then tosses two bricks to Rabies. "Pocket them or tuck 'em around like I'm doing."

Rabies catches the money but doesn't do what Cujo's doing, instead he says, "Any of you ladies got a handbag?"

Cass's mom raises her hand. Then she shows everyone the purse hanging off her shoulder. The purse is faux leather and the size is mini, good for holding two condoms and a fart. I fail to see the point of carrying one at all.

Her mom explains, "I bought it 'cause it goes with my hair."

Some Spanish later Rabies tries Jimbo. "You—White Collar, you got a briefcase of some kind?" The White Collar's reply is negative. To Cujo, the gunman orders, "You're gonna have to make a couple trips to the car. Pop the trunk and dump the money there. Come back and do it again until you empty the vault." He tosses over the car key to the stolen vehicle.

"I'll help," I volunteer. "So he doesn't have to make as many trips."

He's thinking and I'm tucking the money all around my body.

"Okay," finally he agrees, but warns me, "If you don't come back, I'll shoot your girlfriend, you understand?"

"Probably doesn't matter to him." Cass folds her arms, she berates, "He abandoned his daughter in a foreign country. Tells you the kind of man he is."

With the money fastened under my belt, I exit the bank holding up my hands. Cujo opens the door and I back out ass first. I say to Cass and Rabies, "I'll be back."

****

Across the street at the stolen vehicle, Cujo pops the trunk. His head swivels around suspiciously when he's the only suspicious character here. But I can't help but survey the premises as well, and it's all quiet on the western front. No pedestrians, some cars passing up ahead, unlikely to approach the bank. I cower under the trunk lid and drop the first brick inside. Ten thousand dollars in the trunk, then twenty, then thirty…

Cujo does the same, remarking about the money, "Now this is just sexy."

We carried out fifteen bricks. Some are hundred

dollar bills and most are fifties. A total of eighty thousand American dollars.

Cujo jumps, clapping his hands. Then he does this little dance, sliding side to side while snapping his fingers in bad rhythm. A grin wide as his ass.

Suddenly he stops moving and just stares at the money in the trunk. Then, key hanging on a loop on his index finger, he lifts it to eye level. "Oh shit..." Not looking at me, he speaks to the key, "Major, you thinking what I'm thinking?"

Yes, Cujo. I've been thinking exactly what you're thinking. The thing about a heist is you have to devise multiple plans, each catering to a different scenario. Just like an army operation. Plan, prepare, execute, but never stop assessing the situation. Monitor and evaluate the criteria of success at every stage.

The criteria of success is walking away with ten thousand dollars, and the criteria's unadjusted. Now there's eighty in the trunk, for the taking.

So what's left is to execute.

"Major?" Cujo asks again, this time glancing at me sideways, "you thinking what I'm thinking?"

I slam the lid shut and nod. "Let's get the fuck out of here. I'll drive." I reach for the key dangling from his finger but he jerks the key to himself.

"What? What you mean *get the fuck out*?" He frowns, puzzled. "I was thinking maybe we shouldn't leave all the money in this car. I mean, shit, he claimed this car. What if he takes off on us?"

"Not if we take off on *him* first." I roll my eyes in disbelief. "You have the key!" One more time in a whisper, "*We have the key. Let's go!*"

"What, leave him and your girlfriend behind? What

about the rest of the money?"

"Cujo." I want to kick him in his balls so he'll wake the fuck up. "You wouldn't know what to do with all that money if it fell on your head. Now quit arguing and give me the fucking key. That's an order, soldier."

"You're cold, major. You heard Rabies. Man's gonna kill your woman if we don't go back."

I dart a glance to the bank. Rabies is standing there with the gun pointing at Cass. The gunman's patience must be wearing thin. Any second he'll come out and ask us what the hell's taking so long. We'll lose our window to escape with what we already have.

Cujo says, "If anyone gets killed 'cause we failed to go back it's on us."

"He's *not* gonna kill anyone," I say, trying to appease this hardcore gangster, this ex-crew of New Thugs on the Block, LLC, who presently wants to ascertain the wellbeing of every person on the block. "Listen to me, Cujo. We drive off now, we get away safe and sound. Yes, Rabies will be furious when he sees us leave with his ride, but the first thing that'll come to his mind *won't* be to kill anyone. The first thing he'll do is figure out how to escape with what's left in the *vault*—there's still over one hundred thousand dollars in there. What he's gonna do when he sees us take off is *laugh* at us because we're leaving him the majority of the pie. The way I see it, Cujo, if I ever bump into him years from now, like in a bar in Cancun, Mexico, he'll be liable to buy me a goddamn mojito."

Cujo chews on it for a bit. "No, major. You know he's a stone cold killer. What makes you so sure he won't drop bodies after he's taken the money?"

"Why would he?"

"Because," he explains like I'm a kid, "because he said he would."

"You expect me to believe you want to go back there 'cause you don't want nobody killed?"

"Yeah, and you know why? 'Cause *my* mama didn't raise no coward." A belittling scoff. "Is this what the seventy-fifth is all about, huh? You want the key, major? Here"—he tosses over the car key—"scat if you want. We started this and you said no one would get hurt. I'm gonna make sure of that so I'm going back."

I have the key and I have the car—the car filled with eighty thousand dollars.

Cujo backs away toward the bank, saying to me, "That woman, Cassie Rose, she loves you, man. I can tell the way she looks at you. That's *love*, you feel me? Marla never looks at me like that. I'd give anything for her to look at me how your woman looks at you."

"I have a daughter who needs me more, Cujo." My hand is on the car door handle when I say, "I can't choose a woman over my daughter."

He stands in the middle of the street. "Why the fuck you gotta choose?"

I skip a beat. "You expect a woman to wait around while a guy tends his illegitimate child?"

"You missing the point, man. The point is, you ain't gotta choose. You need to accept the fact that they must coexist." He turns around saying, "She still looks at you that way, major. Those eyes, that kind of love, I'm telling you, it's unconditional…"

A woman who loves you unconditionally.

Assess and evaluate.

I close my eyes and adjust the criteria of success.

Accept the fact that they must coexist.

A sigh. *Shit.*

I put the key away and remove my hand from the car door handle.

I follow Cujo back inside the bank.

Chapter Twenty-Five

"What took you so long?"

When we get inside, Rabies is holding the gun at Jim's head. Jim's trembling, looking terrified. Everyone else is gathered around his desk, hands clutched over their hearts like they're praying for peace. They all show their relief over my return by breathing out a sigh.

"Jim, it's okay, I'm here now." I attempt to calm him down. "He's not gonna shoot you."

"Yeah, how would you know?"

"The hammer isn't cocked."

Jim cranks his head toward the gun. He sees the hammer isn't pulled back, and exhales with a scoff. Not trembling any more, he says to the gunman, "Thanks, padre, for making me look like a wuss in front of the ladies."

Rabies lowers his weapon and steps back. "While you two were taking your sweet time, the cops called."

My heart skips a beat.

Cujo's expression is full of regret. He looks at me like he's saying, *Should've listened to you and bailed when we had the chance.*

I act composed and ask, "Are they on their way?"

"You think we'd be standing here talking it over like housewives if the cops were on their way?" The gunman orders the loan officer, "Tell 'em what happened."

Jim flattens his tie. "Right after you guys left the building, the phone rang and I picked it up. It was the sheriff's responding to a call about a robbery."

Another call *about a robbery?*

"Shit," Cujo interrupts. "And?"

"I told her it's a false alarm, like it's been happening all day. I'm sorry," he apologizes to everyone. "He had a gun at my head. What was I suppose to say? That we're being held up? Those would've been the last words out of my mouth before my head got blown to pieces."

"You did fine, Jim." I set him at ease. "I would've done the same thing."

Rabies says to Cujo and me, "What are you waiting for? Empty the vault!"

I tread to the vault with Cujo, passing Ester, Cass's mom and Cass. Cassie Rose, she makes eye contact with me and I try to see whatever Cujo was talking about. *The way she looks at you.* She's looking at me the same way she always has, with those green eyes, sparkling now. Something special there? I don't see it.

In the vault, I pocket ten grand but from the corner of my eye, I see movement out of the vault's opening. I exit the vault in time to see a vehicle park across the street.

Behind the stolen vehicle with the Alabama plate.

My first reaction is to call Cass. She looks to the outside as well. If it's a customer, all she has to do is go out and stop the person from coming in by saying the bank's closed for periodic maintenance. She'd do that because no one would get hurt, it is in everyone's best interest. But Cass isn't moving. She and I, we recognize the car. And we both know that the people in the car are definitely not potential customers.

"Cops," she identifies. "It's that detective from Los Angeles, Grayson, with that woman, the state agent. I forgot her name."

Cujo comes out of the vault, pants stuffed with money. "Someone say cops?"

Rabies turns to me, searching for what to do.

"Yes...cops." I sense the car becoming idle, Grayson pulling the keys...pocketing them.

Evaluate and assess.

Assess and evaluate.

Grayson and Reese get out of the car, close the door. They stare at the car in front of them, the Alabama plate, stare for two, three seconds and then dismiss it. Now they're approaching the bank, where an armed robbery is in progress.

Evaluate and assess.

Adjust the criteria of success.

"I've seen enough men die to last a lifetime," I speak to everyone, calm as can be. "Nobody wants a shootout, right? 'Cause that's what'll happen if someone opens their mouth. You might think you're doing a heroic thing but you'll put everyone's life in danger." I turn to Cujo, Rabies, Jim, and Ester, they nod their heads, all seem to understand. The bank robbers and the bank employees all want the same thing—to rob the bank. Cass and her mother though, they're the unreliable elements.

I say it again, but directly at the mother and daughter, "*Nobody* wants a shootout."

Grayson and Reese walk toward the bank.

****

When the cops are standing by the entrance, Jim is

sitting at his desk like he's never left. Cass's mother sits opposite him acting like a customer visiting for a loan application. Ester sits next to her, the branch manager making sure the client is taken care of, possibly because the loan she's requesting is quite sizable. Cass is at her counter, and I'm locking the vault, turning the wheel after the heavy door's been pushed closed.

Cujo and Rabies are squatting behind the counter, ducked low so they can't be seen from the other side. Cujo on the left side of Cass, Rabies on her right, his gun pressed on her ass. Her hand reaches back and attempts to direct the barrel anywhere but there, but it's no use.

Grayson steps inside, followed by Reese, and the first thing he says is, "Are those Girl Scout cookies?" He means a plate of cookies on Jim's desk. This big cop approaches the cookies, his badge showing on his belt. "I did the Boy Scout thing. Didn't make the Eagle Scout."

Jim offers him a cookie. "Didn't complete the merits?"

American small talk, keeps the country going.

"No." The cop eats. "'Cause I'm black."

And that kills the small talk.

The cops are facing the counter when Cass greets them with a standard teller's smile. "Detective, what a surprise."

"Ma'am," the detective greets back with a nod at me as well. "You remember agent Reese?"

"Of course," I say as I return to my counter from the vault. I give a nod followed by a smile to Reese. "How can I—*we*—help you?"

"Mr. Chin," the woman isn't smiling, "is there

somewhere we can talk, privately?"

That gets me worried. What could they want to talk to me about in private? Nonetheless, I suggest at once, "How about outside?" I come around the counter to halt their casual advance.

"Too hot out." She wipes her forehead. "Is there a break room?"

I shake my head negative. She looks at Cass as well so Cass also shakes her head. No break room, it's true.

"How about an office in the back?"

Yes, there's Ester's office. But no, you can't go in there. To reach the office would involve the cops coming around the counter, and they'd see plain as turds in a toilet bowl, two thugs crouching there, one with a gun to Cass's ass, the other one clearly Cujo, the man they've been chasing all over the state.

But to this request, Ester stands up from over at Jim's desk. "The office is for employees only. Off limits to you people."

Jesus Christ, Ester. Way to use your words.

The big black cop finishes eating cookie and wipes his hands on his jacket; jacket flaps open and close, his shield flashes under the florescent light. *LAPD, Protect and Serve*.

Ester gets smart with the guy, "I don't believe you have jurisdiction in our neck of the woods."

Which is true but his partner, the state agent, does have jurisdiction. She walks to Ester and says in a friendly tone, "Ma'am, I'm sorry, we forgot to introduce ourselves." She makes the introductions and requests Ester do the same. After all of that's said and done Reese flashes a winning smile, showing teeth white as toothpaste. "My partner and I are assisting the sheriff with what happened here last Friday. We meant to come here sooner but we just didn't have the time. I don't mean to get off on the wrong foot with you folks. After all, we need your assistance in a matter of an ongoing investigation."

I ask the cops then, "So you're here about Cujo?"

A pause later Reese replies, "No. Not quite," and she asks again, "Somewhere we can talk?"

Ester gesture's Jim's desk. "If it's related to the robbery last Friday, you can talk here. We all witnessed what happened."

"Ma'am, it's all fine with me, but"—she gazes at the desk—"you have a client." Client meaning Cass's mom.

"Oh don't worry about me." The mother turns around in her chair and the chair squeaks. "I'm just about done here."

"We actually still have a whole lot of documents to go through." Jim piles some papers on the desk, keeping her there. He says to the cops, "Besides, this is a small town, folks will hear about what you say no matter what."

Good. Everyone is onboard.

Nobody wants a shootout.

Reese remarks to her partner, "This is a little unorthodox, but maybe it's better all the witnesses hear what we have to ask."

Hearing this, I lead the cops into the inquiry, so they don't keep pondering where to have this conversation. "I take it you still haven't caught Cujo?"

Cujo is hidden behind the counter next to Rabies.

"He doesn't matter any more." Grayson has his

hands in his pockets, looking relaxed. "Cujo's a small fish. To be honest with you, I drew the short straw coming up here for the chase."

"But he's wanted for murder."

"He shot and killed a criminal—a drug lord. I'm surprised they aren't presenting him a medal. Listen, the point is, small time thugs like him—dime a dozen. The Attorney General agrees with us now that there's a bigger fish in the pond."

"You mean Mad Dog?"

"Not him either," Reese says. "We have reason to believe Mad Dog wasn't at the scene of the crime. He should have an alibi."

Then they must be after Rabies. The *Sicario*. It makes sense. The guy's international, done crime in Mexico and probably Texas. A big fish, for sure. Rabies crouched behind the counter, his gun stuck on Cass's ass.

"We're after an international criminal." There's a hint of excitement in Grayson's voice. "Wanted in at least three countries that we know of. If I catch him"— he looks to Reese and back—"I mean, if *we* catch him…"

"There's a bounty," Reese explains. "An international bounty honored by sovereign nations. Our respective departments could use the monetary compliment, if you know what I mean."

Grayson adds, "Not to mention the international relations effect…"

"But first we have to make sure it's him. So what we want to ask you"—Reese unfolds a piece a paper from her pocket, showing us a grainy picture—"is this the Asian man you saw at the bank?"

Chapter Twenty-Six

"The *Shanghai Bandit*?"

"That's what the media's calling him." Grayson's back is against the counter. "And by the way, I'm only divulging what's already been said in the papers."

"You mean the *LA Times*?"

"*LA Times*, *New York Times*, Mars and Pluto Times, he's been on and off the papers for the past ten years. Notorious for a heist at the HSBC in Hong Kong. He pulled some jobs in LA and San Diego, and then vanished without a trace. But now, if it was the same guy who subsequently robbed Cujo, then he has resurfaced."

Cujo hiding behind the counter, hearing about the Shanghai Bandit.

Jim assures him, "He came in and said bank*er* robber, made it rhyme. Definitely not from around here. And yeah, I think I saw the guy in that picture come in the day before yesterday. He came in, stood around and left. I thought he was your uncle, Chin."

Grayson's back is still against the counter, he's standing at an angle with legs crossed, just chilling with us. "I want a visual confirmation from you, Mr. Chin."

"Why?" I ask. "'Cause I'm Chinese?"

"Your opinion matters." Then he clears his throat somewhat uncomfortably. "Listen, Mr. Chin, I'm a detective so this is what I do. I apologize if I sound prejudiced."

Right then, the phone on Jim's desk rings.

The sudden sound infiltrates my heart. Jim's not picking it up. Who could it be? Sheriff's, again? It's possible. Cass is standing behind the counter, a gun on her ass. She could've slipped her finger to the panic button, pressed it, drew the cop's attention to the possibility of a holdup. Makes sense. She's the one with a gun to her ass. No one would dare jeopardize her safety. No one would dare except herself.

The phone's ringing for a third time. Jim frowns at me like he's asking my permission.

"You gonna pick that up?" Grayson fingers his left ear. "That ringing is piercing."

I produce a tiny nod and Jim picks up the phone, saying "Excuse me," to Cass's mom, his loan applicant. He listens for a moment then speaks, "Yeah okay, next week's fine." The following minute he's just repeating more or less the same thing. Yes, next week, yes, yes. Any time. No, not on Sunday. Christ, it's a *bank*. Anytime other than Sunday.

Finally, he hangs up. "Bell Pacific wants to come in and see about the telephone line."

"Oh that's right," Ester tells us. "I called them and left a message."

The cops glance at each other, nothing for them to get curious about. What telephone line? Who cares? Grayson is staring at me when he brings us back on topic. "So what can you tell us about the Chinese guy, Mr. Chin?"

Just answer their question so they can leave. Leave and we can all finish the heist. So I nod. "Yeah, I think it's the guy in the photo."

"Are you sure? I mean, can you tell me any specific features that match?"

Christ sakes, now he wants to get into details.

"His eyes, ears, and nose." I list body parts like the guy isn't missing any.

"Okay. So, on a scale of one to ten, how likely would you say it's the same Chinese guy? Ten being the most likely."

"I say nine point five."

"Tell me about the other point five."

"Grayson, hold that thought." Reese reaches around her back and unclips a radio from above her ass. "I got a ping."

And Grayson says, "You got signal here?" sounding surprised.

She turns the little knob on the radio and holds it against her ear like it's a portable phone, she listens to it and mouths, "I don't believe it." To Grayson, "They spotted Mad Dog's Pontiac and all units are in pursuit. We gotta finish this some other time."

"Son of a bitch," Grayson utters, then he lingers. "Nah, let the locals handles it. Way too hot for a car chase. Besides, Mad Dog didn't kill Dago."

Reese broods about this proposal.

Then I say, "You guys for serious? The guy shot at me."

The agent gives Grayson a wistful look and to me a bashful one. "Mr. Chin is right. Mad Dog's gotta be running from something. All units, Grayson, let's go."

Grayson appears sullen at first, then he says, "Shit. You're right." Now with conviction, "*You're* driving."

I breathe out a mental sigh of relief. The uninvited guests are finally leaving. Time to Charlie Mike.

They hustle to the door, and Reese tells me, "We'll return tomorrow. I want you to know, Mr. Chin, you've been tremendously helpful." She brushes her hair back as a breeze come through the door. Her hair smells good.

Before her hair lands on the back of her shoulder, there's a sneeze.

"*Escheeew!*"

The cops turn around a third of the way.

Silence, in the bank.

As if one isn't enough, another, "*Escheeee-choooo!*"

Aw, shit...

So close.

Grayson and Reese, standing by the exit, scan the bank in a one-eighty. No one appears to have sneezed. Everyone appears to be terrified. Everyone except me. My shoulders slack. Feeling like a captain of a sinking ship.

"Who the hell was that?" Reese's eyes fix on Cass, who stands near the origin of the sneeze. Reese's hand goes for her gun, steel clipped and holstered on her waist.

Her fingernails are on the grip but her thumbnail fails to unclip the holster in time. Rabies springs up from behind the counter, his left arm around Cass's neck in a chokehold position. Right hand pointing the gun at Cass's temple.

"Move a muscle and the next thing you see is her brain all over the fucking floor."

Chapter Twenty-Seven

So we have a Mexican standoff. Nothing to do with the original sense of the phrase but one which involves an actual gunslinger from Mexico. Rabies's gun, looking mighty large next to Cass's head, has its hammer cocked back. With two armed cops just across the room, the guy isn't fooling around. "Don't even think about it, Chocolate Pie." Chocolate Pie means agent Reese, who's frozen and has yet to draw her weapon. "I want you to unclip the holster and drop the gun to the floor. Then kick it over." To Detective Grayson, "You too, pig."

Grayson flashes a wrathful look like Danny Glover in *Lethal Weapon*.

There must be some kind of protocol. Cops must be taught how to deal with this kind of situation at their academy for their training. And apparently, the way to deal is to do as told. Hostage's safety comes first, I reckon. The two cops unclip their firearms, drop them to the floor, then kick them over.

I step back two, three paces.

"Who the fuck are you?" Grayson interrogates unarmed. *Lethal Weapon* without a weapon. "Let me rephrase, you know who you're fucking with? You're fucking with the LAPD and the state's Bureau of Investigation." He turns a little so his badge is showing. "You're fucking with the wrong people, asshole."

Rabies ignores Grayson and appears to be kicking his partner. "Go around and get their guns, Cujo."

The cops exchange confused glances. *Cujo*?

Anton *Cujo* Samuels, ex-New Thugs on the Block, LLC, now the Notorious BRG—bank robbing gangsta, rises from behind the counter holding his nose. "Anyone got a tissue?"

"Jesus Christ," Grayson, in shock, peers at him and the vault. "You're robbing this bank, *again*? You're a brand new kind of dumb criminal, Cujo."

Cujo decides to wipe the mucus on his ass before moving around the counter and picking up the guns. Grayson's and Reese's legally ordained firearms are now in the possession of the brand new kind of dumb criminal. Cujo sneers, a gun in each hand. "I got your guns. Who's dumb now, punk?"

Jim shakes his head and says to the cops, "You should've just left and let them rob us." Cass's mom, opposite Jim, is covering her mouth with her stubby hands, as if to contain the hysteria within. Nonetheless, she nods her head in earnest agreement.

"So what's next?" Agent Reese asks with hands in surrender. "What do you plan on doing with all of us?"

Rabies tell her, "We're gonna empty the vault and then lock your asses inside. Then we're gonna take this one for a ride." This one means Cass.

"I'm sorry," Grayson apologizes sarcastically. "But once again, who the fuck are you?"

Guy introduces proudly, "I'm Rabies."

Grayson turns to Cujo. "You bit him?"

"Why does everyone say that? Why would I bite him?"

"Don't take her. Take me instead," I say,

reminding him what we agreed on. This is my extraction plan.

However, Cass rebuts, "No, take me. Don't take him. Take me, please." She peers at me with those green eyes.

"Cassandra!" Cass's mom stands up from the chair and the chair falls back. "Are you crazy? Let them take *him*." She turns to the cops. "Officers, please don't let the bad black man take my daughter. Let them take the gook instead."

"Ma'am, it's *detective*." Grayson flashes her sour expression. "I wasn't aware she's your daughter." Now he's studying the daughter and mother as if he's trying to link any resemblance. "Don't worry, ma'am. They're not taking anyone hostage."

"Says the guy who got caught in his panties." Cujo clacks the gun barrels together. "I heard you say you're not after me for Dago's murder no more. But let me tell you somethin', cop, I would've done it. I got what it takes."

"Your mother must be proud," Grayson says.

"I lost my gun but now I got two, yeah, *what*, motherfuckers."

The cops say nothing.

I assess and evaluate the new situation. There are two cops here in an open heist. We don't want them harmed and we don't want them around. Even unarmed, they're huge obstacles. Assess and evaluate.

Evaluate and assess.

I tired, Daddy. I hungry. I no have home.

I know, Daughter, I want to say*, your daddy's gotta remove some obstacles.*

"Attention, Grayson," sounding military, I say to

the detective, "you've forfeited your service weapon, yet you and your partner's presence in the bank is still an endangerment to the occupants' safety"—I gesture to Cass, who is being held at gunpoint—"if you decide to make a tactical retreat, I'm inclined to believe the robbers will not only permit you to do so, but also spare everyone from harm." To Cujo and Rabies, I ask, "Am I right?"

Let them retreat and let things be as they were.

Cujo nods with the guns. Rabies releases his chokehold on Cass, a gesture of good faith.

Cass cowers behind the counter, safe.

"What you saying, major"—Grayson says, not addressing me as Mr. Chin, but as my rank—"you're saying we walk on outta here, like we didn't see a robbery in progress, like we pretend we never stepped in here at all?"

"Affirmative. This way, the robbers don't have to lock anyone in the vault, and nobody gets taken hostage." A pause for effect and I say it again, "It'd be a tactical retreat, detective."

Grayson wets his lips, pondering it over.

Silence for some odd heartbeats.

"All right"—he lowers his hands and turns to Reese—"we can do that for the good of the general population here. A tactical retreat—there's no shame in that. *However,*" to Cujo, he relates, "there *is* shame in something else."

Cujo frowns. "What you looking at me for?"

Grayson rubs his hands and chuckles. "Just hear me straight out, all right, brother?" he says, sounding ebonic all of a sudden. He takes a step closer, acting casual. "You ever been laughed at by somebody? You know how that feels, right, being jeered at? Well this thing right here?" He gestures around. "This is embarrassing, man. Got caught with dick in my hand. I'd go back to the precinct and I'd be hearing people laughing behind—"

"Don't nobody gotta know what happened here," Cujo points out.

"But they *will*. Just hear me out, my man." Grayson smiles, showing patience. "Let me ask you this, you know how hard it is to make it as a black man? You think being black in the LAPD is a stroll in the park? *Shit*, think again." He says *shit* the same way Cujo says it, *she-it*. "You understand I'm the third black detective in the history of the precinct? What you're doing, you're setting me back—"

"Man, cut the shit and tell me what you want."

"I want my gun back."

And there it is. This is Grayson's play. I did not see this coming at all.

Grayson goes on, "Ain't no conclusive story gonna justify how I got no gun. Yeah, I can tell nobody what happened here, don't gotta say nothin' about no tactical retreat. But how am I gonna tell my captain I ain't got my *gun* no more? What, I lost it? Left it on a bus? Forgot where I put it?" His head cocks to the side. "What was I, high?"

Cujo thinks for a moment. "Why don't you tell 'em you got mugged?"

"How could I get mugged if I was packing? *She-it*, you ever heard no detective got mugged on the street? Packing a steel as big as his dick?"

Cujo gazes up the gun end to end, appraising its size in comparison to his dick.

"If you give the gun back to him," Rabies chimes in, "I'm liable to tap him in the head."

"Hey, *amigo*, you mind?" Grayson turns. "You got no part in this discourse. I'm talking to my *man* here."

Cujo peers past the detective and asks, "What about the sister? Don't she need her gun back as well?"

"Man, she a woman, she probably looses a gun every other week, you know what I'm saying?" And he laughs. A big, haughty laugh.

"Yeah, yeah." Cujo lets out little chuckles. "I know what you're saying."

Agent Reese cringes, annoyed at these two.

"So I get to keep *this* gun?" Cujo waves the smaller gun—a Sig Sauer. "And give you back *this* one?" *This* one means the gun big as Grayson's dick.

"Yeah, that's right, that's right, my man." Grayson steps forward.

"Man, back the fuck off!" Cujo points both guns at the detective. "I said, back the fuck *off*. Trying to trick me? We gave you a chance to quit and you play me for a fool, asshole? Get on your knees and hands behind your back. That's what you pigs like to tell folks, ain't it?" He walks over to Reese. "You too, bitch. I *said*, get on your pretty knees like you're 'bout to blow me. Don't be acting no high-class cunt, *bitch*."

Reese kneels.

Fuck. I had the situation under control and now, the situation has gone FUBAR. I was so close in removing the obstacles. So fucking close.

Grayson gets on one knee but decides to stand up. "Listen brother, this black-on-black crime has *got* to stop. I'm—"

"Shut the fuck up!" Cujo says, sounding out of his

mind. He aims the guns, one at Reese and one at Grayson. True to his gangster prose, he's about to let the cops feel the wrath of his menace. "Don't talk to me and do as I say! Get on your fucking *knees*!"

"Cujo, my brother—"

"Don't *brother* me."

"Listen—"

"One more word outta your ass I swear I'm gonna hit 'em up."

"Hit what up? I'm only trying to help—"

"Not another *word*."

"Anton…"

"*Eschew-ee!*"

At the same time, *BANG*.

Chapter Twenty-Eight

The gunshot echoes.

The place is still and everyone appears confounded. No one expected a gun to go off. *No one*, meaning Cujo as well. He's frowning at the weapons in both hands, his hands are shaking, as if he can't believe it. I remember I told Grayson once, *Cujo shot anyone it'd be an accident*.

Some flakes fall from the ceiling. They land on Cujo's bald head like sprinkles on a chocolate cupcake. Some land on detective Grayson's body too.

Grayson dusts off the flakes and looks up to the ceiling.

I look up as well.

There's a hole the size of a baseball.

"Can I get a word in here?"

Now everyone directs their attention to the voice at the entrance. There stands a scar-faced man in a suit holding a Beretta. Its barrel smoking. "Anyone care to update me as far as the robbery is concerned? I waited outside for like an hour now. You have any idea how hot it is outside in these clothes?" He does a quick survey and remarks, "Jesus, the whole town got invited to this little soiree?" To Rabies, he speaks something along the line of *como estas*? Their guns pointed at each other.

Seeing how the situation has changed, not for the

better, not for the worse—just changed—Reese finally gets up from her knees. She straightens her pencil skirt and states to the newcomer, "You're Roberto *Mad Dog* Ramirez."

"Is that what you do, lady? Go up to people and tell them who they are? Walk up to a person on the street and say, you're William *Billy Bob* Roberts, like he doesn't know?"

"I'm a cop." She reveals the badge clipped on her skirt. "I charge you with attempted assault of a police officer." She looks up at the ceiling. "Assault with a deadly weapon."

"And you're gonna overcome me with what, your silky panty hose?" Mad Dog sneers. "I don't think you're charging anyone here *without* a deadly weapon." To Rabies, "You gonna rob the joint for me, or what?"

Rob the joint for *him*? So he's not here to partake, he's here to *take over*.

"I guess you spilled the beans after all?" Rabies says to me and then to his superior, "No matter. This here is *my* score. I'm running this shit on my own. This has nothing to do with you, Mad Dog. No offense intended."

"Then why do I feel offended?"

Rabies and Mad Dog, two Mexican gunslingers in the bank, guns pointed at each other talking about what's not offensive.

Caught in the crosshairs, Grayson mutters, "Need the Animal Control for this kind of shit."

"Is this how it's gonna be, Rabies?" Mad Dog asks everyone this: "I brought you to the states and this is how you repay me?" He's asking like he expects other people's input. "I made you, *esé*, don't forget that. I *made* you."

The heist has slipped out of my control but it's still a *heist*, yet; no one is doing the robbing. I must steer the criminals back on track, so I suggest, "Why don't you rob the bank first and figure out the details later?"

Let's go, people. I got a daughter waiting for me in a fucking sweatshop.

No one appears to have heard me.

"Yo, Mad Dog," Cujo gets his attention, calm now that he realizes he didn't fire the gun by accident. "Where's Marla, man? Where's my girl?"

"She's leading a car chase. I was monitoring the joint from afar, out of sight. When I saw these niggers park their car I knew something was up, so I sent Marla off in the Pontiac to draw the cops away. If it wasn't for me looking after your black ass, the place would be swarming with townie clowns. You owe me your share, nigger boy."

Grayson and Reese hearing the n-word, unarmed, both take a heavy breath through their nose, suppressing their anger.

Their nostrils flare.

Cujo shakes his head. "So you're using Marla as a bait?"

"It's called a diversion, dumbass."

"I know what a diversion is. What I'm saying is, you're sacrificing her to the po-pos? 'Cause she ain't gonna get away, you know? Your Pontiac ain't no getaway mobile."

"Cujo," Rabies calls his attention and reminds him. "He's here to highjack us. He got a gun on me and you got two guns. You need to take him out."

Take him out or he's taking over. Cujo looks at the

two guns in his hands, thinking about it. And I want to tell him, *Just rob the godforsaken bank.*

"Now hold on a second." Grayson's palms are out, acting the peacekeeper. "No one's shooting anybody. Let's calm down and think about this. Cujo? You ain't gonna shoot nobody in front of the police. Look at me, son. You wanna go to jail that bad? You wanna hang with them hard-piping brothers down in Lompoc penitentiary? Doing twenty-five-to-life? You think it through?"

"Cujo, you forget he ordered me to execute you?" Rabies saying, "I bet if I told you what him and Marla were doing in the sack, you wouldn't hesitate to drop him, not for a second."

Grayson's getting nervous. "Cujo, listen to me—"

"No-no, go back." Cujo rolls his guns in a backward motion. "Marla and him were in the sack?" To Mad Dog, he says, "You hooking up with my girl, man? You said you wouldn't hurt her. What you doing with her in the sack?"

"What you think, sexual healing?" Rabies paints the picture. "No slow-ebb penetration there, *homes.* They were doing it like rabbits on crack."

"She wouldn't..." Cujo raises the gun, the big one.

"Oh yes, offering him that grateful pussy. She a fine piece of ass, you know it."

"Cujo," Mad Dog finally explains himself, "she was the one who insisted I shouldn't let you talk to her on the phone. She was over you, you understand? I know it's hard to hear but it's true. You can ask her."

"Take him out, Cujo," Rabies urges. "Smoke his ass."

"You think Rabies is gonna let you live after this?"

Mad Dog says, doing what he can to talk sense into Cujo. "You seeing what he's doing here? He's *betraying* me. *Me*—his *hermano*. What makes you think he won't double-cross you once he's used you? You think he's gonna split the money with you? You better check your head, my friend. Better see it clear who you're working with. I got a new proposition here, you drop him and I'll split the money with you 50/50, call it a new partnership, yeah? What do you say? Point your gun at him. Smoke *him*."

"I spared your life once, Cujo, don't you forget," Rabies says. "Why would I kill you if I'm generous enough to have spared your life?"

"You can't trust him, Cujo. You know how many people he's killed in cold blood? Two I know of he shot just for fun."

Grayson and Reese exchange an expression. Then they step back a little so they're out of the guns' crosshairs. The two cops stay quiet; no choice but to be content about these criminals turning on each other.

A complete derailment. A full FUBAR.

For the first time today, I'm thinking about blowing my cover. I'm thinking if I ought to scream some sense, *Let's finish this and be gone already!* Thinking if I ought to get a gun and get some action going once and for all.

The Mexican gangsters continue saying, Cujo this, Cujo that. Cujo do him. No, Cujo, do *him*.

Cujo has heard enough, finally. With both guns up, arms straight, one pointing at Mad Dog, the other pointing at Rabies, he says, "I ain't splitting the take with nobody. And if I *have* to I'd split it with the chink over there."

The chink over there obviously means me.

Now Grayson and Reese are looking at me funny; Grayson scratches his head, Reese's neck jerks back and her chin tips down, frowning at me. Everyone else is glazing at me perplexed, except Cass. She's hiding behind the counter and I can't see her face.

At last, Cujo orders me, "Empty the vault and drop the money in the car like before. If you think of running, man"—he smacks his lips and points out—"just look at them guns here, all locked and loaded and ready to pop. There'd be a shootout for sure. You wanna bet on that?"

A step in the right direction.

Mad Dog's M9 is on Rabies. Rabies's six-shooter switches between Mad Dog and Cujo. Cujo with two guns, has one on Mad Dog and one on Rabies. All gunmen are ready to fire, yet no one dares to go first.

This time, we have an actual Mexican standoff.

I turn to the vault and just as I'm treading toward it...

BOOM, a blast followed by glass shattering.

Ears ringing, I turn to the entrance and find one of the glass doors is gone. From the distance a faint sound of racking—that one-two operation of a pump action shotgun is heard. My first thought is: I'm imagining this; my ears are ringing, I couldn't possibly hear well. But then I realize the shattered glass on the floor and I know it's real. *We're getting ambushed.*

People scream in the background.

Sounding like mass casualty.

My dear daughter, what have I done?

Before another blast is heard. I yell over the confusion, "Everyone get on the floor!"

BOOM.

Like a bomb went off.

"Ah! I'm shot!" Cujo drops, crying, "Motherfucker shot me!"

The other glass door of the entrance is gone. No one's outside. *Where did the shot come from?* Grayson and Reese are on the floor, arms over their heads. Mad Dog is in the fetal position. Jim and Cass's mom are out of the blast range hiding under the desk. I can't see Rabies, he must be ducked behind the counter with Cass. Cujo, lying on his back, leans up a little, teeth biting his tongue in pain. He points the gun at the entrance and, *pop pop pop*, lets off three rounds, not hitting a goddamn thing. He falls flat against the floor, bleeding in the abdominal area.

There are no more blasts and I hope the attacker isn't reloading.

The smell of gunpowder lingers.

Composed, I direct the occupants of the bank, "Everyone, crawl behind the counter, *now*. Keep your head down!" My head comes up a little as I crawl next to Cujo. I try to flip him over in order to get a sense of his wound.

I can't move him, not with my chest against the floor. Grayson crawls next to me and erects to a squat. He lifts Cujo by the shoulders while I sneak a peek under. Cujo screaming profanity.

"Single pallet entry below the rib-cage. No exit wound," I relate to Grayson as he tries to drag the fallen thug behind the counter to safety.

"Ah shit!" Cujo screams at the top of his lungs. "Let me rob the bank, *please*! Oh Lord, why won't you just let me rob the fucking bank? *Another* gunshot wound? I ain't got no *insurance* for this shit!"

"You won't be needing none in lock-up," Grayson assures him, dragging his ass.

Reese is crawling next to them, dumbfounded. "Who the hell fired at us?"

Then, we all hear the announcement from outside the building. A guy shouting, "E-everybody on floor. I-I am banker robber!"

The place is quiet for what seems to be a long ass time.

Everyone chewing this piece of information.

Then Cujo, no longer being dragged away, tilts his head up. "Isn't that who you cops were talking about?" He gazes from Reese to Grayson, eyes bemused. "Is that the Shanghai Bandit?"

Chapter Twenty-Nine

The heist's turning out to be a crime convention for cops and robbers.

We have a LAPD detective and a state agent; the agent is from the state capitol and the detective is way out of his jurisdiction to attend the show. We have two members of the cartel, all the way from Mexico, representing. One former member of New Thugs on the Block, LLC, presently known as the Notorious BRG. Lastly, we have an internationally wanted man, the surprise guest of the event, a celebrity known as the Shanghai Bandit.

Pop-click-pop-click-pop. Rabies shoots blindly with his revolver, his head ducked low with just a hand on the counter.

"Stop wreaking havoc! You shot up the fucking phone!" Reese looks like she wants to choke Rabies. "Why don't you let me have a go at it," she says, asking for the gun.

"Yeah, nice try." Rabies moves sideways crab-style, hugging the weapon to his chest.

All of us are cowered behind the counter now. Ester and Cass's mom are embracing each other on the floor, trembling, next to them are Cass and Reese—the women grouped together.

Us men are banded around Cujo. Grayson putting pressure on Cujo's wound while I rip Cujo's orange underwear/mask to make a tourniquet. Cujo aims at anyone who tries to take his guns. Rabies and Mad Dog turn their guns on each other. Jimbo crawls on the floor escaping to the other side, to where the women are.

Then suddenly, Mad Dog's aim moves away from Rabies. He fires, making the women go *Ahhh*! "Drop it," he says.

I turn and find Reese's hands in the air. One hand holding her radio. She drops it.

Pop. Mad Dog shoots up the radio from six feet away.

Ester and Cass's mom start crying. So does Jim.

"We're under siege and I was gonna ask for back-up." Reese is fuming at Mad Dog. "You wanna be killed by the Shanghai Bandit, is that it? You wanna die?"

"I rather get killed than walk out of here in handcuffs." Then he turns to Rabies. "Look, we have to work together. Blast our way outta here with the money. You remember Juárez?" He runs his finger up and down that scar on his face. "It'd be like old times. Shit, will you point your fucking gun somewhere else? I'm talking to you."

I let the Mexicans argue and direct Jim, "Take the women to the vault and close the door. Jim"—I snap my fingers—"you hear? The vault's bulletproof, take shelter in there. Jim, you're in charge of keeping the ladies safe."

Jim comes around by pulling his own hair. "What a goddamn nightmare." After a shaky breath, he utters, "C'mon, ladies. Keep your heads down, let's move away from this insanity."

"Mom," Cass says, "go with Jim. I'm staying."

Cass's mom wants to argue but Cass assures her, "Just go. I'll be there in a minute. There's something I want to talk to Chin about."

Now's not the time to talk. Ester's ass is already in the air, crawling to the vault. Jim assumes the position and Cass's mom has no choice but to follow. She says to her daughter, "I love you, Cassandra."

The three of them are lost to sight when the special guest shouts from the outside, "I want money. All of it! Hurry, I no have time!"

Grayson, finishing up tending Cujo's wound, lets his voice boom from behind the counter. "This is LAPD detective Grayson speaking. You're holding civilians as well as two members of law enforcement inside this bank. And I know who you are. You're the Shanghai Bandit!"

Grayson just introduces people, not even asking the man to yield.

"Who?" the immigrant says. "I-I what?"

"You're the Shanghai Bandit! You're wanted in three countries for multiple robberies and homicides, not to mention the devastation you've caused on a certain national monument!"

"Mon-you-what? No-no, I'm not, okay? You make mistake."

That gives everybody pause, especially Grayson. He's frowning now, considering if he's actually made a mistake. "You're *not* the Shanghai Bandit?"

"No idea who you talking about. Just give me money, quick *now*! Or I shoot!"

"*Wait*...did you not rob the Grand Lisboa in Macau, let see"—he counts with his fingers—"eight, nine years ago?"

After a moment, he replies, "I robbed casino. So?"

"And the HSBC before that?"

"No see what your point is?"

"How did you escape from Hong Kong that one time?"

"I took the ferry to Macau. I think so. It too long time ago."

"The *ferry*," Grayson mutters. "But the manifest didn't have anyone unaccounted for!" Then to us, he explains, "I studied his robberies—"

"I remember. Yes. I jumped from pier. S-swimming to a ferry boat. I hug rubber tire."

"What tire? You mean the boat bumper?"

"I hug tire. One hour later, I'm in Macau."

"Shit, you *are* the Shanghai Bandit! And two years after that, you held up a bank near LAX! A guard died of a heart attack!"

"I'm no Shanghai Bandit!"

"Yes you *are*!"

"I'm *not* from Shanghai!"

Grayson is looking at me for some reason when he asks, "Okay, so where you from?"

"I-I'm from Kaohsiung."

Again, Grayson is looking at me when he asks, "Kao-shit-what? Where the hell's that?"

I enlighten, "It's in Taiwan."

The bandit shouts, "I never been to Shanghai! Why call me Shanghai Bandit?"

"Gotta give him that." I shrug to Grayson. "It's like calling a man from Canada the San Antonio Bandit. It'd confuse people."

"Man, who cares where he's from. Shanghai Bandit, Peking duck—same shit." To Agent Reese he winks. "Looks like it's gonna be *us* bringing in the Shanghai Bandit. C'mon baby, it's promotion time."

"How we gonna do that?" Reese darts a glance to her radio shot up on the floor. "We're besieged and *unarmed*. Plus, what we gonna do about those three?" Those three meaning Rabies, Mad Dog, and Cujo. "I think the best we can do right now is *stall*."

At which time the bandit prompts, "I want money, now now now!"

And I'm thinking, *fuck, man, so do I*.

"If we stall," Grayson points out, "he might get away. We'd lose the chance of bringing him in *ourselves*. C'mon, opportunity like this is what we've been waiting for. You and I, we've climbed the highest we can, no matter how many thugs like the ones in this room we apprehend. But the *Shanghai Bandit*? Shit, I'm thinking we'd be decorated by the AG, if not the *Governor*."

Agent Reese is chewing her lip, contemplating what he said. Then her gaze shifts to Mad Dog and Rabies, who are listening to the discussion. Again, she asks, "What about them?"

"Them?" Grayson casts a pitiful glance at the criminals beside him and scoffs. "I say fuck 'em."

"Says the man with no weapon," Rabies mocks.

And I interject, "Detective, might I make a sensible suggestion?"

Grayson thinks it over. "You outrank all of us, major. Go ahead."

"If you aren't gonna arrest Mad Dog, Rabies, and Cujo, if you'd let them go in exchange for the apprehension of the bigger fish, then perhaps we can all work together to get what we want. What you and

Agent Reese want is the bandit." And to the gangsters, "What *you* want is to get out of here with the money. Do I have that right so far?"

"*My* money," Rabies corrects. "I'm not sharing."

"Work that out once you *have* the money. Right now, we all need to cooperate, do you agree?"

Reese eyeballs Grayson then me. "Assume we agree, for now."

Reluctantly, Rabies nods. "How should we do it?"

"First off, we need to do everything on the double, before sirens blare and scare off the bandit. He'll flee and be picked up by the sheriff or CHP, which will make you two cops look downtrodden instead of victorious. What do you think?"

"With all due respect, major," Grayson says, talking fast. "Will you just get on with it?"

"I'll go out with the money—"

"I want the Dog outside with the money!" the bandit demands. "Just the Dog, only him! Dog, bring me money!"

What the hell? I stand up a bit and peer over the counter. "Which dog?" I shout to the bandit. "We got three dog related individuals in the bank at the moment!" *Cujo, Rabies, Mad Dog.* It's a goddamn veterinary in here.

"Mad Dog," the bandit narrows it down. "I want Mad Dog!"

Now everyone is looking at Roberto *Mad Dog* Ramirez. Grayson's squeezes his forehead as he asks the guy, "You know the Shanghai Bandit?" A hint of awe.

"Not that I recall," Mad Dog admits, a little shrunken. "In fact, I don't know any chinks from

China."

"He says he's from Taiwan."

"There's a difference?"

I come between the two. "This is all the more reason for us to work together. Okay... So Mad Dog will go out with the money—"

"Wait-wait just a minute." Mad Dog lifts his hand and thumbs back at himself; panic in his eyes. "The bandit called *my* name and wants to meet face to face, sounds like he's got something against me. Who's to say he won't blast my ass to pieces the moment I step out of the goddamn door?"

"We're letting you go," Grayson says. "Why don't you take one for the team?"

"What team? Why don't you take one for the fucking team?"

"You scared, *hombre*?" Rabies's squats with his back against the wall, the gun against his forehead like he's praying or something. "Thought you wanted to shoot our way out. Isn't that what you said? It'd be like Juárez, no?" He moves the six-shooter from his forehead to his chest. "I'm ready to blast the fool. Let's go."

"Go where? C'mon, that was before he called on me. Now I'm trying to remember when did I ever cross a chink." To me, he clarifies, "I mean a *Triad* chink. You know, Chinese organized crime? Fukienese Phoenix, Panda Union, Bamboo Sticks United... Man, those chinks don't mess around."

"Far as I know, the Shanghai Bandit has no ties to the Triad," Grayson assures him, "or any other Chinese crime syndicate for that matter. Besides, he's out there *alone*, ain't he?"

"With a *shotgun*." Looking at Cujo wounded on the floor, Mad Dog recoils. "Fellas, I'm gonna have to think this over." Now he's whimpering to himself in *español*.

"What kind of cartel are you, Scarface?" agent Reese scolds. She looks like she wants to bitch-slap him. "Don't be such a rear echelon motherfucker. Get your ass out there and burn that Latin fire."

"Bitch, fuck that Latin fire crap, you know how much mad shit I had to do to just live up to that stereotype?"

"Listen to me, Roberto." I face him and grab him by his collars. "This is what I'm gonna do. I'm gonna get the money and go out for a meet and greet. At the same time, you stay here but you need to speak for me." Now I'm shaking him. "Make him believe it's *you* who's coming out, you understand?"

He ponders. "What about you?"

Rising to my full height, I look down on him. "I'll improvise."

At full volume, Mad Dog announces, "Okay, I'm coming out. Don't shoot!"

"Anyone want to give me their weapon?" I explain. "He's gonna expect me to be packing, so I might as well."

Cujo on the floor volunteers, "Take mine." He means the smaller weapon of the two—Reese's Sig.

"You'll have it back in one piece," I assure Reese as I wedge it into the back of my waistband. Then I open the vault and check that everyone's okay before I say to Jim sitting there hugging his knees. "Give me some money." To the cops, I explain, "He expects me to go out there with money, so I'll carry this by hand, seeing how we have no damn moneybags." Having exhausted the hundred dollar bills and the fifties, I pocket five bricks of twenties—ten thousand—and leave the vault's door ajar.

Rabies and Mad Dog sniff the air, smelling the money scent from inside the vault. Couple of dogs nod a couple of times, satisfied there is still plenty of cash left for them. Then the latter shouts on my behalf, "I'm coming out with the money! Don't shoot!"

With the money and the gun, I take a deep breath and step toward the door of the bank. I'm picturing what could unfold. Maybe I'll shoot the bandit. Or maybe no one gets shot. He'll take the money and go. Then what? Run after him? Bail on my own? Maybe not. Maybe he'll shoot me instead. Who knows? I'm improvising.

Three steps to the exit.

A voice behind me says, "Chin."

I swivel around and find Cass standing behind the counter, right at her station, her nametag on her chest, like this is any ordinary day. If I just came in the bank and saw her, I probably wouldn't have noticed anything's wrong.

"Chin…promise me you'll come back?"

I turn my back to her and I say nothing. A faint sound of a snivel reaches my ear.

Two steps to the exit.

One step at a time.

Soon as I'm outside, I mutter to myself, "Jesus Christ."

Something unexpected.

The man, the Shanghai Bandit from Kaohsiung, Taiwan, is lying flat on his back.

I kneel next to him and take off his ski-mask.

His eyes stare blankly at the sky. Spasms shake his lower body and his torso twitches. He's foaming at the mouth. The shotgun lies next to him, unattended and unreachable, the last thing on his mind. He's making sounds like he's choking on his own vomit.

Like he's dying.

First thing that comes to mind is this guy's trying to pull his routine again. But then I study him up close, and I'm second-guessing.

I remember men dying in 'Nam. There's two types of dying men. Type one has the knowing expression, the despair in their eyes telling you, *this is it*. Type two is the opposite, they don't know or don't want to admit it. Their expression is begging you to save them.

Shanghai Bandit is the type two.

He's not crying wolf, this guy's for real.

I look from him to the car across the street. The car with eighty thousand already in the trunk. The key is in my pocket. Ten thousand more on my person.

FUBAR at the bank. Right now I just need to cross the street, climb in the car, and get my sorry-ass out of Dodge.

The Shanghai Bandit on the ground is suffering like an insect under a magnifying glass. I'm thinking about what Cass said to me, *Promise me you'll come back.*

I'm remembering the phrase adorning the Alabama plate, *God Bless America.*

Thinking about the American thing to do.

I'm wondering if I'll ever regret my act of humanity as I face the entrance of the bank, shouting back in, "We got a man down!"

Chapter Thirty

Twice I've missed my getaway. Don't know if I'll get a third chance.

I pick up the shotgun.

Now, Rabies, Mad Dog, Grayson, Reese, and Cass are all outside gathered around the Shanghai Bandit. Cujo's wounded so he's still inside the bank. Mad Dog shakes his head saying, "No, definitely don't know this chink." The others are diagnosing the patient's symptoms. Cardiac arrest? Seizure? Cerebrovascular accident? Poisoning? Grayson says, "Who said poisoning? Stupid ass." Two or more people ask the detective for his take. Grayson's reply: "I look like a fucking doctor?"

"What's going on out there?" Cujo props himself up behind the counter, trying to see or hear what's happening outside.

"I'm telling you it's poisoning," Mad Dog tells everybody. "My uncle got bitten by a snake and died. He was exhibiting the same symptoms. Foaming out of the mouth"—the guy points at his own mouth and draws circles—"foaming and jerking before he choked on his tongue. Listen, I bet he can't talk."

Yes, the patient isn't talking.

"I bet if you check his temperature, it's gonna feel normal."

Cass kneels and checks his temperature. "It feels

normal."

"*My* temperature's normal, asshole," Grayson says, peeved. "*Everyone's* temperature is fucking normal. You saying we *all* got bitten by snakes?"

Cass points out, "We do have lots of snakes in this area."

Reese goes bug eyed. "See any bite marks on his body?"

"Man, the guy's faking it!" Cujo's heard us and is shouting from inside the bank. "He's doing it like last time! I thought he was having a stroke and tried to save him! C'mon, major, you saw what happened. You tell 'em. Tell 'em!"

"He isn't faking it, Cujo." I study the patient. He's so old and so fragile. So helpless. "It's real this time." Then to everyone I suggest sincerely, "Whatever he's got, we gotta take him to the ER."

"Man, this is bullshit! Just leave him be, we must finish the bank job!" Cujo shouts, "Come back here and empty the vault like we were suppose to! Gotta get this show on the goddamn road!"

"We'll stay and rob the bank," Mad Dog distributes the tasks. "You niggers take him to the hospital." Grayson and Reese scowl at the guy and he keeps going. "Get him outta here. Otherwise he's gonna die a most miserable death. My uncle…I saw him die. No one should go through that kind of pain." He checks his wristwatch. "Man has an hour at the most."

Cujo shouts in disbelief, "You dumbass motherfuckers, y'all being played, fuck! Look at my gunshot wound, I'm leaking something relentless here. Ain't nobody talking 'bout taking *my* ass to the hospital!"

Mad Dog yells back, "Hey, will you shut your stupid mouth! You're giving me an ache from head to ass, fucking nigger!"

Grayson and Reese glaring hard. Eyes look like they're scorching sockets. Grayson takes a step forward but Reese holds his hand, yanking him back. They're unarmed so it's better to keep quiet.

"What you called me?" Cujo, however, isn't letting it go this time. He maneuvers around the counter and holds up the weapon—Grayson's BFG. "I don't think you're dropping slurs for no identification purpose."

"No, I'm dropping slurs for what it's for. Get it, stupid ass nigger?"

"Let me tell you somethin', Mad Dog," Cujo explains it to him after a heartfelt sigh. "You may use the n-word for identification purposes *only*. You get it?" he says, reciting what I told him that one time. "They ask you, where's Cujo? You tell 'em he's the wounded nigger over there. The n-word is then used as an ID-ing purpose, and I ain't got no beef with that. But if you say Cujo? That stupid ass nigger who should've been left behind in Africa, we got ourselves a serious problem, *hombre*. You feel me?"

Mad Dog is looking at us as if asking, *What kind of retarded logic is that*? Cass, the Caucasian female, offers no input on the matter. Perhaps it's the PR thing to do. Rabies, Grayson, Reese and I—minorities—all look like we have something to say, or at least *should* have something to say. But we say nothing. Just stand back, letting this play out by itself.

Mad Dog goes, "Cujo, you're the stupid ass nigger who should've been left behind in Africa together with these good for nothing niggers here." The good for nothing people meaning detective Grayson and agent Reese. "In fact, now that I think about it, it's exactly what Marla told me while I was fucking her wild. She was screaming how she wished you'd taken a boat ride back to your motherland where your moronic black ass belongs. Then she moaned as I busted a nut in her butthole." Mad Dog chuckles at us, like he said something clever.

No one's amused in the slightest, and agent Reese intervenes this time by stating, "You're a racist."

"Seriously?" Mad Dog turns to her. "Is this a habit of yours? Telling people what they know? Go up to a cripple and say, 'You're a cripple.' Are you sure you're a certified cop?"

At the same time, Cujo adjusts his body to the fire ready position. Engaging his muscle memories: one arm straight the other in ninety-degrees; one eye shut and another aiming astute. No flaws in his stance except that below his ribcage, he's pouring blood. "Mad Dog," he exhales, calm. "Take back what you said, homie, you hear? Don't be talking about Marla and don't be talking 'bout where I belong."

Shotgun in my possession, I consider intervening. Then I remember the racist trucker whose nose I busted. And I recall what my colonel said to me, after 'Nam, Sometimes, it really is better not to intervene.

I step back two more paces.

Mad Dog disrespects, "Can't keep a job, can't stay in the army and your sorry-ass gang. Face it, Cujo, a nigger will always be a loser."

"You're wrong, Roberto."

"And you know what else?"

Cujo warns him, "Don't say it, man."

"You shall *never* overcome."

Pop pop. Cujo shoots.

Double taps him in the chest.

Mad Dog bleeds from the heart. He drops.

Rabies speaks a string of Spanish as he takes cover, his back against the building's wall, once again, he has his gun barrel vertical on his forehead, like he's praying to it, though Cujo has lowered the gun and slumped to the floor. Wasn't about to shoot Rabies to begin with.

Mad Dog was here to take over the heist. Now, sideways is how his body lies, and so is how the heist has gone.

Reese sticks her leg out at Mad Dog's body and pokes him with her pointy heel, making sure he's a corpse. Then she eyes from Cujo to Grayson, and asks, "Why didn't you stop him, Grayson?"

"From what, killing a drug dealing racist asshole? I had the gun I would've done the same thing." Grayson kneels next to the corpse trying to free Mad Dog's Beretta.

I aim the bandit's shotgun at the cops. "Don't even think about it."

Chapter Thirty-One

"What the hell you doing?" Cass is gazing at me with those eyes, then her eyes shift from the tip of the shotgun to what it's pointing at—the cops. She looks like she wants to freak out or cry. "Chin, put down the gun, please." Her lips are trembling. Overall she's having a bigger reaction than she did to Mad Dog getting put down.

"You done praying?" I ignore her and direct Rabies, "Get over here and retrieve Mad Dog's weapon before the cops have us in a standoff again."

A total of five firearms are involved at this point and I must keep track. Rabies has his own six-shooter—gun *numero uno*. Cujo still has Grayson's BFG—gun number 2. I have Reese's Sig and the bandit's shotgun—guns number 3 & 4. Mad Dog's down and his M9 is up for grabs—gun number 5.

Rabies seizes Mad Dog's M9 and belts it on his side. "You blowing your cover?"

Like I have a choice? I admit, "Keep the charade going any longer we may never pull out of here." I eye the bandit on the ground, his body still twitching from time to time. According to the late Mad Dog, the guy has less than an hour. *Empty the vault then take him to the ER.* Got to make haste. "Rabies, notice the shoulder bag on him? Grab it and take it to the vault and ask the folks inside to fill it up on the double."

"Mr. Chin, what are you doing?" Reese asks with her hands up, on the other side of the shotgun barrels. "You realize you're helping them with the robbery?"

Jesus Christ, Mad Dog was right. She *does* like to state the obvious.

"So that's why Cujo said he'd split the money with you." Grayson has his hands up as well. "Let me guess, you're their inside man. What'd you do for them, trip the alarm?"

"Detective…" I sigh to the guy as if I'm relieving stress. "How many times have your hands gone up in surrender today? I'd be tired by now if I were you." To Reese as well now, I suggest, "Why don't you just forget about that promotion, stay quiet and watch us rob the bank. Don't do anything stupid and no one else has to miss supper today."

Rabies frees the shoulder bag from the bandit before returning to the bank and marching toward the vault. Cujo collapses, exhausted.

"But you work here. Chin…" Cass is standing on the side of the cops. She takes a step. "*We* work here."

"And who did that stop?"

She knows as well as I *everyone* working here is robbing the place, taking advantage of last Friday's robbery, scamming the FDIC. She contemplates what I said, then says, a bit too quickly, "Okay, so let me help."

Before I protest she lets on, "I don't want the money. I just want to do what I can to help you succeed. Will you let me do that, Chin?" She bats her eyelashes.

Okay, but, "Why? Aren't you angry at me for robbing the bank?"

"I'm not angry at you for robbing the bank." Her voice is trembling but she keeps it at full volume. "What I *am*, is *disappointed* that you didn't tell me about it. You didn't trust me with your plan. Didn't *trust* that I possess a heart big enough to be by your side." Now her eyes are misty, their color a lighter shade of green. "Why didn't you just *tell* me?"

"Because I know you too well, Cass. You're all about doing the right thing."

"The *right* thing"—she scoffs and then swallows some saliva—"listen to me, Chin, the *right* thing is to support the man I love in whatever endeavor he embarks upon."

Cass and I stand over Mad Dog's body talking about what it means to do the right thing.

A woman who loves you unconditionally…

A moment later I reveal, "My daughter is in a Vietnamese sweatshop… I need ten thousand dollars, Cass. I need it to purchase her freedom."

"Okay—so why didn't you just *tell* me?" Blinking, her tears drop. "Why didn't you let me *help* you?"

"You…you're not angry that I have a daughter?"

"Are you fucking deaf?" She slaps me on the chest. "Didn't you hear what I *said*? I *said*, I'm not angry about whatever it is you kept from me, what I am is *disappointed* that you didn't *tell* me. Why didn't you just tell me you have a daughter? Why didn't you tell me you need help? Why not? What are you afraid of? You coward!"

Cujo's words ringing true. *You ain't gotta choose. You need to accept the fact that they must coexist.*

Rabies comes out with a stuffed duffle bag. Finally, the contents in box 56 and box 57 are emptied.

He approaches the scene and prompts, "I got everything. We're good to go."

"We don't have everything." Then to Cass I say, "I'm gonna go inside and drag Cujo out so I can set him in the car. Can I trust you to point this thing"—I present her the bandit's shotgun, gun number 4—"at the cops? They move, shoot them."

"*Hey-Zeus*, you're not thinking clear. You don't know what she's gonna do with that shotgun. She might turn it on you."

Reese interrupts, "Wait. Who's Zeus?"

I ignore the agent and to Cass, I ask again, "Can I trust you?"

Rabies shakes his head in disapproval. "*Hey-Zeus,* she might shoot your ass instead. In which case I got no complaints. You get taken out due to your own fault and I get to keep more of the money."

Reese says again, "Can someone tell me who the hell is Zeus?"

"Chin…" Cass moves forward. "If you don't trust the woman who loves you no matter what, then you're with the wrong goddamn woman." She steps forward and seizes the shotgun.

Raises its barrels and points them at me.

Grayson and Reese, both holding elated breaths, are ready to let out sighs of exultation at the turn of events.

Then, the barrels swing around and are pointed at them.

"Luckily," Cass says, finger on the trigger, "I'm the right woman for you." The way she's looking at me now, *the way your woman looks at you*, I see it.

I see it so clear.

237

"Oh my God." Grayson's having a revelation. "You people are a bunch of psychopaths. Ya'll gone lost your fucking minds."

"C'mon Rabies, let's help Cujo." To Cass, I say, "They move, shoot 'em."

"*Psh*. Don't have to tell me twice."

In that light, I think she looks so gallant.

And so beautiful.

****

There are three matters to decide upon now that we have the money and the cops in check. First, what to do with Cujo. Second, what to do with the Shanghai Bandit. Third, what to do with the cops.

Mad Dog's body lies on the sidewalk, none of our concern.

The first matter Rabies is kind enough to assist me in resolving. We're taking Cujo. Not to a hospital but we aren't leaving his wounded ass behind. We're taking him to safety and that's that. Matter of professional courtesy. So we lift and prop him on our shoulders, then drag the fallen comrade from the battlefield, out of the bank. Along the way Cujo spits on Mad Dog's corpse and sneers. Once across the street, he calls shotgun and Rabies lets him have it. Shotgun the ride, not the weapon.

On to the second matter: what to do with the Shanghai Bandit. We're settling it the American way— by voting. Cujo voices his objection despite his previous conviction to uphold professional courtesy. Rabies, overjoyed by the duffle bag full of money, isn't hard to convince into being a Good Samaritan. Cass has the deciding vote, and she says to me, "I'll do whatever you tell me to, Chin." *A woman who loves you unconditionally*. So we drag the Shanghai Bandit from the sidewalk and lay him in the backseat of the car.

Now the last matter: what to do with the cops.

Rabies suggests, "Let's just kill 'em," like there's nothing to it.

"No." Cass, shotgun pointed at the cops, presents a better option, "We lock them in the vault with my mother and the rest."

I tilt my head to the cops, as if asking for their opinion on the matter. They exchange sideway glances and nod back at me, saying, "We'll take the vault." It's the better option.

So the three of us escort the cops to the vault and lock them in there together with Ester, Jim, and Cass's mom. The mother asks Cass as she closes the door, "Honey, aren't you coming in as well?"

Cass, with the shotgun, says, "No, Mom. I'm locking you in."

"But I don't understand...where are the bank robbers?"

"You're looking at them." She pushes the vault to a close and turns the wheel.

Jim shouts from the inside, "What is happening? I need to use the bathroom!"

The wheel locks in place and I say, "All right then, let's get the fuck out of here."

Part Three

Shanghai Bandit

Chapter Thirty-Two

The heist was supposed to be an in-and-out deal, done in fifteen with zero casualties. Now the operation is two hours past the original timeframe. One dead, one wounded, and one is having a heart attack or stroke or seizure or whatever the fuck. What a fucking travesty. On the bright side, we were supposed to take one hundred thousand from the vault. Now we have eighty thousand in the trunk plus a hundred thousand in the bag—the duffle bag Rabies is hanging onto.

I'm driving the stolen vehicle because I told the gang I know an escape route cops won't track. Cujo is slumped in the passenger seat, hands applying pressure on his shotgun wound. Rabies is in the back squeezed between the bandit and Cass. The Shanghai Bandit's eyes are shut tight, he's wheezing, foam drying around his mouth. Cass is behind me. She leans forward and massages my shoulders. It feels good. In the rearview mirror, I catch the bandit's shotgun between Rabies' thighs. Its barrels point down.

The plan is to pull up to the hospital's emergency driveway, honk and kick the bandit from the moving vehicle. Cass and Rabies agree, it's the least we can do. Cujo, on the other hand, wants to be let out as soon as I drive past the town limit. He'll take his share and bounce. Now he's talking about where he wants to go spending that money. Speaking with eyes squeezing shut.

I ask him, "What about Marla?"

He opens his eyes and breathes with difficulty. "I don't want to talk about her right now." Changing the subject, he says, "What about you, major?" Then his head cranks back a little. "And you, Rabies. What you gonna do with your share? You're clutching that bag pretty tight there, ain't you?"

We're still in town so I keep the speed under forty-five mph. At the stop sign, I halt completely and look left, look right, and left again, going through the motions, drawing no attention. Being cautious is much better than getting caught, especially now. I steer west on Citrus Street passing the post office and its empty parking lot, heading for the train track, to the county medical.

A slight sense of déjà vu.

I glance at the rearview mirror and find Rabies sitting stoic. Both hands on the duffle bag, shotgun still between his thighs. His own handgun is lost to sight. After a moment he exhales. "Now that you killed Mad Dog, Cujo, the reality that he's actually gone, it's having an effect on me."

"You got the money and you're alive. What you complaining about having an effect?"

"Mad Dog is gone. Dago is gone. Their drugs are gone. I just realized that I'm in charge now and I have to restart the enterprise, build it from the ground up."

"Yeah?" Cujo tries to turn all the way, intrigued. "How you gonna do that?"

"When I was a young boy in Mexico, I was a mule. Used to deliver products from A to B on my bike. You know who gave me the job? Mad Dog, that's who. I was fifteen years old."

And I'm thinking about my daughter, what it's like to grow up in 'Nam.

Rabies goes on, "After I moved to Texas my nephews took my place. First thing I'm gonna do is bring them across the border, I need people I can trust, then I'm gonna squeeze out the fucking Columbians..."

His voice fades as Cass massages my shoulders with both hands. She asks, "Can we send some money to my parents? You know, for my sister? Now I've forfeited the FDIC scam."

Forfeited on account of me.

There should be at least seventy thousand after a three-way split. I only need ten thousand so I tell Cass, "Of course." I try to catch a glimpse of her in the rearview mirror but the headrest is raised too high. Can't see her face. "I should write your folks a letter and explain myself."

"Without a return address, right?" Her voice is soft and light, not angry. "If you have trouble expressing yourself, perhaps you should write a letter to me as well, like the one you wrote to your daughter."

I think. "Yeah, I can do that." After a pause I say, "Cass, I'm sorry I kept it from you."

"That's messed up, Rabies." Cujo coughs. "You'll start a gang war on the streets."

Cass and I working on our relationship.

Rabies and Cujo discussing the drug trade.

Rabies goes, "It'll be over before you know it, 'cause I'm gonna drop the bomb on their roofs. You know, like Hiroshima. Fuck the Columbians."

"Shit, you got a bomb?"

"It's a figure of speech, dumbass."

Keeping the car speed steady, three blocks before the train tracks. I see the light.

"So you got little kids as mules. Then what about logistics here?" Cujo rubs his head, smearing blood on at the neck. "How you gonna bring the drugs from over at the border?" sounding interested in cartel business. He tries to turn around again to look at Rabies.

"Don't move, you're getting blood on the seat."

"Man, this ain't even your car."

Ahead, the light turns from green to yellow to red. I ease my foot off the gas and let the vehicle coast before I step on the brake, halting just behind the crossing.

In the complete stop, Rabies leans forward parallel to us; his head is in that space between Cujo's and mine. He's mesmerized by the train tracks when he murmurs, "How do I move the drugs, you ask? If you pay attention, Cujo, the answer to your question may just be right in front of you."

We're staring right in front of us. Staring at the railroad in silence.

When all of a sudden, Rabies is shot in the head.

Chapter Thirty-Three

The guy's brain splatters on the windshield. His dream shattered along with it. An eyeball sticks to the glass beneath the rearview mirror like chewed-up gum. His body is caught between the driver's seat and the passenger's, the shotgun propping him up like a puppet with cut-off strings. Red is splashed everywhere, reminiscent of when Marla tampered with the dye pack and made it explode. Talk about a strange sense of déjà vu.

But this isn't dye. It's Rabies' blood.

I've seen dead bodies plenty of times, this is nothing new for me to gag about. But here in this car I expect to hear a scream, from someone, anyone, a scream at the gore, at the grotesque body without a head. Yet no one is screaming. No one's hysterical. I suspect we're all too shocked. But I do hear a whimper from behind me.

"Chin…"

Cass has stopped rubbing my shoulders. I turn back, looking past the headless corpse and find her sitting there. The gleam in her eyes is gone. The six-shooter is pointed at her head, hammer cocked, a finger on the trigger.

Cass looks terrified.

The Shanghai Bandit wipes his mouth with his other hand, wiping off the dried foam around his lips.

Then he pulls on the strap of the duffle bag, finally freeing it from below Rabies' belly. He places it on his lap. No spasms. His legs aren't twitching or jerking. He doesn't appears to be choking. It was all a show.

Well, shit. He duped us, again.

Son-of-a-motherfucking-bitch.

Gun pointed at Cass's head, a head which now I find to be so beautiful, a head I do not want to see get blown away, a head way too pretty to be goo.

The bandit demands of me and Cujo, "Ejaculate now."

"*Excuse* me?" Despite his wound, Cujo turns all the way around to face the backseat, coming out of shock due to something even more shocking. "What you say?"

"I say, ejaculate now," he says.

"What the fuck?" Cujo, profoundly bewildered, asks, "*Now*?"

"Yes. Now! Ejaculate now, now! Or I shoot!"

I appease my grandparent's one-time country man, the Shanghai Bandit from Taiwan, in a language I haven't spoken in years, "*Bie sha ta.*" Don't kill her. "*Qiuqiu ni.*" Please don't.

"*Hao.*" Okay. Then he switches to English again, "You must ejaculate." He looks at me down there, at my belt, where Reese's Sig is wedged.

"All right man, I've been to prison. I know how this goes." Cujo unbuckles his belt, shaking his head. "But I gotta tell you, this is beyond bizarre, even by prison standards."

I withdraw Reese's Sig nice and slow and unclip the magazine. The cartridge falls under the seat. I say to Cujo, who's unzipping his fly, "Don't ejaculate, Cujo.

He means *eject*." I eject the remaining bullet in the chamber. The bullet pops out and I let it drop to join the magazine under the seat. The Bandit nods, satisfied.

I attempt to correct the guy, "The word is *eject*, not ejaculate." By all means it's got fewer syllables, should be an easier word to pronounce.

"Yes, ejaculate. Now you." You meaning Cujo.

"Shit man, you had me worried." Cujo withdraws his weapon as well, pops the last bullet in the chamber and let it fall to the ground. We were soldiers. We eject in style.

Traffic light turns green, yet we aren't moving.

"Good. You ejaculate beautiful," the bandit compliments. "I teach you something, okay? You have one, two, three, four, five—five guns. No good. They in wrong people—no good. Too many guns don't know who got whose gun. You do not throw guns away. You do not have to take guns. You only must tell people to ejaculate. Because after you ejaculate, you empty, no? And you no use and not good. Like now."

"Yeah, I see what you saying." Cujo plays along but eyeballs me like, *What the fuck is this guy yammering about?* "Yeah, I feel you. After I ejaculate, I feel real empty, like on the inside, yeah."

"Out the car, now," the Bandit orders, and to Cass, "You out with me, this way."

The bandit keeps the gun on her as they exit to the side facing the curb. I climb from the opposite side, no gun and too far from my girl. With Cass's life in the balance, I dare not do anything stupid. Cujo's closer but he's wounded. He's incapable of doing anything stupid.

"Hijacked *again*. What'd I tell you, major?" Cujo steps onto the sidewalk and squats, must be excruciating for him to stand up straight. He removes his hands from his wound and I see blood congealed with that of Rabies. "We should've just left his stroked-out ass at the bank. Now we're gonna get our heads blown to pieces like Rabies in there. Man, I was starting to like that dude."

I join Cujo on the sidewalk facing the bandit and Cass, the latter a hostage to the former. But then he pushes Cass toward me; she runs forward and crashes into my embrace. I turn her away from the gun's aim, shielding her with my body. I kiss her head.

The three of us are opposite the bandit. The bandit with the gun pointed at us.

"You have the money and you can take the car." I gesture to the car parked with the driver's door open.

"You stupid?" the bandit says. "The car from Alabama."

"Please, spare our lives."

Gun pointed upright, he says, "Give me one reason."

One reason? I recall that time on my driveway, when Mad Dog held me at gunpoint, the only thing I wanted to do before I die was read the letter my daughter wrote. Now, held at gunpoint by the Shanghai Bandit, the only thing I want is to see my daughter personally. I'm holding Cass's hand, hugging her tight when I tell the gunman, "I—no, *we*—we have a daughter."

"A daughter?" The guy appears surprised. "Why you rob bank if you have daughter?"

A pause later I tell him, "I was doing it *because* I have a daughter."

He thinks about it and nods. With that accent of

his, he states, "You are *not* a good father, yes? I had daughter too. I forty year old when she born." Now he looks sad. "She the best."

Cass, hearing his tone, withdraws from my embrace and faces the guy. Some kind of sympathy in her eyes, she asks, "Why are *you* robbing banks if you have a daughter?"

The bandit says nothing.

"Is it for the same reason? Are you robbing banks *because* of your daughter?"

"I…" the bandit utters, "I no rob banks." Says the guy with the duffle bag full of money, money fresh out of a vault from a bank.

"Okay, you're not robbing banks." Cass nods like she's gets it. "So what happened to her, your daughter?"

"Why?" He aims at her now. "Why you ask what happened?"

"You said you *had* a daughter, or was that your English—"

"I was no good father, okay?" The guy is trembling, so is his voice. "I was bad father, like him." Him meaning me. "I always away rob bank after bank in Taiwan, Hong Kong, Macau, because I want money to take her to America, to give her good life. Finally, I come, and I keep rob banks—it all I know how. LAX, a guard heart attack and died. Then I realize, okay? I no rob bank no more. I take my daughter to school. I pick her up from school. I stay home. She safe. Then she grow up, she grow up smart and she go to college—my dream come true. But American college—USC—is a bad, bad place. Very, *very* bad. There she meet bad friends." The guy appears hateful for a second and then goes back to being melancholy. "She meet friends and they do drugs."

"Aw, shit." Cujo gets tired from squatting and sits his ass on the sidewalk. "I think I know where this is going."

"Her friend Marley sell cocaine. Make her buy. Make her spend her money. Make her *addict*. Then one day…" He looks about to break down. "One day she no call me. But police call me. They call me, I ID her body."

Now I recall the night at the library when I read the *LA Times*. A headline had caught my eye. *Chinese coed found dead in dorm, possible drug overdose.*

In the distance, sirens wail.

"Stupid cops," Cujo remarks from the ground. "Guess they finally figured out what was going on at the bank."

"I am not bad guy," declares the Shanghai Bandit. "Everyday I see family from China and Taiwan, from Korea, Vietnam, everywhere, in LA, in San Fran, and I want to tell them, go back! This country is no safe. They do not know danger. But I know… I know Marley, I know her father is drug dealer. What I do? I kill him. I protect more family from drugs."

"You…you killed him," Cujo, the ex-soldier, now career criminal, looks up at the bandit. "Dago had sixteen holes in him but he wasn't shot sixteen times with a *handgun*. He was shot with that *shotgun* of yours. What you got, *double-aught* buck-load? Eight or nine .33 pellets in standard shells?"

"Eight," the bandit admits.

Double-barrel shotgun, two times eight is sixteen.
Sixteen holes.

"Now I know what caliber pellet I got caught with." Cujo inspects his wound. "Hooray for me."

"I no rob banks," the bandit says, justifying his actions to us. "I do right thing. So I phone police, but they no come the bank."

I recall, Cops said someone *phoned-in* about a robbery. "So it was you. But…how on earth did you know the bank was going to get robbed?"

"I stay in town to find Mad Dog. I walk pass bank and I saw cop run to bank, I saw cop run to bank again, I saw cop run to bank three times. It's the girl cried wolf, yes? A very old trick. I know stories. Girl cry wolf many times then nobody come, wolf eat her. I know how to use the story. I use before in robbery."

"Wait," Cujo asks, "you're saying where you're from it's a *girl* who cries wolf?"

"I no rob banks, okay? I rob drug dealers. I take drug money so no one buy more drugs to sell. You understand? Mad Dog, he is drug dealer. The man I kill, he is drug dealer."

Cass steps forward. "*We* are not drug dealers."

Sirens wail louder and louder.

The cops are near.

"Will you let us go, please?" Cujo huffs in pain. "We're out of time. All of us."

The bandit directs the gun at Cujo. "You took drugs. Are you drug dealer?"

"Shit, me?" Cujo attempts to stand but gives up just inches off the ground. "Truth is, Mr. Shanghai Bandit, I was a *user* and I *wanted* to be a drug dealer. Yeah, I took Dago's stash after you killed him and I was gonna sell 'em. But I never did. Then somethin' else happened. I started robbing banks and you know what? I like it, a lot. It's like the *ultimate* American dream, man. You ask me if I'm drug dealer, my answer is: *hell* no, yo. I ain't no drug dealer. I'm straight up bank robber, mister. I don't got a daughter so I think I'm qualified, right? Shit, think I'll call myself the Harlem Bandit. *HB* for short. What you think?"

"You from Harlem."

"Nope, never been there, but that's the point, Mr. *Shanghai* Bandit."

The sirens stop. I figure the cops have arrived at the bank. In a matter of minutes they'll figure out we're on the way to the hospital. Matter of minutes they'll show up at this forsaken juncture.

"Friday you took me to hospital," the bandit recalls. "I thank you, Mr. Harlem Bandit." To me, "How about you? You drug dealer, or bank robber?"

The ground seems to give off subtle vibrations.

I must be imagining things. "Neither." I shake off the sensation and say to him, "I'm a father."

"Good." He lowers his gun. "Be a good father to your daughter."

"You said you're only robbin' drug dealers." Cujo squeezes his eyes shut in pain, bites his lip, then finishes his thought, "Now that you see we ain't no drug dealers...you don't gotta take that money from us." He opens his eyes and tilts his head at the duffle bag.

"You know what they call me?" Guy starts to back away.

"They call you..." Cujo huffs. "They call you Shanghai Bandit."

"I no from Shanghai."

"That I heard."

"They make mistake."

"Ignorant Americans."

"However…" Guy turns around. "I *am* bandit."

Sirens wail again.

Five, four blocks away.

Only one way out of here and that's across the tracks. Just as the bandit's about to bail, something unexpected is heard. A sound forgotten. A sound I never thought I'd hear again in Abisko, California, for as long as I live.

Gong gong gong gong.

The lights—four of them, are flashing red and out of synch; the arms of the level crossing drawing down.

Gong gong gong gong.

The arms stop lowering and form a saltire—an *X*. They're stuck. The lever mechanism must be in dire need of lubrication.

"What the hell?" Cass exclaims. "Since when have they reactivated the—"

Chugga chugga and a thundering horn drown her words and sirens and silence alike.

Vibration is felt from toe to head. Ground rumbling.

A train is coming.

Chapter Thirty-Four

In front of the level crossing, the stolen car with the Alabama plate is parked with Rabies' corpse inside. The four of us—the bandit, Cujo, Cass and I—stand facing north, facing the train.

I turn back and make out shapes in the distance of the vehicles approaching. Their size appears bigger and bigger. Their numbers increase. Cops, the whole sheriff's department plus CHP, they're all heading this way.

All of a sudden the Shanghai Bandit drops the shotgun and darts southbound along the train tracks. He's an old man carrying a duffle bag. Steps later he appears out of breath, but his speed isn't slowing a bit, a steady 15, 16 mph. His head bobs like a tired old pigeon. Arms flail high with each thump of his feet. His figure diminishes and he doesn't look back.

I look back, and...

SWOOOOSH.

A yellow metal beast with monstrous wheels rolls past the crossing, making hairs fly. A smoke pipe at the tip of its nose blowing steam black as coal. An old-school freight train. Not boxcar style but wagon variant with intermodal containers in stacks of two. I catch the letters on one of the containers: "COSCO." The engine must be pulling at least fifty wagons—one hundred containers.

I watch the Shanghai Bandit. He's racing with the train and the train is winning. It rolls past him but he doesn't stop running. He keeps up and glances right, then, just when their speed differential seems to reach zero, he reaches out, grabs hold of something on a wagon, and...he leaps.

"My God, did that just happen?" Cujo's jaw drops. "Did the Shanghai Bandit catch a ride on this motherfucking train with all that money, PFM style?" *Pure fucking magic.*

Yes he did. "But he didn't take *all* the money." To Cass, I say, "Quick, help me get the money from the trunk."

As we empty the trunk, from the corner of my eyes I see half-a-dozen Grand Fury's, two, three blocks away, approaching fast and mighty furious. The sound of their sirens increases as they near, volume rivaling that of a train.

"That's enough, Cass." She's taken five bricks and I say, "Leave the rest. It belongs to him." Him meaning Cujo. "C'mon, we gotta catch a ride as well."

Stuffing a brick of money down her blouse, she says, "We leaving him?"

"See the cops?" Cujo smiles. "They're gunning for us, that means they either captured Marla or she escaped. Long as she's fine, I got no complaints." He moves his hand from his wound up to his heart, fingers crossed. "Gotta have faith."

No time to stay and chat. Stepping away from him, I say, "Fare thee well, soldier."

"Major, haven't you heard? Call me Harlem Bandit." To Cass, he says, "Miss, you take good care of him, all right?" He waves. "*Adios.*"

I grab Cass's hand and we run.

A brick pops out from her bosom and I order her to leave it.

I hold her hand tight.

"Keep running and don't look back!" I huff and puff. "We're gonna catch the last wagon!"

"How will we know it's the last wagon if we don't look back? It'll be too late!"

"The last wagon will be a locomotive—a *head*! Do you trust me?"

Running beside me, she shouts, "I do!"

"Then grab my hand and do not let go!"

"I won't!" She takes my hand. "I won't let go!"

A wagon with two containers rolls past us. Then another, then another…until finally, a yellow beast that looks just like the one pulling the wagons, attached backward.

I reach up, and I shout.

"Jump!"

Chapter Thirty-Five

The last wagon is often a locomotive as it saves from attaching one on its return journey. Sometimes, the last locomotive *pushes* the wagon forward, but that would be easy to spot because it would've been blowing steam from the rear. I grew up around the railroad, seen trains pass by all my childhood. I know how it goes. Presently, the head serves no specific purpose, which also means that it's unattended.

We occupy the locomotive, facing forward but being pulled backward. Traveling on the railroad my ancestors built. *Mom, Dad, do you see?* The rails are not obsolete.

"Chin!" Cass pats me on the arm. "Look!"

Out of the window, with everything appearing smaller and smaller, I see a figure crossing the tracks. *Cujo.* Another figure helps him get in a car—a red car—Pontiac, *Marla.* They get in and the car swerves ninety degrees, heading north along the rails.

Off-road.

Seconds later, an army of police cruisers cross the tracks, heading west, not stopping.

I blow a sigh of relief. "Everything will be all right, Cass."

"I really want a smoke, but...I won't." She sits on a stool that's probably reserved for the engineer, and asks, "Where is this train going, anyway?"

It's heading south, with a freight full of containers that are marked COSCO—China Ocean Shipping. Best guess, "Long Beach." It has one of the largest shipping harbors on the west coast.

"So we're going to Long Beach." She taps her lips and repeats, "Long Beach. Yeah, I can do that."

"I'm not going to Long Beach, Cass. Just gonna get off there, then I'm gonna board a boat that's gonna sail across the Pacific, so I can make my way toward Vietnam."

"To see your daughter?"

She may or may not be mine, but, "Yes. She was sold for ten thousand dollars. That's why I robbed the bank, Cass. I need to purchase her freedom."

She retrieves a brick of fifties from her bosom. The she gropes herself up and down, frantic. "Shit, this is all I got." Her hands goes around her butt, her waist and her breasts, she says, "Must've dropped everything in that jump. I only got five thousand."

"Don't worry." I empty my pockets, that also hold five bricks, but of twenty dollar bills, ten thousand dollars. "They gave me these to meet the Shanghai Bandit with." Plus the five thousand Cass got, "We have fifteen grand in all. Ten for my daughter, the rest for your sister."

All this for fifteen grand.

"So just enough." Looking at the bricks, she asks, "Then what?"

"Then...I don't know." A shrug. "One step at a time, I guess."

"Are you going to bring her to America?"

"I'll tell her what America's like." Thinking of what the Shanghai Bandit said, *America is not safe.*

"I'll tell her the good and bad, then let her decide."

She stands from the stool and looks at me with those green eyes, eyes gleaming ever so bright. We say nothing for a very long time. The train passes the service station where I found Mad Dog and Marla, where the phone is working and the clock is telling the time. My car abandoned with the flat tire.

"Tell me, Chin." Cass frowns like she's debating internally. "You love me or what?"

"Well..." I've accepted the truth—that the woman I have feelings for, and my daughter, must coexist, so I say, "Look at it this way, if I don't love you, would I ask you to come with me?"

"You mean...to Vietnam?" She blushes a little. "Are you asking?"

"Aren't you gonna tag along with me anyway?"

"No—What? Are you asking me to go with you or not?"

"Are you gonna invite yourself or not?"

"Stop it." She looks like she wants to knee me in the balls. "One last time, are you inviting me to go with you or what?"

First, I kiss her.

Then, I say, "I just realized the Shanghai Bandit is on the train with us."

A word about the author...

Eric Qiao was born in Dalian, China. He moved to the United States with his family when he was twelve years old. His debut novel, *The Only Girl in China*, is also published by the Wild Rose Press. He's currently working on his third novel in San Diego, where he has just settled.

Thank you for purchasing
this publication of The Wild Rose Press, Inc.

If you enjoyed the story, we would appreciate your
letting others know by leaving a review.

For other wonderful stories,
please visit our on-line bookstore at
www.thewildrosepress.com.

For questions or more information
contact us at
info@thewildrosepress.com.

The Wild Rose Press, Inc.
www.thewildrosepress.com

Stay current with The Wild Rose Press, Inc.

Like us on Facebook

https://www.facebook.com/TheWildRosePress

And Follow us on Twitter
https://twitter.com/WildRosePress